SEDUCTIVE SIN

BELLAMY BROTHERS THREE

HELEN HARDT

HS
HARDT & SONS

SEDUCTIVE SIN

BELLAMY BROTHERS THREE

Helen Hardt

This book is an original publication of Helen Hardt

Cover Design: Shepard Originals
Edited by Eric J. McConnell

Paperback ISBN: 978-1-952841-32-3

PRAISE FOR HELEN HARDT

"Helen Hardt is a master at making you fall for the bad boy."
~**Words We Love By** on *Savage Sin*

"Hardt spins erotic gold..."
~***Publishers Weekly*** on *Follow Me Darkly*

"22 Best Erotic Novels to Read"
~***Marie Claire*** **Magazine** on *Follow Me Darkly*

"Intensely erotic and wildly emotional..."
~***New York Times*** **bestselling author Lisa Renee Jones** on *Follow Me Darkly*

"With an edgy, enigmatic hero and loads of sexual tension, Helen Hardt's fast-paced *Follow Me Darkly* had me turning pages late into the night!"
~***New York Times*** **bestselling author J. Kenner** on *Follow Me Darkly*

“Christian, Gideon, and now…Braden Black.”

~**Books, Wine, and Besties** on *Follow Me Darkly*

“This red-hot tale will have readers fanning themselves.”

~**Publishers Weekly** on *Blush*

“Scintillating…”

~**Publishers Weekly** on *Bloom*

“An absolute must-read. With its engaging plot and enthralling characters, this novel keeps you hooked from start to finish.”

~**The Llama Library** on *Bloom*

“Helen's intelligent writing style and skills have made this story a must-read.”

~**FireSerene Reads** on *Bloom*

“It's hot, it's intense, and the plot starts off thick and had me completely spellbound from page one.”

~**The Sassy Nerd Blog** on *Rebel*

“*Craving* is the jaw-dropping book you *need* to read!”

~***New York Times* bestselling author Lisa Renee Jones** on *Craving*

"Completely raw and addictive."

~**#1 *New York Times* bestselling author Meredith Wild** on *Craving*

"Talon has hit my top five list...up there next to Jamie Fraser and Gideon Cross."

~*USA Today* **bestselling author Angel Payne** on *Craving*

"Talon and Jade's instant chemistry heats up the pages..."

~**RT Book Reviews** on *Craving*

"Sorry Christian and Gideon, there's a new heartthrob for you to contend with. Meet Talon. Talon Steel."

~**Booktopia** on *Craving*

"Such a beautiful torment—the waiting, the anticipation, the relief that only comes briefly before more questions arise, and the wait begins again... Check. Mate. Ms. Hardt..."

~**Bare Naked Words** on *Craving*

"Made my heart stop in my chest. Helen has given us such a heartbreakingly beautiful series."

~**Tina, Bookalicious Babes** on the Steel Brothers Saga

"This book was fantastic! It was steamy, funny, romantic, and just about any other emotion you can think of..."

~**Steamy Book Mama** on *Lily and the Duke*

"The writing was fast paced and *hot* for a historical romance...with lots of chemistry...and a lot of fun!

~**Bound by Books** on *Lily and the Duke*

"An enthralling and rousing vampire tale that will leave readers waiting for the sequel."

~**Kirkus Reviews** on *Unchained*

"Dangerous and sexy. A new favorite!"

~***New York Times*** **bestselling author Alyssa Day** on *Unchained*

"A dark, intoxicating tale."

~**Library Journal** on *Unchained*

"Helen Hardt has some kind of skill I don't have the words to describe. Her writing is addictive. She sucked in my mind and I just don't want to read anything but her right now!"

~**OMGReads Blog**

"Helen Hardt...is a master storyteller."

~**Small Town Book Nerd**

For my readers

PROLOGUE

SAVANNAH

"You're not coming anywhere near me!" I glance around quickly, looking for something, anything, to use as a weapon.

I pick up the Jane Austen I was reading, using it as a shield.

"Put that down, Savvy," Miles says. "Eat your damned dinner. I can't have you fainting from hunger."

He's right. I can't faint. I want to be completely conscious for whatever he has in mind for me. If I'm unconscious, I can't fight back.

"Eat," he says again.

I take the tray and set it on the small table in the living area.

A fork.

Good.

And a spoon.

No knife.

The salmon is flaky and doesn't require a knife. Not that he would have given me one anyway.

I force myself to ingest the food. All of it. And the water.

I rise. "I have to go to the bathroom."

He blocks the door to the bedroom. "You're not going anywhere."

"Would you rather I piss on you?"

I regret my words as soon as I say them. With my luck, I just turned Miles on with that threat.

"Fine. Go."

I head into the bathroom and close the door.

Of course there's no lock.

And of course he can see everything I'm doing anyway.

Fucking cameras.

Is it really that important to watch me take a crap?

But I'm glad I ate the food. Already I'm feeling stronger. Healthier.

I made a deal, and I'll see it through, but I won't make this easy or enjoyable for him.

Then I laugh out loud.

Enjoyable for *him*? He's already enjoying this. Whether I lie like a dead fish or fight him to the end, he'll enjoy it. He'll get off.

I flush the toilet and look in the mirror once more. My skin is pale, my hair is stringy, and the anxiety of the last several hours is imprinted deeply into my eyes.

I see myself as whoever is watching me sees me.

A pawn.

A weakling.

A mere thing.

I can't escape. I made my choice.

I chose the wellbeing of Falcon over my own.

And as much as I hate what's about to happen to me, I can't bring myself to regret it.

I leave the bathroom, enter the bedroom—

Miles is there already, standing by the bed, naked, his hard cock jutting out and ready.

I swallow, forcing the food to remain in my stomach.

I lie on the bed, and he lifts my satin gown over my hips, hovers over me, his face menacing.

"Tonight you're mine, Savannah Gallo. Welcome to hell."

1

FALCON

In every prisoner's life there's that one day they can recall that changed everything. That put them on a different path.

For me it was the day Zion came to my cell block.

Zion, I knew, would be trouble.

Different from the way Fletcher or Bruno had been trouble for me.

It only took me that one time in the cafeteria to get Fletcher in line, and Bruno? After I freed Tommy Ortiz from his tyranny, he stayed in line as well.

But Zion...

The first day I saw him, I knew.

He was as burly as they come, solid muscle, but a good five inches shorter than I was.

Already I saw it in him. Small man's complex. He's the guy who has to exert his dominance over everyone to compensate for his lack of height.

He had a shock of sandy brown hair, and a nearly pretty face —one that would've made him a target if he weren't so burly.

You can tell a lot by how a man walks. Especially on the inside.

A lot of new prisoners come in with a hunched posture, which doesn't bode well for them. Those who can come in while walking upright with a straight back are trying to look brave so they won't be a target.

They walk briskly, swinging their arms freely. They look straight ahead while not making eye contact with anyone.

If they're good at this act, they won't see a lot of trouble in prison.

These are the guys that fly under the radar, are left alone.

The ones who look at the ground, shoulders slumped—those are the targets. The ones whose screams I try to ignore at night. The ones for whom prison is a whole different experience.

But then there are those like Zion.

*Those who come in walking upright, a slow even gait, and they look everyone—*everyone*—in the eye.*

The kind that assesses everyone with a single glance. Separating the strong from the weak. Ready to assert dominance over the situation, whatever it may be.

That was Zion.

He walked past Bruno, eyeing him. And then past Fletcher, who is bigger than I am.

Until he got to me.

He looks me up and down, his gaze taking in everything about me. Judging me. Sizing me up as a competitor. I curl my hands into fists, my gaze never wavering from his.

I look him in the eye. Always in the eye. These criminals only take about a millisecond to respond to that split-second you take your attention away from them.

I don't speak to him.

I don't speak to anyone until they speak to me. It's kind of my calling card.

But he sizes me up, cocking his head.

He's waiting for me to say something.

He'll be waiting a long time.

Finally, he speaks. "How's the fucking food here?"

"We just hired a new gourmet chef. He used to work at a Michelin three-star place," I say with sarcasm.

He raises an eyebrow. Interesting. Not everyone can do that. But I can. However, I keep my eyebrows right where they are.

"What are you in for?"

"Killed a motherfucker."

The lie I've learned to tell. I'm innocent, but innocence on the inside is a sign of weakness. Plus I don't mention that it was manslaughter. I let them think it was fucking murder.

He waits for me to ask why he's here.

I don't.

Larkin stands on one side of me, Tommy Ortiz on the other.

Zion gestures to Tommy. "He yours?"

"He is. Hands off."

Tommy suffers from the same problem that Zion himself does. Pretty features. The kind that make prison hell.

But Tommy is under my protection now. And Zion won't get anywhere near him.

He gestures to Larkin on my other side. Larkin isn't pretty. He's rough, with a crooked nose that's been broken so many times it no longer looks normal. He has a scar slashed across his face. He looks mean enough, but he's a softy on the inside. The man's all beta, which is why he hangs with me.

"What about this one?"

"I'm nobody's bitch," Larkin says gruffly.

"Did I ask you?" Zion closes the distance between himself and Larkin.

Do not step back, I say to Larkin subliminally, hoping he gets the message.

He does.

He's a natural beta, but I've shown him how to survive in here.

"What about the rest of these losers?" Zion asks.

"Nobody touches anybody in my cell block," I say. "You want to shove your cock up somebody's ass? Get yourself transferred."

The eyebrow again. This time, I use my height to my advantage. I shove my shoulders back, lift my chin. Because what I say is fact. Nobody gets fucked on my block. It's bad enough I have to listen to the screams from the other ones.

I run a tight ship. But sometimes, when we're all locked up at night, things can go wrong. A rogue guard sometimes finds an inmate he likes, or he takes a bribe from another inmate.

Then it's up to me, the next morning, to take care of things. But I don't always know who's at fault. I rely on my men.

The grapevine in my block is pretty damned good.

"I don't answer to anybody," Zion says.

"Good enough. Don't fuck up, and you won't have to."

A sly smile curls his lips. "I don't think you understand what I just said."

I cock my head, turn my jaw into granite. "You think I don't? I went to college. Did you?"

"As a matter of fact, I did."

"Then I think we both know what I meant and what you meant. Only one problem." I glance around for a second and then fix my gaze back on Zion. "All these men here? They're on my side."

"You think?"

"I know your type. You think you're the first little guy I've seen come in here and try to make waves?"

"Five minutes alone with me, and you'll no longer think I'm so little." He grabs his crotch.

Seriously? He's threatening me? With his fucking dick size?

No cock gets near me.

"I'm thinking five minutes alone with me, and you'll be a dead man."

He grins, and I swear to God if I look closer I'd see saliva in the corners of his mouth. "I'd like to make you shriek like a fucking wildcat."

Yeah. I'm done with this piece of shit. "You're going to want to get the fuck away from me now."

"I don't take orders from a pretty boy."

I hold back my chuckle. The only pretty boy here, other than Tommy, is fucking Zion himself. Trying to be the tough guy. Keeping muscle on that tiny frame so people take him seriously.

If he's thinking about raping anybody in the cellblock, he'll be sorry.

And he sure as hell won't get anywhere near me.

"You show Savage some respect," Larkin says.

"How about I show your ass my cock?" Zion taunts him.

"Make all the threats you want," I say. "You mark my words. You even try *to carry any one of them out? You won't see the light of the next fucking day."*

"Big words."

I lift an eyebrow. "You think you know what big is? Think again."

That gets him. His eyes go wild, as if he's mad. "You watch it, Savage. Yeah, I know who you are. Falcon Bellamy. And I know you ain't in for no murder."

"You did your homework," I say. "So fucking what?"

"You think you're so fucking tough. You don't know what it's

really like to be a criminal. What it feels like to shove a knife into someone's flesh, watch them bleed out. After you've fucking taken their pussy and ass in every way possible."

So he's a rapist. Good for him. He won't get along well here. Not in my cell block. We don't take kindly to rapists.

They're only above child molesters on our totem pole of who are the worst degenerates of humankind. Even murderers fare better. At least their victims don't have to live the rest of their life in fear.

"Keep talking," I say. "You're close to signing your own fucking death warrant."

"Big words," he says again.

"Original words on your part."

The irony seems lost on him.

He finally backs away, standing straight and tall, still meeting my gaze. "You need to watch it, Bellamy."

"His name is Savage," Larkin says through gritted teeth.

"The only thing I'm going to call him is fresh meat." He grabs Tommy's arm, yanking him toward him. "And I'm taking you."

"Maybe I didn't make myself clear." I stalk toward Zion, force him to let go of Tommy, and then lead him to the concrete block wall, where I grab a fistful of his orange jumpsuit. "You don't touch any of my men. Have I made myself clear now?"

With his right hand, Zion grabs my wrist.

And I'll give him one. He is fucking strong.

But I'm stronger. And meaner.

I wasn't always mean like Zion, but you learn to be mean on the inside. You do it for survival. You do it to protect those who are too weak to protect themselves. And you do it to put shitheads like Zion in their place.

"Quite a grip you've got," I say. "But it won't get you anywhere here. Stay away from all of them...or I'll fucking kill you."

My words aren't even menacing. I say them matter-of-factly. I've found they have more effect that way.

Let them think I'm a little off my rocker. Let them think whatever they want.

All I need to do is watch my back, and the backs of the rest of the men on my block.

Not too difficult.

Not for Savage.

"ALL WIRELESS ALARM systems rely on radio frequency signals sent between door and window sensors to a control system that triggers an alarm when any of these entryways are breached," Leif says quietly. He points to several circled areas on a blueprint of the McAllister estate. "The signals deploy any time a tagged window or door is opened, whether or not the alarm is enabled. But when enabled, the system will trip the alarm and also send a silent alert to the monitoring company, which contacts the occupants and the police."

I shake my head. "How is this even possible?"

"It is. All the systems use different hardware, but they are essentially the same." He scans the immediate vicinity. "This isn't that advanced. It's been around since the nineties. I can jam the signals to prevent them from tripping an alarm by sending radio noise to prevent the signal from getting through from sensors to the control panel."

"It all sounds like gobbledygook to me."

"It did to me at first too," Leif says. "But it's actually pretty simple once you understand how the tech works."

"Right."

Leif plays with his gadgets, listening intently. A few lights flicker on and off, and he taps in different codes. This goes on for several minutes until he smiles. "Got it. The whole thing is disarmed, including the cameras and microphones. But now we have to get in and out before they discover this."

"How could they discover it?"

"Depends. If they have actual humans manning the cameras, they'll see it quickly. If they don't, it'll be a while."

"And how do we know whether people are watching?"

"We don't, Falcon. That's why we fucking hurry." He pulls out another gadget. This one looks like a small pistol with several pointy metal rods sticking out of it.

"What's that?"

"It's a lockpick gun, just in case disabling the system didn't unlock the gate."

"Why wouldn't it?"

"Sometimes the gate is on a different frequency so cars can come and go via a remote control without unlocking the whole system. That's probably the case here."

We walk toward the gate, staying in shadows as much as we can. In the distance, several dogs bark.

"Where do you think the hounds are?" I ask.

He cups his hand around his ear and listens. "Could be in the back, but they sound farther away than that. There's probably a couple dogs in the back and one or two in the house as well." He pats the bag of jerky in the pocket of his hoodie. "We'll take care of them."

"Just how quickly does the doggie downer work?"

"Too damned long, but it'll do the job."

Leif and I make it to the gate.

"Yeah, it's still locked." He pulls out the gun, clicks it a few times. "We're in."

My heart is racing like a fucking madman's. I don't even know for sure that Savannah's here, but I feel like she is.

I feel like she's close.

And I feel like she's in danger.

The moon hangs low in the night sky, and it casts a pale glow over the sprawling mansion. I follow Leif as he slowly opens the wrought-iron gate and enters the property. He follows the shadows, keeping us cloaked. Our black attire blends seamlessly into the darkness. A cool breeze sweeps over us, makes the trees in the yard rustle.

"Armed guards?" I whisper.

"Probably," he says, his voice so low I can barely hear him. "But they won't know security is down yet. We just have to stay out of their sight. Stick to the shadows."

"Won't they see the security lights are out?" I ask.

He shakes his head. "There'll be a backup generator that takes over the main system."

"Then how the hell are we going to get into the house?"

"Leave that to me," Leif says.

2

SAVANNAH

W*elcome to hell.*

I close my eyes, prepare my body for what is about to happen.

No gun is being held to my head, no knife to my heart.

My life is not in danger.

What am I supposed to feel?

Disgust?

Yeah, I feel that.

But fear?

No. I'm not afraid. He won't kill me. He has to marry me first, for whatever reason his family deems important enough to force this.

I just wish I were stronger, capable of overpowering Miles and his horrid body.

His breath is minty fresh, which only angers me. He's a rapist, damn it. His breath should smell like rotted garbage.

Falcon won't be coming for me. He doesn't even know where I am.

Besides, I did this for him.

I made this deal with the devil to make sure he doesn't go down for murdering Abel, and Miles had better damned well keep that promise.

Falcon.

Think of Falcon.

It's Falcon about to fuck me.

Not Miles McAllister.

Only Falcon.

My Falcon—

My eyes shoot open.

Except this isn't Falcon, and not even the best imagination in the world can convince me that the man ready to thrust into me is anyone other than who he is.

Miles McAllister.

His shoulders are narrow, and while he clearly goes to the gym often, his muscles don't rip out of his shirt the way Falcon's do. His hair has an oily sheen to it, like he's skipped a few showers. But even with those physical differences, I could close my eyes and imagine Falcon.

But I could never get past his face. He's not a bad looking guy, but even the handsomest man in the world would look ugly if he had a heart as dark as Miles's. Especially his eyes. They're like two bottomless whirlpools, waiting to swallow up any unsuspecting swimmers that come within their grasp. Eyes that could kill with a simple glance.

I stare straight into those mean blue eyes. "So you're a rapist now?"

"You made a deal," he says through clenched teeth.

"I made a deal to marry you. Not to be raped by you."

He cocks his head. "What the fuck do you think marriage is, Savvy? We're going to fuck."

"Yeah. After we're married. This wasn't part of the deal, Miles."

Will he buy it?

Probably not, but at least I've got a moment's reprieve.

An extra moment to try to figure out how to get out of this mess.

A moment ago I wasn't regretting this decision, but now?

The idea of anyone inside me other than Falcon Bellamy has me ready to hurl. My belly cramps—an intense pain, like a knife slicing into my stomach.

Acid rises in my throat, but I swallow it down.

Big mistake, because rhythmic contractions start in my gut and diaphragm.

The salmon, the salad, the—

All of it.

All of it's coming.

Then it explodes with projectile force out of my mouth and right into Miles's face.

I retch once, twice, three times until Miles, the bed, and I are all covered in puke.

"My God!" Miles spits the vomit from his mouth. "Fucking disgusting. Jesus!"

He scrambles off the bed and into my bathroom. I hear the whoosh of the faucet on the sink.

The acrid scent of puke erupts around me. I wrinkle my nose, feel nauseated again, but then I inhale once more.

Still disgusting, but in a way it's sweeter than a rose in bloom because it got Miles McAllister off of me.

I've no doubt he'll be back because for some reason he needs to marry me.

Some reason I need to figure out.

But it's not going to happen tonight.

My green silk nightgown is covered in barf. I get off the bed, pull off the comforter.

It looks like it didn't seep through to the sheets, so that's good.

I'm not sure what to do, because I won't be able to open my door to get the comforter out of here. Still, the stench will overwhelm me eventually, so I need to at least get it as far away from me as possible. I drag the soiled comforter out of the bedroom and through the sitting area to the door and—

I gasp.

The door is cracked, but only slightly. No sliver of light from the hallway is visible. Only about an inch of the wood is visible, with no actual crack where I can pull it open.

He really fucking didn't make sure the door was closed and locked? Anyone could have walked in on him raping me?

Maybe that's it. Maybe he *wanted* someone to walk in on us. Just the chance of being caught would have added an extra layer of thrill to this sicko. Any unwitting servant who accidentally walked in would catch an eyeful of him dominating his woman, his rightfully won conquest.

Jesus.

Could I open it the rest of the way? There's no doorknob on this side—only a brass plate with a keyhole.

The water is still running in the bathroom, and then I hear Miles turn on the shower.

He'll clean himself up and then no doubt come back for me and throw me in so I'll be clean when he finishes what he started.

I have to be gone by then.

I leave the comforter in a heap on the floor and try to

figure out how to get the door open without making it close back on itself and click the lock into place.

I glance around the room at the books, the desk, the tables, the couches.

Nothing.

I've already gone through all the drawers. There's nothing in this room that I can use as some kind of lever to pry it open. I'm going to have to just hope that I can get enough of a grip with my fingers to pull the door back enough to open it and get out.

I try and—

"Damn!" I say out loud, and then cover my mouth.

Sure enough, all I did was loosen it enough and then lose my grip so the door closed back on itself, the lock clicking in place.

Tears spring in the bottom of my eyes. My one shot, and I blew it.

I draw in a breath, sniffle, and force the tears back.

There's got to be another way. All I have to do is find it.

I can't give up. Falcon never gave up in prison, and I won't give up now.

I swallow down nausea as it creeps back up on me.

I feel like I need to throw up again, but there can't possibly be anything left in my stomach. Not after everything that spewed all over Miles.

I can't help a slight smile at that thought.

Miles covered in puke. My puke. That's how he'll always think of me from now on... Even if I don't escape, I'll always have that.

Of course, that might just make him more pissed, which doesn't bode well for me. My smile fades.

Damn it, Savannah. Think!

Ugh. All I can think of is Miles, who will be coming out of the shower at any moment—

I drop my mouth open. Miles! Of course!

He has to be able to get out of here. He has a key. Where are his clothes?

I sneak back into the bedroom. The bathroom door is open, but he can't see me from the shower. At least I hope he can't. The shower door glass is frosted, right now it looks like his head is down and he's washing his hair.

Still, I'm as careful as I can when I find his pants. I shake as I go through the pockets. First I find his wallet. Good thing to have. Then, in another pocket, his phone and a key chain with a few keys on it. I grab the keys and hurry back to the door.

I turn back and snatch his phone as well. Don't want to make it easy for Miles to call for help once he realizes I've escaped.

I run back to the door and shakily lift the keys to the lock.

First key doesn't work.

Fuck.

Second key—

Yes!

The lock disengages, and because I've got the key in the lock, I'm able to pull the door open. I turn the key again, locking the mechanism, and then close it from the outside, locking Miles in. I have his key, and there's no keyless entry on this door. I suppose they couldn't take the chance that I'd guess the code. After all, what more is there to do in a room than go through every permutation? I'd eventually get it after days and days of doing the same thing.

I look down at my vomit-stained nightie. Why didn't I think to change my clothes? Why didn't I think to grab my purse?

Because all I could think of was escaping. There's nothing in my purse to help me anyway. They took my wallet and my phone.

At least I have Miles's wallet and whatever's inside plus his keys and phone. I don't have time to look through it now. Miles won't be able to get out of the room, but he'll be able to use the intercom and get someone to let him out quickly.

I need to get out of this house. But first things first. I need to find something to wear, or at least to cover my nightie.

I walk quickly through the hallway, and once I'm away from my door, I no longer hear the shower running. In fact, I hear nothing.

Is that good or bad?

I have no idea, and I can't take the time to ruminate on it. I need to find something to—

I jerk at a sound coming from down the hallway.

I grab the first doorknob and I say a silent thank you to the universe when it opens.

I slip inside.

It's dark. Probably another guest room like the one where they were keeping me. Will I find clothes in the closet?

Once my eyes adjust, I look quickly at the door. It's the same. No knob. No way to lock it or unlock it from the inside without a key.

I can't think too much about that. Most likely there will be bars on the windows, just as there were in my room. At least I can hide here for a moment and check the closet.

I walk through the sitting area to the bedroom, not daring

to turn on the light. The bed is empty, thank God. I open the closet door and—

Nothing.

Fucking nothing.

I don't dare speak. What if someone monitors these rooms? What if the intercom is on?

Holy shit, what if there's a camera?

I slide along the edges of the room until I'm back to the door. I draw in a deep breath, not even caring that I smell like puke.

I need to get out of here soon, so no more looking for clothes. It's this nightie, puke and all, or nothing.

And it sure as hell won't be nothing.

I swallow, gather my courage, and—

Fuck, fuck, fuck!

The door is closed, and with no knob, I can't open it, even though it's not locked.

Maybe I can use Miles's phone. I grab it.

It's locked. Of course. With an eight-digit code.

I can still make a call to one of his emergency contacts. Of course, they're all going to be family.

And I can't call 911. Any cop who ended up coming to my rescue would surely be one who's been bought by the McAllisters. Plus their sirens would alert all of the family members and servants that something is up.

Damn it!

I throw the phone across the room.

I shake my head, my heart falling to my gut. I lean into the wall on the left side of the door and slide down into a sitting position, burying my head in my hands.

I'll be punished for this.

I told Miles I'd come with him willingly, and the first chance I got, I tried to make a run for it.

They'll find me soon, and God only knows what they'll do to me.

I sit in the crouched position, my stomach empty, my hair a mess, my nightie caked with dried vomit.

And I accept my fate.

3

FALCON

Still walking in the shadows, Leif and I case the mansion. We pace all the way around, looking at each point of entry as Leif assesses it.

We don't encounter any hounds, but Leif throws a piece of the tainted beef jerky every couple of steps to ward off any who might show up.

"I think this one," Leif says when we find a door.

"Why this one?"

"It appears to be a door to the servants' entrance. It's far less grand than the main entrance, and off to the side. The McAllisters wouldn't want any of their distinguished guests to enter through here. We'll be less likely to run into anyone we can't buy off."

"Christ," I say under my breath.

"Hey," he says. "None of that shit. We're going to get through this." He pats me on the shoulder. "We're going to get your lady back, man. The Phoenix always rises."

I hope to God he's right.

I sure as hell don't want to go back to the slammer, but I'll do it if it means saving Savannah.

Leif messes with his lockpick, and within a few seconds, the door is open.

I'm expecting a couple Dobermans to lunge out and go for our throats, but they don't, thank God.

"All right," Leif says. "No talking at this point. Not even a whisper."

"How do we communicate then?"

"With our hands."

Yeah, right. That's not going to work, but I don't want to be the one to tell Leif.

We walk in and are greeted with the hallway and two staircases, one going down and one going up. The servants' quarters are clearly not as elegant as the main part of the mansion. The entryway is small and dimly lit. The floor beneath our feet is weathered and scuffed linoleum and the walls are plain and painted in muted, peeling colors. It's an area of functionality rather than beauty, a stark reminder of the social hierarchy within the mansion.

I raise my eyebrows at Leif. This place obviously has a first floor, but we can't access it from here.

"If they've got her here," Leif says. "She's either in the basement or on the second floor. She's definitely not on the first floor."

"Thought you said no talking," I say.

"I did. But we need to figure out where to look first."

"Is she a prisoner?"

"I don't know. You know more about these people than I do."

I look at the floor. "Except I don't, man. I don't know shit about the Texas Mafia. I didn't even know there *was* a Texas Mafia."

"They came for her," Leif says. "They came to your house, with guns, for her. So yeah, I'd say she's a prisoner, but probably not the kind of prisoner they keep in the basement."

I say no more, because I know exactly what he means. She is definitely a prisoner, but her chains will be invisible. Invisible bindings of husband and wife.

Over my fucking dead body.

"Second floor," I say, my teeth gritted.

He nods. "I agree."

We stealthily walk up the stairs.

It's dark outside, but not that late yet. Servants are probably going to be wandering these hallways, so we have to be ready.

I run my hands over the gun in my waistband. I can fire any piece, but I prefer to be dealing with a gun that I know. I've never fired this one.

Still, if I have to, I'll do it. For Savannah.

I'll gladly go back to hell to free her.

She's come to mean so much to me in such a short time. I love her. She's the other half of my soul.

We reach the top of the stairs. Leif looks around. It's a hallway, with doors speckled on each side. Servants' quarters, no doubt.

They wouldn't be keeping Savannah here. She's a prize and would be kept in the highest luxury. This is just a way for us to get into the house.

We walk through the hallway and get into the main wing. It is as plain as the entryway. Simple overhead light fixtures flicker throughout, and the air has a sterile tinge to it.

I peek into one of the rooms. It is furnished with simple wooden tables and chairs, unadorned dressers, and beds with simple white linens. The walls are scuffed.

As we continue, we come across an empty communal area with a plain dining table and a few chairs. On the other side of the room is a door, this one in a dark cherry, much grander than those of the servants.

That must be how to get into the main part of the house.

That's where we'll find Savannah.

If she's even here.

And if she's not? It will be my fault. I'm the one who told Leif to start here, at the senior McAllister's house.

Why does the McAllister family want her so badly?

There's got to be a reason. Maybe Savannah herself knows. After all, she kept her family history from me when we first met.

I don't fault her for that, though. Neither of us expected to fall so hard and so quick.

But she's going to have to level with me about it. That's the only way I'll be able to help her.

We managed to get through the hallway without encountering any wayward servants. The day servants are probably in their rooms already, and the night servants are in the other wing of the house.

Which means we will probably encounter them there.

Fuck it all.

Leif grips the doorknob on the large cherry door with his gloved hand.

And he looks as surprised as I am when he finds that it's unlocked.

He raises his eyebrows at me, and I do the same.

But at this point, no talking. We both know we're going to encounter people behind this door.

He cracks it open just a bit.

This is *my* woman we're going after, and I feel like I should be taking the lead. But Leif and I both know he's better equipped to do this job. If we end up behind the slammer, I'll take the lead there.

Walking into this mansion hallway is like walking from steerage up to first class on the Titanic.

Plush carpeting under our feet instead of cold tile, which actually works in our favor, as it's easier to disguise our footsteps.

White and gold wallpaper, as opposed to flat gray paint on the walls.

And the doors are solid wood and ornate, with brass fixtures.

Where to look?

It doesn't escape my thoughts that we could very well be on a wild goose chase.

It's possible she's not here at all.

It's possible she's on a plane on her way out of the country.

In which case? Leif and I are both going to prison if we get caught.

Leif begins checking each door.

First one is locked. Second one too. Third one—

Thud thud thud. "Let me out of here!"

I cock my head.

Leif simply nods at me, turns to the door. "Mr. McAllister?" he says, disguising his voice so it's a bit higher than normal.

"Yes, it's me, damn it. The bitch locked me in and the intercom isn't working."

I raise my eyebrows.

Leif smiles. Ah...so the intercom is down because it's part of the system that Leif dismantled. Nice.

"Get me out of here, damn it. Open this door!"

"Right away," Leif says. "Give me just a minute, sir, to find the right key."

I look around hesitantly. If there's anybody else in any of these rooms, surely they can hear him.

Or perhaps not. I would imagine most of these rooms are soundproofed.

Bitch locked me in.

Savannah.

He'll pay for calling her a bitch.

But if he is talking about Savannah, that mean she's escaped.

Thank God.

Whoever is behind that door finally stops pounding on it, obviously thinking we're going to find someone to let him out.

We only have about five minutes before he starts pounding again.

"We need to hurry," Leif whispers softly.

I nod.

4

SAVANNAH

My heart thumps wildly, and I try to bring back a memory of a happier time. Something to get me through this.

And I think of it.

A time with my mother—before I knew who our family really was.

Late spring. Mama always said it was her favorite time of the year. I liked the fall, when the leaves changed colors and then fell to the ground. When the breeze got cooler and I wore a scarf around my neck to stay warm.

But for Mama, it was spring.

One time, because we were the only girls in the family, we went on a picnic. Mama took me to a meadow, where flowers were just beginning to bloom and the grass was a lush green. A tiny stream flowed through the meadow and the waters were so clear I could actually see my reflection in it, kind of like a mirror, except it was blurry and changed a lot because the waters were moving.

It was a warm enough day that Mama let me take off my shoes, and I walked in the soft grass and looked up at the sun. It wasn't a hot summer day, just a warm day. The sun felt like it was giving me kisses on my face. The warm spring breeze made the trees rustle.

Mama spread out a checkered picnic blanket, and inside the basket were sandwiches, fruit, and homemade chocolate chip cookies.

We had a maid and a cook, and Cook usually made our food, but Mama made all of this herself. I watched her prepare it this morning. Even the cookies.

I breathed in, and I could smell the outdoors. The wildflowers, the grass, all mingling with the chocolate chip cookies, which smelled best of all.

Mama filled a plate for me. A peanut butter sandwich on sourdough bread, which was my favorite. Apple and orange slices, and because it was a special occasion, she gave me potato chips as well. Mama didn't allow much junk food in the house, but every so often we could have things like potato chips and pretzels and popcorn.

Then we sat together on the picnic blanket, and once I had eaten everything she gave me, I got a chocolate chip cookie.

Mama patted me on the shoulder. "Look, Savannah. It's a butterfly."

Sure enough, a butterfly had landed on her checkered picnic blanket. It was an interesting butterfly—black with some purple and blue spots on it.

"Life is full of beautiful moments like this, sweetheart," Mama said. "Whenever you're feeling down, remember this day, this meadow, and how much your mama loves you."

"But Mama," I said, "I don't ever feel down. Only when I'm sick or something."

She smiled at me and pulled me onto her lap. "I know that, Savannah. You're such a special little girl. You'll find out that sometimes, when you grow up, life isn't always quite so happy. So remember this day."

~

FUNNY. I haven't thought about that in a long time. Not since I found out Michael had died.

But I think of it now.

Perhaps a sweeter memory would be a newer one—one involving how much I love Falcon—but I can't go there.

If I think of him, I'll never be able to get through the rest of my life as Miles McAllister's wife.

I'm going to have to erase all images of Falcon, all feelings of the love I have for him.

In my troubled moments—and I know there will be many —I'll go back to my mama in the meadow and our special picnic just for the girls.

That is all I'll have to uplift my spirit.

I close my eyes, bury my head again, and—

A gasp escapes my throat as I hear something.

The movement of the doorknob.

Miles has found me.

And now I'm going to be punished.

I rise, determined to accept my fate with strength and fortitude.

I will stand tall and proud, and I'll—

The door opens.

I gasp again.

The light in the hallway shines not on Miles McAllister, but on Falcon Bellamy.

The tightness in my chest loosens, and a wave of immense relief washes over me.

I let out a breath I didn't realize I was holding, and fear drains away from my body. My legs still tremble, but this time not in fear.

I run into his arms.

"Oh my God, Vannah. Baby." He kisses my forehead, my face, my cheeks, my lips.

I swallow. "I'm covered in my own vomit," I say quietly.

"Do you think I care about that?"

Another man tugs on Falcon's arm. "This is all great," he whispers, "but we need to get the fuck out of here. Someone's going to let shithead out of his room soon."

"Leif?"

"Yes, it's me." He points out the door. "We need to go."

I lean down and pick up the wallet, phone, and keys. I hand them to Falcon.

"I locked him in," I say. "And I have all these keys. And his wallet and phone."

"You're a genius, Vannah." He shoves the stuff in the pocket of his black jeans. Then he pulls off his black hoodie. "Put this on."

I nod, throwing it over my head.

"I wish I could give you something to cover your legs," he says.

"I'll be all right."

"Damned right you will."

He takes my hand, and together we follow Leif out of the room, closing the door quietly.

Thump thump thump.

"Guess he got tired of waiting," Leif says in a whisper.

We walk briskly through the hallway to a door, and then through it.

The hallway is now different. I know from my grandfather's house that we've entered the servants' wing. All of these organized crime families are the same. Live in opulence but keep the help in the unkempt wing of the house so they know their place.

The good news is we'll be safer here.

When we reach the stairs, Falcon takes me in his arms, holding me as we go down.

Then a door.

And behind it...

A barking dog.

"Damn," Leif says. "I guess this one didn't get any beef jerky."

He opens the door carefully. "Hey, boy."

The dog snarls.

"Got something you're going to like."

Leif takes some beef jerky out of his pocket. The dog takes interest, sniffing. Leif throws the beef jerky, and the dog scrambles after it.

"I don't think that's a guard dog," Leif says, "but just in case, let's get the fuck out of here quickly. They're bound to realize the system's down any time now."

Falcon is still holding me, but he puts me down. "We can probably move faster if you walk. You okay, Vannah?"

I look down at my bare feet. "I'll do my best."

"Let me know if you can't. If you need me to carry you, I will."

"I can do it, Falcon."

Inside I'm at war with myself. I should tell him to put me back. That I did this for him. That he's in danger now if I don't marry Miles.

But I can't leave him.

I absolutely can't.

I'll tell him everything, and we'll deal with the fallout. Together we can do anything.

Falcon and I follow Leif, who keeps to the shadows until we finally reach the wrought-iron gate.

Leif pushes it open. "Good," he says, "they haven't gotten the security system back online yet."

We walk past the gate, still keeping to the shadows when—

A siren blares, making my blood run cold.

"Fuck," Leif shouts over the sirens. "They figured it all out. They're going to be looking for you, young lady."

"How far is the car?" Falcon asks.

"It's about a block. We're going to have to run for it."

"Savannah isn't wearing shoes."

"Can you do it?" Leif asks me.

"I swear to God. I can do anything you need me to do."

I keep my hand in Falcon's, and I take a deep breath, ready to run my ass off.

And I do it. I run, keeping up with the two men. I step on several small jagged rocks, but I don't feel the pain. Too much adrenaline. When we finally reach the car, I look down at my feet. They're covered in small cuts and a lot of dirt, but I'll live.

Leif unlocks the car and I launch myself into the back seat.

Leif gets us the hell out of there, the tires screeching.

"How much time do you think we have on them?" Falcon asks Leif from the front seat.

"Not much. But they won't call the cops. They were obviously keeping someone under duress. Kidnapping and false imprisonment."

"No," I say quietly. "They weren't."

"What the hell are you talking about, Vannah?" Falcon asks.

"I went willingly, Falcon."

He turns around, glaring at me. "Why the fuck would you do that?"

"I… I made a deal. For you."

His eyes widen. "Fuck."

"I made a deal so you wouldn't be charged with Abel's murder. Miles can take care of it. I thought I'd go with him, marry him." I grab his arm and squeeze it. "I didn't want you to go back to prison."

He whips his arm out of my grasp. "Vannah, I'd go back to prison for a thousand lifetimes for you."

"But I don't want you to."

He crosses his arms. "I didn't kill the motherfucker anyway. They can't pin it on me."

I shake my head. "You don't know the kind of power these families have. They have judges in their back pockets. Cops in their back pockets. They can pin *anything* on you."

"She's probably right," Leif says.

"Then what the hell are we going to do?" Falcon says. "Because she is *not* going back to that degenerate."

"Falcon, I—"

He holds a hand up to quiet me. "Absolutely not, Vannah. You belong with me. I belong with you. And if we have to stay on the road our whole lives, so fucking be it."

A smile spreads across my face. "I don't want that for you, Falcon. But I love that you're willing."

"Are you kidding me? I have no life without you."

I look down at my puke-stained nightie and wrinkle my nose. "I'm covered in my own vomit."

"I don't care."

"It actually... It actually saved me."

"What do you mean?"

"Miles. He... He was on top of me, about to—"

"Vannah..." he says through clenched teeth.

I put my hands in front of me. "He didn't, Falcon. He didn't. I was ready for it. I had accepted my fate, but then... They fed me a meal. Salmon and some vegetables. And I didn't feel like eating, but I knew I had to. I knew I had to eat to keep up my strength, to be tough. To get through this for you. And I..."

"You puked all over him?" Leif says, laughing.

"It didn't seem so funny at the time, but yeah. I puked all over him. And he didn't get into me, Falcon."

"But he fucking touched you."

"Yeah. But he didn't kiss me. All he was going to do was fuck me. Rape me. But he didn't. I projectile vomited all over him."

Leif is laughing in the front seat.

Falcon glares at Leif. "I don't see what's so funny about this."

"Falcon, don't you see? She did what she had to do. Her

body did what it had to do. She kept him off her. This is a *good* thing."

Falcon grits his teeth. "But he had her there. He was going to take my woman."

"But he didn't," Leif says. "She didn't let them. Even if it wasn't conscious, Savannah's stomach had the tools to get her out of the situation, and it used them to its advantage. It's amazing what your body can do if you just let nature take over. Trust me. I followed my body's lead more times than I can count when I was in the Navy."

Falcon turns around again, looks at me from the front seat. "Are you okay, Savannah? Please tell me you're okay."

"I am." I press my lips together. "He scrambled off that bed so fast and into the bathroom to take a shower. And then... I tried to get out. But the door, it doesn't open from the inside. There were no doorknobs. He had left it slightly ajar, but when I tried to pull it open the rest of the way, I couldn't, and it ended up closing. But then I looked in his jeans, found his keys, and was able to open it."

"I'll be damned." Falcon pulls the stuff out of his pocket. "We have Miles McAllister's wallet. And his phone."

"We do," Leif says. "Savannah, you're one smart little lady."

"She's damned brilliant," Falcon says.

"I only did what I had to do."

"Listen to me, Vannah." Falcon glares at me. "Don't you ever put yourself in harm's way for me again. You got that? We're in this together now."

"I only thought—"

"I know what you thought, and I love you for it, baby. But you will *never* give yourself to another man. Is that clear?"

I nod. Following orders has never been my strong point, but I have no problem obeying Falcon.

I want him to be happy. And if keeping myself safe is the price for that, I'll do it.

"But what if—"

"I will *not* go down for the murder of that fucking degenerate," Falcon says. "I have sources too, you know. You don't spend eight years behind bars and not make some friends on the inside."

"But friends on the inside can't help you now, Fal." Leif says.

"You'd be surprised. A lot is going on in those prisons that the guards have no clue about. But even if they're not helpful, my father has friends too."

"They couldn't help you the first time," I remind him. "Plus, we've just made more enemies, and I'm not just talking about the McAllisters."

"Who else then?"

I close my eyes, breathe in. "My own family."

Falcon wrinkles his forehead. "What the hell are you talking about?"

"My father wants me married to Miles," I say. "I thought I had talked him out of it, gained my freedom. But I haven't. There's a reason why I have to marry Miles McAllister. And it's not just to forge an alliance between the McAllister and Bianchi families. There's something else at play here."

"What is it?" Falcon asks.

"I wish I could tell you. I don't know." I scratch the side of my head. "There's something behind this. Otherwise, Miles wouldn't have gone to such trouble to get me."

"But you gave yourself to him," Falcon says. "To secure my freedom."

"I did. That only means I went willingly. He was going to have me no matter what. He sent two gunmen to your home. He wouldn't have resorted to that unless he had to have me for a reason bigger than a simple familial alliance."

"I don't understand," he says.

"I'm afraid I don't either," Leif says.

"I'm glad you both don't. I know you've both been through your own private hell. You in prison, Falcon, and you in Afghanistan, Leif. I don't pretend to understand what either of you went through. I will never understand it, and I accept that."

"Neither of us want you understanding that, Vannah," Falcon says.

"I know that. What I'm telling you is that my family and the McAllister family... Something is brewing. I don't have a clue what it is yet, but somehow it involves me being married to Miles McAllister. They're not going to give up without a fight."

5

FALCON

At my instruction, my brother Hawk had a safe house constructed eight years ago after I went to prison.

I haven't actually seen it yet, though I was planning to go there with Savannah after Abel and Giancarlo came after her.

But we both decided we couldn't run.

Now?

With Miles McAllister after my woman?

We're going to the safe house.

Hawk gave me blueprints of it. It's not on our property. It's on adjacent ranch property, and it's made to look like an abandoned ranch hand dwelling. Seven other houses encompass the small neighborhood, all abandoned. The dwelling that serves as the safe house is marked with light orange stucco and clay shingles. It's slightly set apart from the other residences, but not so much so that anyone would take notice.

Access is completely restricted and protected by multiple layers of security. The doors are reinforced, the locks are electronic, and video surveillance shows every point of entry to the home. Entry requires a thumbprint, and only Hawk and I have access. Once inside, I can add Savannah's print to the database. Leif's too.

We arrive, and when I get us into the house, instead of a foyer, there's a security room where I can monitor every surveillance camera and control access to the house. I can also communicate with anyone outside the house through satellite technology. The room is equipped with a secure landline and encrypted communication.

We leave the security room, though, and we enter into a comfortable living area. Living room, dining room and kitchen. The living room is furnished with leather recliners and a leather sectional. There is also a flatscreen TV and a bookshelf.

The kitchen is stocked with nonperishable food items, bottled water, and cooking utensils. I texted Hawk on the way and had him stock the fridge with a few weeks' worth of fresh food as well. Bread, fruits, vegetables, lots of meat. The basics.

The garage off to the side of the kitchen, built for two cars, is another fortress of security.

Five years' worth of survival food and water take up all the space. The two electric vehicles are actually stored underground, accessed from a tunnel that connects to the main part of the garage.

The house has three bedrooms. Blackout curtains cover the windows to ensure privacy. Each bedroom is equipped with a wall safe as well, for storing important documents or sensitive materials. A large closet houses medical supplies, and the security room has access to telemedicine if necessary.

Attached to each room is its own en suite bathroom facility with a shower, toilet, and basic toiletries.

And of course, the most important thing—the house possesses a massive backup generator in case of interrupted powers or power outage. We're in Texas, after all, and keeping the house cool is necessary.

Candles, matches, everything else. It's all here.

The house has been soundproofed and has extraordinary measures to prevent any kind of eavesdropping.

The basement is an underground bunker, complete with a shooting range—including myriad firearms and other weapons—and a home gym.

Escape routes and safe exits are built in, allowing us to leave discreetly in case of emergency.

Hawk did not staff the house with security personnel, and I don't plan to either.

The fewer people who know we're here, the better.

So far, only Leif knows.

"I can't thank you enough for taking care of the dogs," I say to him once Savannah and I are securely in the house.

"Not a problem. They'll be safe and well-loved until you can come back for them."

Savannah bites her bottom lip. "I'm going to miss them so much."

"I know, baby." I touch her cheek. "But they're in good hands."

"What if someone sees you coming here?" Savannah asks. "What if..."

"No one will see me," Leif promises. "Besides, I shouldn't have to come back here. Falcon and I can communicate as necessary on secure lines, and you have everything you could possibly need to last for the next five years."

"Sammy will be all grown up by then," Savannah says, her lips in a frown.

"Vannah," I say, "listen to me. Listen good. We will *not* be here for five years. I'm hoping we won't even be here for five *days."*

She scratches her arm anxiously. "You don't understand, Falcon. I need to figure everything out. I need to figure out why my family is so adamant that I marry Miles McAllister. Why *he's* so determined to marry me. Until we know that, they will continue to come after me."

"They won't find you here," I say.

"How can you say that?" She grabs the sleeves of my shirt. "They know you and I are together. They know we're in a relationship. They already sent Abel and Giancarlo to your home."

"Which is why the safe house is not on our property."

"Who owns this property?" she asks.

"A corporation," I say. "A corporation that cannot be traced to me or anyone in my family."

"To the outside world," Leif says, "this looks like an abandoned ranch house on a small ranch surrounded by other abandoned homes."

"A ranch that has no crops or animals," Savannah says. "Isn't that a huge red flag?"

"An abandoned ranch wouldn't have any crops or animals. It's true that there's no evidence of them ever being here, but that's only something we need to worry about if they come looking," I say. "They won't, Savannah. This place is secure. Hawk made sure when he dropped off the supplies."

She swallows, her lips trembling. "I want to believe you."

"Then believe me," I say. "Because no one will come near you. Not a single person. They'll have to get through me first."

"And me," Leif adds.

"You can't be doing this," I say to him. "You're a newlywed. Your wife needs you."

Leif lays a hand on my shoulder. "My wife understands. This is you and me in a foxhole, buddy," he says. "And I won't let you down."

I grab Leif in a bear hug and we say our goodbyes.

"You know where I am if you need me."

I nod. Then Leif leaves.

I grab Savannah, crush my mouth to hers—

But she pushes me away.

"No way," she says. "I'm covered in my own vomit. I need a shower."

6

SAVANNAH

I simply stand under the water for the first few moments of my shower.

I have the water set to the hottest temperature I can stand, because I want to burn Miles McAllister off of my flesh.

I specifically asked Falcon not to join me.

This is something I need to do alone. Wash the dirtiness from me, the contamination.

I almost feel like I'm under one of those decontamination showers, the kind you use when you've been contaminated at a hazmat plant.

I grab the shower pouf, squirt gel into it, and scrub myself.

Then I scrub myself again and again and again.

My skin turns red from the heat and the scrubbing, but I don't care. I want to scrub every bit of Miles McAllister off of me.

When I'm finally done scrubbing, I scrub some more.

Then I slide down the wall, sitting on the shower floor.

Tears want to come, but they don't. Because I know my fight is far from over, and I can't let weakness take hold.

Still, I let a few tears fall.

Just a few, and then I force myself to stand, and I wash my hair.

By the time I'm finished, the shower is no longer scalding. It's merely hot. And it's time to get out.

I didn't ask how large of a water heater this place has. I didn't ask anything.

Because though I'm happy to be here—happy to be with Falcon because it's where I want to be more than any place in the world—I know what lies ahead of us.

My family and the McAllisters will not stop. They won't stop until they achieve their goal.

I need to find out why this marriage is their goal. Then I might be able to find a way to get out of it.

If only I could speak to my mother alone, but I know that can't happen.

My father will keep tabs on her.

My father.

I step out of the shower, grab a towel, wrap it around me. Then I dry my hair with another.

My father.

My father who I know loves me, whose first instinct is to protect me. It's why he let me out of this after college, and why he allowed me to leave Austin and move to Summer Creek to work as a parole officer, no longer doing the family's bidding.

But something happened between then and now.

Something to make him change his mind.

He lost both of his sons, and I know he wouldn't give up

his only daughter without what—in his mind—is a damned good reason.

Fatigue takes over then.

What time is it anyway? Sometime in the middle of the night.

Will I be able to sleep?

It's not like I have a choice. I need sleep to be able to function. For my strength. The same reason I forced myself to eat dinner earlier.

Turns out my dinner served a better purpose than I'd anticipated. It got Miles off of me and facilitated my escape.

But if Falcon and Leif hadn't come, Miles would have eventually found me huddled in that closet, still covered in my own puke. He would've forced me into a shower, probably had servants scrub me clean.

Then he would've strapped me down, probably gagged me so I wouldn't puke again.

And then he would have forced himself on me. Raped me. And he wouldn't have been gentle.

And sometime tomorrow—probably it's today already—I would've been forced into marriage.

A marriage I agreed to for Falcon.

Even now, I don't regret that decision. I assumed I would have to go to bed with Miles after the wedding, but his mother assured me he wouldn't come to me tonight.

She was so wrong.

He wasn't going to take me in love. Of course not. He doesn't love me and I don't love him.

No, he was taking me in anger. Rage.

Which means...

He doesn't want this union any more than I do.

It's our fathers...

And I need to figure out why.

"Vannah?" A soft knock as Falcon's voice comes through the door. "You okay in there?"

What a loaded question. I'm so far from okay.

But I'm a hell of a lot more okay than I would've been had Falcon and Leif not come for me.

I clear my throat. "Yeah. I'll be out in a minute."

"No rush, baby. Just checking."

I wipe the steam off of the mirror with the towel.

Small beads of condensation form on the glass instantly, but at least I can see myself. A sort of blurry image of me.

Kind of how I truly see myself right now.

I want to be with Falcon more than I want anything else, but even more than that? I want his freedom. I want him to have a good life.

If he goes back to prison...

God, I can't go there.

He said he would serve a thousand more prison sentences for me. But doesn't he understand that I don't want that for *him?* I want him to have the life he deserves.

He wasn't born into the mafia.

That's me, not him.

While I can't escape the circumstances of my birth, he can. He doesn't have to be bound by it.

Maybe one day he'll tell me what really happened that day. That day that young cop got shot, and Falcon took the heat for it.

I'm pretty sure he's protecting one of his brothers. Perhaps even one of his sisters.

I don't know. I don't know who else Falcon would go to prison to protect.

All I can think of is his family. Well, his family and me, apparently. He would gladly go back to prison to keep me out of the McAllisters' clutches.

He would definitely do anything for Raven, too. I've seen how much he loves her, how much her illness is killing him.

And now?

He doesn't even know how Raven is doing because he came after me.

He came after me when he should be with her.

I discard my towels and wrap a dry one around me, my hair falling in damp waves around my shoulders.

I leave the bathroom.

Falcon's eyes turn to fire when he looks at me. "God, Vannah. I'm not sure I've ever seen you look more beautiful."

I have to let out a short chuckle. "Falcon," I say, "we need to talk."

"We do," he agrees. "But first, I'm taking you to bed, Vannah. I need you."

I hold my hand out to stop him. "Falcon, I need you to check on Raven. See if her bloodwork came back."

His face twists in anguish. "I can't think about that right now, Savannah."

"We both have to be thinking about that. We have to remember that there are other people in this world. Not just us and our problems."

"You're more important to me than anyone," he says.

"That doesn't mean Raven isn't important to you. It doesn't mean you can just—"

He stops me with two fingers to my lips. "I adore Raven. I'm worried sick about her. But Leif will get the information, and he'll let me know as soon as he knows anything. It's the middle of the night, Savannah. We're not going to get any news right now."

I sigh. He's right, of course.

"We have a lot to talk about, both of us," he continues. "But it can all wait until morning."

"You don't understand." I pace the room. "The McAllisters won't wait until morning. Neither will my father. They'll be out looking for me. They won't stop until they find me."

He grabs my shoulders and stops me in my place. "They won't find you here, Savannah. And if they're even close, I'll find out, and we'll get you the hell out of here."

"You don't understand." I try to wiggle free, but he keeps his hands firmly planted on me.

"Perhaps I don't understand everything," he says. "I don't know exactly what your family is into. But what I *do* know is that I will move heaven and earth to keep you safe, Savannah. If it means I burn down the city, so be it."

I don't know what to say. I'm too tired to say anything, really. I've told him it's not what I want. That I want his safety above all else.

"It seems we're at an impasse then," I say. "Because you want to protect me more than anything, and I want to protect you more than anything. Falcon, those two goals are at cross purposes."

"I'm the man," he grits out. "It's my job to protect you."

I roll my eyes. "Don't go all alpha on me, Falcon. I love you for who you are. I truly do. I wouldn't change a hair on your head. And I love that you want to protect me." I close the already short distance between our two bodies. "But know this. I want to protect you just as strongly."

He tightens his grip on my shoulders to the point it almost hurts. "God damn it, Vannah. God damn it all to hell."

His mouth is on mine then, prying my lips apart.

I don't have the strength to resist him. Because I want this as much as he does. I need to lose myself in his strong body. And for just a moment, I want to let *him* be the strength.

Because I've been through the wringer tonight.

We kiss hard—hard and passionately. Minutes pass, I don't know how many.

With one hand, he wrenches the towel from my body, and it falls into a puddle on the floor.

I stand before him naked, our mouths still fused.

He's still wearing his black shirt and black pants and black boots. His hoodie is gone, of course, because he gave it to me.

Almost as quickly, he rips his mouth from mine.

"Get on the bed, Savannah."

I'm too tired to disobey him.

In fact, I don't want to disobey him. Even if I had all the energy of a steam engine, I wouldn't disobey him. I like when he gets dominant in the bedroom.

I like it a lot.

And right now? I need him. I need him inside me, cleaning the rest of Miles McAllister from my body. Because even after the scrubbing I took in the shower, I still feel tainted.

I crawl onto the bed, and I wait for him.

He sheds his clothes more slowly than I imagine, but he's still undressed within a moment.

His cock is hard and ready, and he covers me with his body.

"Listen to me, Vannah," he says, his gaze searing into mine. "I'm going to fuck you now. I'm going to fuck you hard, and I'm going to fuck you fast, because I need it."

"I need it too, Falcon. We both do, after the hell we've been through."

"When my cock is inside you, I want you to remember." He stares through my eyes directly into my soul. "Remember who you belong to. You're *mine*, Savannah Gallo. You will never be his or anyone else's. Do you understand me?"

"Falcon, I was always yours. It didn't matter what he was going to do to me, or anything else—"

He puts his hand over my mouth, clamping it shut. "Stop right there. No other man will ever touch you. Do you understand me?"

His hand covers my mouth, so I can't answer him.

I want to nod. Because I want to believe it.

But I know better.

They won't stop.

"Tell me you understand that," he says again. "You fucking tell me *now*, Vannah."

So I nod.

I nod because I want it to be true. I desperately want it to be true.

He removes his hand from my mouth.

"Good. Now say it."

"I'm yours, Falcon," I say. "No other man will ever touch me."

And as I say those words, they're more like a prayer. A prayer to God and the universe and everything almighty.

I cast a spell into the heavens.

Please...

Please don't let any other man touch me except Falcon Bellamy.

Then he thrusts his cock into me.

"Feel this?" he says, his teeth gritted. "This is me taking you, Savannah. This is me making you mine. Only mine. No other cock will ever get inside this pussy. No other cock will be inside your ass. No other cock will be in your mouth. Or anywhere near you. You belong to me. This pussy is mine."

I let out a soft moan.

"Say it, Vannah." He thrusts, thrusts, thrusts. "Say it. Say this pussy is mine."

"Yours," I say, my breath coming rapidly. "My pussy is yours, Falcon. Only yours."

"Damned right it is."

Thrust, thrust, thrust...

"Always mine, Savannah Gallo. You were made for me. Created in the heavens above just for me. It's clear emotionally and spiritually, and it sure as hell is clear physically."

Thrust, thrust, thrust...

I writhe against his ministrations, arching my back, lifting my hips, trying to get him farther and farther into me.

I want him branded on me.

Not only on my heart, but on my soul.

I want to be his. I want any other man who looks at me to know I'm his.

God, if only that were possible...

He thrusts and thrusts and thrusts, and though I'm exhausted, and also hungry, and also completely drained, each time his pelvic bone hits my clit, a match is struck.

Ignition is started.

And when he thrusts deeply, something inside me implodes.

The climax is different this time, less intense, yet in a different way from before. It's an emotional climax. And with that, I vow to never let another man touch me.

No matter what I have to do.

7

FALCON

I release everything into Savannah.

Everything I have to offer her. My fortune, my love, my life.

Because I would give up my life in a moment for her.

I stay deeply embedded inside her for a moment, relishing her tightness and my climax.

A moment later, I roll off of her, onto my side, so that I'm looking at her.

"Open your eyes, Savannah."

She obeys me and rolls onto her side so we're facing each other.

"Understand this," I say, my voice as serious as I can get it. "You belong to me, and no other man. Tell me you understand."

"Falcon, we've been through this."

"Yes, and you said it. But you were in the heat of passion. I said what I did also in the heat of passion. But I want you to say it to me now, now that we've both climaxed. Tell me that you understand. That no other man will ever touch you."

"That's what I want more than anything," she says.

"It's what I want more than anything too, but that's not what I said."

"Falcon, I—"

"Tell me now, Savannah. You will not go running off to Miles McAllister thinking you're making my life better. Because you won't be. You won't be making my life better if you're with another man."

"But if it means you don't go to prison…"

"Savannah."

"No, Falcon." She flips over, turning her naked back to me. "You're not being fair. I love you. I love you just as much as you love me. Believe that."

I roll her back over so she's facing me again. "I do believe that."

"Then understand that I can't have a life without you anymore than you can have one without me."

"If you're with Miles McAllister, what good does it do to keep me out of prison?"

"It makes your life better."

"My life will never be better if I can't have you." I grip her arms firmly. "If I have to spend every moment thinking about you in someone else's arms, in someone else's bed. I'd rather be in prison than have that."

She gulps then, audibly. "All right. I understand. But I can't bear the thought of you back in that prison."

"Trust me, Savannah, it's not what I want either." I take her face in my hands. "But do *not* give yourself to another man thinking you're helping me. Because you're not."

She nods, and in her eyes I see the truth. She believes me.

"But Falcon," she says, "they will *not* stop. The McAllisters will come back. They will search all over until they find me."

"How can you possibly be that important to them?"

She bites her lip. "I wish I knew. Something's going on that you and I don't know about. And until we figure it out and put an end to it, they will not stop. They will not rest until I am married to Miles."

"I don't understand."

"I know you don't, Falcon. I don't understand a lot of it myself, but I do know that they would not be pushing this if it weren't necessary. At least necessary as far as they believe."

"I can have Leif look into this. He's a great PI. He investigates for the Wolfe family in New York."

"No, Falcon. Please. It's enough that he's taking care of our dogs while we're here. Please don't ask him to do anything else. He and Kelly are still newlyweds. They need to have their time together."

"There's no one else I trust, Vannah."

"What about your brothers?"

"I trust Hawk," I say.

"Not Eagle?"

I shake my head vigorously. "Eagle's a loaded pistol. I love him. But no, I do not trust him."

"Hawk then."

"Hawk isn't a detective, Savannah. Leif is the best at what he does."

"All right."

I pause and scratch my chin. "Actually, there is someone else."

"Who?"

"Lance at the tattoo shop. He's a hacker. His skills are different from Leif's, but he might be able to help."

"Why not him then?"

"Because I don't want anyone else to know we're here. Why we're here. What good does it do to be hiding in plain sight if you tell people you're here?"

"Then I don't know what to do," she says. "You need someone who can find out what's going on with my family and the McAllisters. Why they need Miles and me together."

"It can't be you," I say.

"Funny that you say that, because I was just going to suggest me."

"Yeah, that's not happening."

"It has to be someone who can get into my home, who can look through my dad's documents."

"And there's no one else?"

She bites her lip.

"Who, Savannah? Who can do it?"

"There's one person, but I don't know how to get in touch with him. I haven't heard from him in a while. I don't even know where he is."

Jealousy erupts in my gut. "He?"

"It's not what you think. I'm talking about my brother Vinnie."

"Perfect," I say. "You don't want Leif involved in this, but this is something he can do from the safety of his own home. He can find your brother."

"No one knows where my brother is," she says. "Don't you think my family has tried to find him?"

"Are you sure he's still alive?"

Her eyes close, and when she opens them, a lone tear falls out of one.

I gently wipe the tear from her cheek. "I'm sorry, Savannah."

"It's something that's crossed my mind more than once," I say. "But I do truly believe he's alive. I think we would know if he'd died. I'm sure he's put something in place so that we'd be notified. Or at least that *I* would be notified."

"But you're not sure?"

"He's my big brother, Falcon. He's always held a special place in his heart for me. When he left the family, he and I had a talk. He told me that even though he wouldn't be here, he would always be in my heart and I'd be in his. That it killed him most to leave me."

"Were you close to your other brother?"

"Not quite as close, though Michael and I were closer in age. But Michael's gone, after he married Miles's cousin. So it makes me wonder..."

"Makes you wonder what?"

"I always assume the McAllisters had something to do with Michael's death. But I think maybe I was wrong."

"Why would you think that? Why would they have Miles's cousin's husband killed?"

"Because that's the way it works sometimes in these families. They don't care whose spouse they're knocking off. To them it's just business. But because they're coming so hard after me, it makes me think Michael was the key, and someone else had him offed."

"I'm sorry this is so hard for you to talk about."

She closes her eyes, takes a deep breath in, and then exhales slowly. "He was my brother. I loved him. And yes, it's hard to talk about, but I think I have to. We need to figure out —" Her stomach lets out a growl.

"Hungry?"

"Yes, I am. I threw up my whole dinner. So now my stomach's a void."

"Come on. Let's go to the kitchen. I could eat as well." I rise from the bed, go to the closet, and find bathrobes for Savannah and me. I hand one to her. "Come on. Put this on."

"Is it okay to have the lights on?" she asks.

"Yeah. No one can see the lights from the outside. The windows are lightproof and soundproof."

"You guys really thought of everything."

"Hawk did." I frown. "God, I hate to bring him into this."

"If Leif can find Vinnie, maybe we won't have to," she says.

But already I know.

I'm bringing Hawk in.

He's the most like me, and he'll be able to help.

When we get to the kitchen, I open the refrigerator. It's full of fresh produce, so that's what we'll eat first. The freezer is full of meat. "I've got bread and deli meat," I say. "Sandwiches?"

"Sounds perfect."

"Good, because we have to eat all the stuff in the refrigerator before it spoils. After that, unless we can get someone to bring us fresh food, we'll be getting into the survival food."

"Survival food?"

"Freeze dried stuff. The kind you take when you go camping."

"I've never been camping."

"Really? Well then, Savannah, when we get out of this, I'm taking you camping."

"You eat freeze-dried food? You don't live off the land?"

"Oh, we do. But you always have to have a backup plan. Sometimes the hunting and fishing is bad. You have to have backup so you don't starve."

"Why don't you just go home when the hunting and fishing is bad?" she asks.

I let out a chuckle. "You really don't get camping."

"How could I? I just told you I've never been."

I pull out the loaf of bread and some deli meats and cheese. I grab some mustard, mayonnaise, lettuce, and tomato.

"Here, let me help." Savannah takes the tomato from me. "You know where anything is?"

"Nope. We'll just have to search, but the kitchen should be fully stocked with everything we could need."

She begins opening and closing cupboards and drawers until she finds a cutting board. "Voilà." Next she searches and finds a knife, and then slices the tomato and pulls leaves off the head of lettuce.

I go through the cupboards until I find plates. Soon, we each have a sandwich ready. I grab two bottles of water out of the fridge.

"Is there any booze here?" she asks.

"I don't think Hawk would've left bourbon out."

"I could sure use a drink," she says.

"I could too, Vannah, but it's the middle of the night. Let's eat our sandwiches, and then let's try to get some sleep."

"Yeah, you're right." She takes a plate and sits down at the small table in the kitchen. She opens her water and takes a drink.

I take a bite of my sandwich.

The meat is a peppery turkey breast. Pretty good, but certainly not gourmet fair. Hell of a lot better than the food in prison, for sure.

We finish our sandwiches quickly.

"You sure you should have eaten so quickly?" I ask.

"Yes, I'm fine. Trust me, that nausea and vomiting was because Miles was making me sick." She rubs her stomach gently. "Literally sick."

I caress her cheek. "God, Savannah. I'm so sorry about all of this."

She looks up at me and her eyes light up. "Falcon, you came for me."

I take my hand away from her and scowl. "But he had his hands on you."

"He did, but his cock never got inside me. And that's thanks to you."

"I think that's thanks to you and your throwing up."

"Yeah, but he eventually would've found me. And he would've finished what he started."

Just the thought of that makes my hands curl into fists.

She covers one of my fists with her hand. "Easy. It's over. It didn't happen."

"And it never will," I say, my jaw clenched.

I'm still not sure she believes me, but that's okay. I know the truth.

Because if that degenerate ever comes near my woman again?

I will kill him with my bare hands.

8

SAVANNAH

I take our dishes and put them in the dishwasher.

"Do you want anything else?" Falcon asks. "There are some apples in the fridge."

"No, I'm good." A yawn splits my face. "Maybe we should just go to bed." Then I look around. "I feel so naked without my purse and my phone. Miles has everything. He has my ID, for God's sake."

"But you have *his*. Maybe you can make some use out of it. His phone won't do you any good, though. And even if you had yours, your regular phone wouldn't work here anyway. Signals can't get here, so we use satellite."

I nod, yawning again.

"Let's go to bed," Falcon says.

"Okay."

He doesn't have to ask me twice. I'm exhausted. Now that my stomach is full, all I can think about is a soft bed and Falcon's shoulder.

HILLS AND VALLEYS...

The meadow with my mama. Our picnic together, mother-daughter style.

My room, my own bed, my stuffed dog that I affectionately call Puppy.

I look for a safe space, but I can't find one.

Because of my brother—the only brother I have left since Vinnie left.

Michael.

My Mikey is dead.

Shot in his own home.

Michael, who played by the rules. Who stayed and did his duty to his family. Who married Miles McAllister's cousin Elizabeth.

Sadness sweeps through me—sadness laced with anger.

Laced with regret.

Because I know what's going to happen now.

They're going to want me.

I push that to the back of my mind, because right now I need to mourn my brother.

There was a time when I was a little girl when I knew neither of my brothers would ever leave me.

Especially Vinnie. Big brother to both Michael and me. The perfect older brother—he protected us without fail whenever we needed him.

But then he left.

Never to be seen or heard from again, so I turned to Michael. Mikey, my rock. My big brother.

"I want to see him," I said to my father.

"No, Savannah. Absolutely not."

My father's ice cold. His face is frozen. No expression at all. This demeanor... As if all feelings and emotion have left him.

His son is dead, for God's sake.

His fucking son is gone, and he's a damned ice man.

My mother is weeping.

As any mother would.

I always thought I wanted to have children. Ever since I was a little girl and played with dolls, mothering them—feeding them, diapering them, rocking them to sleep.

I wanted to have my own real live baby doll.

Now, as I watch my mother mourning her son, her baby doll, I rethink that.

It nearly killed her when Vincent left, but at least we know he's alive. Or we can at least imagine that he is.

But Michael?

Michael is undeniably gone. His heart no longer beats. He's dead.

The D word.

No mother should ever have to refer to her child with that word.

I won't have children.

I won't bring them into this world.

Then it occurs to me.

If they force me into marriage? I may not have a damned choice.

"I want to see him," I say again.

"Savannah, I said no." My father's voice is still icy.

"You should at least let Mama see him."

"I will not. Why would I want to put her through that?"

"Because maybe she won't believe you. Maybe she won't believe you unless she sees him with her own eyes."

My father's hand comes out then, and he strikes me across my cheek.

I drop my jaw, my hand going to my stinging cheek. I can feel it turning red now.

This is my father. A man who has never laid a hand on me my entire life.

"I'm sorry I had to do that," he says, "but you gave me no choice, Savannah."

"There's always a choice, Daddy," I say. "There's always a choice."

I've heard those words from somewhere, but at the moment I can't remember where. Perhaps I read them in a book, heard them on a TV show or movie. Maybe in a class.

But they ring in my mind now.

There's always a choice.

So I make a choice now.

I choose not to get entangled in this mess. Not to bring children into this family.

My father doesn't reply to my words. Just gives me his icy stare.

My father, Vincent Gallo Senior.

My father, who was forced into marriage to my mother. Not to join a family. The Gallo family, as I understand it, is nothing compared to the Bianchi family.

But Caroline Bianchi, my mother, needed a husband who would be loyal to the Bianchis. They found that in my father.

My father does whatever my grandfather tells him. He's a good lackey, and a strong man in his own right.

No weakness there.

But I see him now as my grandfather must see him.

He just struck his only daughter. For the crime of asking to see her dead brother.

I see my father in a different light now.

I'm still his little girl, and in a way, I still have him wrapped around my little finger.

But here, it's family first. And by family I mean the business of family, not individual family members.

I will be watching my back.

Every step of the way.

When my father finally goes into his office to deal with the fallout, I go to my mother, sit in her lap like I did when I was a little girl, nuzzle her shoulder.

And we cry together.

I WAKE UP, tears in my eyes.

I was dreaming, but I can't remember what about, until it hits me like a brick.

My brother's death. The change I saw in my father that day.

What I fear I may see in my father now.

He'll do more than slap my face this time.

In his way, I believe my father loves me. Loves all his children for that matter.

But when you're born into this kind of family—and this kind of business—you learn that it's *all* business. Family is business. Nothing is personal anymore.

Vinnie is gone, and Michael is dead. I'm all that's left to bind these two families.

But I'm not sure why it's so important.

Does it have something to do with Michael's death?

I wasn't told any of the details—if any of the details are even known.

That's how it is in these kinds of families. Women are treated as second-class citizens. As chattel to barter with, to use as pawns when necessary. But they're never told why. They're never told anything.

Even in the twenty-first century, it still happens.

I think of that day when I was locked in a room by my own father. Unable to escape as he and the McAllisters negotiated for me.

Somehow, that time, I got through to him. He got me out of it then and set me up to help the family as a parole officer in Austin. Five years later, I thought they had finally let me out.

But no.

It was a temporary reprieve at most.

And my father fucking knew it the entire time.

I reach toward the nightstand to find a tissue to wipe my eyes and sniffling nose, but there's nothing there.

Seriously? No tissues? They must be here somewhere.

In the meantime, I scramble out of bed, head to the bathroom, and use toilet paper to wipe my face, blow my nose.

"Vannah?" Falcon's voice.

I leave the bathroom. "I'm here."

"You okay?"

I rub my eyes, hoping he won't know I was crying. "Yeah. Just a bad dream."

"About what?"

"My brother's death. The day I started to see my father for who he truly is."

"Come here."

I crawl into his arms. "I'm all right."

"You've been through so much. Almost being raped by that piece of shit."

"Thank God for puke." I force out a chuckle.

He takes my face in his hands. "I don't want you to worry about him anymore, Vannah. You're *my* responsibility now."

I pull away from him then. "I don't want to be your responsibility."

He furrows his brow. "What the hell do you mean by that?"

"I don't mean anything bad. I just don't want to be *anyone's* responsibility." I look away from him. "I'm tired of being treated like a thing."

"I would never treat you that way."

"I know that. I know you wouldn't on purpose, anyway. But for God's sake, I can't be your responsibility or anyone else's. I have to be responsible for myself."

He chuckles then.

"I don't see what's so funny about that."

"You don't want to be *my* responsibility," he says, "but what did you do? You made a deal with the devil himself to keep me out of prison. You made me *your* responsibility, Savannah. And I don't want to be *your* responsibility either."

I draw in a breath, and then I smile. "You're right."

"Damned right I'm right." He draws me closer and puts an arm around my waist. "But I'll never stop protecting you."

"Then I'll never stop protecting *you*. If we love each other, Falcon, we have equal responsibility to each other."

"But I'm the—" He stops abruptly.

"You're the what? You're the man? Well, here's news for you. I'm the *woman*."

He smiles again. "Yes, you certainly are."

He comes closer to me, brings his lips to mine, but I push him back.

"I'm serious. I understand the differences between men and women. Men, in general, are physically stronger. Women, in general, have to watch their backs. But I grew up in a family where women were devalued. Used as pawns in a dangerous and vicious game. I made a choice a long time ago —when my brother died—that I wouldn't play that game anymore. Of course, they forced me into it anyway."

"No one will force you into anything anymore, not while I'm alive and breathing."

I bite on my lower lip.

He doesn't understand my family, and he never will.

"I wish I could explain this to you," I say. "But they won't think twice about eliminating you if you stand in the way of getting what they want."

Then he chuckles again. "Savannah, I may not know the ways of families like yours. I may not know the ways of organized crime. But I know the ways of life in prison. And I'm pretty sure it's not all that different."

I widen my eyes at him.

"You think I didn't see people being used as pawns? I nearly took a guy out just to save the poor guy he was keeping as his bitch." His face darkens. "I had to fight my way to the top, Savannah. And trust me, it was far from pretty."

"Yeah? I get it, and I'm so sorry you had to go through all of that, Falcon." I place my head against his chest, feeling his heartbeat. "But there were no guns in prison."

"There were shivs. I got several more years tacked onto my sentence because I used a shiv when I needed to."

"I know, but—"

He puts his fingers over my lips to quiet me. "Let's just agree to disagree. I don't know everything about how your family works, and you don't know everything about how prison works." He looks upward. "God knows, I hope you never do. But my guess is that they're more similar than you think."

I don't try to fight back, because frankly, he's right.

"The women in your family are prisoners," he says.

"You're right," I say. "We are. The difference is that we can't fight our way to the top like you did."

"Maybe you can."

I widen my eyes, staring at him. "Falcon, with all due respect, we can't."

"What if you could, though? What if you could buy your own freedom?"

"What are you getting at?"

"You say there's a reason they need you so badly. And it's for more than a simple alliance."

"Yes. It must be."

"Do you think Miles McAllister is in love with you?"

"Absolutely not. He doesn't want me any more than I want him."

Falcon draws in a breath. "Something sinister is at work here."

"You think?" I say sarcastically.

"No. I don't mean it in the way you mean." He strokes his chin. "When I was in prison, Vannah, I learned to sniff out the true evil. Then I learned to watch my back and stay the fuck away from it as much as I could. When I was in that house, rescuing you with Leif, I had this feeling the entire time. That pecking at the back of your neck that you can't quite describe, but you know is there. That sixth sense that tries to warn you of something. Some kind of impending danger."

"Well," I say. "You broke into a mobster's home. Of course there was danger. For the life of me, I don't know how the hell you got all three of us out of there safely."

"That's not what I'm talking about, Savannah. In prison, there was always impending danger. Everyone was a threat, and not just the other inmates. The guards. More than one of them looked at me with lust in their eyes."

"Oh my God, Falcon..."

"No, it never happened. Because at that point, I had figured out how to determine someone's intentions at just a glance. The tenseness in their bodies, the coldness in their eyes. They didn't have to say a word to make it clear what their intentions were. I figured out what they were after, and then I made it clear that any such advances would not be tolerated. You see, Vannah, when you're in prison, you feel like you have nothing left to lose. So I would've let them kill me before I let them fuck me."

"And the guards knew that?"

"They knew. In their way. They stayed away from me because they knew I would fight back. Even in the end, if they'd gotten what they wanted from me, they'd have paid dearly for it. They all knew that." He saddens then, his eyes going somewhere else.

"Falcon?"

"But I couldn't always protect my men."

"I'm so sorry."

"I did what I could. If any other inmate messed with one of mine, he paid for it. But not everyone else in the prison had my gift for reading other people. I think it's something you're born with, something that can't be taught. So I never made any effort to teach any of the other inmates on my cell-block how to detect danger before it gets to you. I didn't think I would have to, anyway. If some sinister-looking fucker made his way into the prison, I made sure to put him in his place as quickly as I could." He casts his gaze to the ground. "The guards were another story. There wasn't any way I could make them pay. So I taught my men as best as I could to deal with it the way I did. To make sure the guards knew, in no uncertain terms, that they wouldn't go quietly."

"But they weren't all you."

"No, they weren't. They didn't all have my strength and determination, and they sure as hell didn't have my instinct."

"What exactly are you getting to, Falcon?"

"I'm getting to this." He looks deep into my eyes. "You and I both agree that there's something larger at work with your family and the McAllisters, and you need to be able to protect yourself. I don't know if you can learn how to detect danger on instinct alone, but I'm going to teach you what I taught those men. When danger *does* rear its ugly head, you're going to know how to *not* get fucked with, Savannah."

9

FALCON

I haven't shown Savannah the basement of this place yet.

It's an underground bunker—part of it, that is.

The other part is a gym. Weights, cardio equipment, everything anyone would need to stay in the best shape ever. If disaster strikes and anyone is forced to stay here for five years, they'd better stay in shape.

That's what I will teach Savannah.

I'm ready to tell her this when my satellite phone jingles.

I take a look at it. It's ten a.m. Not that we could tell, since the lightproof shades are drawn.

My brother Hawk is calling.

"Hawk," I say.

"Leif got in touch with me."

"Good. You're the only one I trust, brother, other than him."

"I hear you. But I've got some good news for you."

"I could use a little good news right now."

"Raven's bloodwork came back. She's still in remission. She just has a virus."

I can't say all the weight has been lifted from my shoulders, but a tiny bit of it has. "Thank God."

"I know. They're taking her home this afternoon. What am I supposed to tell Mom and Dad about why you're not there?"

"I don't fucking know, Hawk. I wish I knew."

"I'll think of something," my brother says.

"Thanks. I owe you."

"Falcon, you don't owe me shit. You've paid your dues. You deserve a break."

"This isn't about me. How much did Leif tell you?"

"All of it, dude." He chuckles lightly. "She must be one special lady."

"That she is, brother. I'm going to need you to watch out for Raven. And Eagle."

"Christ, Fal."

"No matter what, he's our brother."

"Yeah, I know it, and I love him. But it's because of that spoiled little shit that—"

"Hawk, I made my own decision eight years ago."

"Yeah, but you made it to protect him."

"No regrets. I'd do it again."

"Really? Would you? Knowing what you know now?"

"Back then, at twenty-two, to avoid watching my seventeen-year-old little brother go down? Yeah, I would. And if I could go back in time to that exact moment, I'd still do it. But now? All these years later? After all I went through to protect him the first time? If he hasn't learned his lesson at this point and fucks up again, I think he's on his own."

Even as I say the words, though, I'm not sure I mean them. I've waffled on this since I've been out. He's still my baby brother.

"Good to hear you say that, bro," Hawk says.

"You need to keep him out of trouble, Hawk."

"He's twenty-five years old. What the hell can I do?"

"Do whatever you have to, man. Kick the shit out of him if you have to."

"I might enjoy that," Hawk says.

That's Hawk. His quiet fortitude, his sense of justice, but it turns into fucking raging mania when he's pissed off because someone else isn't following the rules.

But I don't worry about it. He's still my brother, and he'll still watch out for Eagle.

"Let me know what you end up telling Mom and Dad," I say.

"Will do. I don't want to call too often, though."

"I understand. Take it easy."

"You too, brother." The call ends.

"Good news?" Savannah asks.

I nod. "Raven's okay. Her bloodwork came back. She's still in remission. Her white cell count is only up because of a virus."

Savannah heaves a sigh. "I'm so glad, Falcon."

"You and me both, Vannah." I pause and look at the phone in my hand. "We can't use this phone very often, but I do need to call Leif."

"Please," she says. "I'm serious. I don't want you bothering him with trying to find Vinnie."

"He's our best shot, Savannah."

She sighs again. "All right. But Kelly is never going to forgive me."

"I'll give Leif the choice. If he can't do it, I'm sure he knows others who can."

She frowns. "How many others do we want knowing about this?"

"They won't know. Leif won't tell anyone why he's looking for Vinnie. And he certainly won't tell anyone about us or where we are."

She nods then. "All right."

"But Savannah, what makes you think your brother might know anything about this? He left the family."

"Yes, but he was the firstborn son. Things were shared with him that were never shared with Michael and me. Which is probably why he left the family."

I look deep into her eyes. "Savannah, do you really think he'll know anything? Or do you just want to find your brother?"

She gnaws on her lip.

"I will help you find your brother. No questions asked. But if he's not a good source for this…"

"He may not be," she says. "But I don't know who else to ask. My father won't tell me. I can't get in touch with him anyway, because then he'll know where I am."

"I see your point. So it's either find Vinnie or try to figure out how to get the information some other way."

"Exactly," she says, "and I honestly don't know how to get it without asking Leif to hack into something."

"Yeah, I know a hacker, but like I said, we don't want anyone else to know about this other than the people who already do—Leif and Hawk."

"Right."

"I have sophisticated equipment here in the safe house. But I'm no hacker."

"Neither am I," she says.

"Tell you what," I say. "We're going to have some breakfast, and then we're going to have a workout session."

She frowns. "Yeah, there's something you should know about me and exercise."

"You hate it?"

She looks down at her feet. "I'd say hate is too weak a word."

"Too bad how sad, Savannah. I'm going to get you into shape. But first..." I slide on top of her, my cock hard and ready. "First, I'm going to make love with you."

A soft sigh leaves her throat, and her eyes close.

I slide my cock into her wet heat, slowly this time.

She's already wet, and though I'd have liked to take my time with her, give her some awesome foreplay, all I could think about was getting into her hot cunt.

I stay embedded inside her for a moment, relishing her tightness, her sweetness, her complete perfection.

Then I pull out and push back in.

Another sigh escapes her, and she wraps her arms around my shoulders.

God, her touch.

Just her fingertips on my flesh can get me moving.

I pull back, push back in once more.

But then I go crazy.

Definitely time to fuck her.

So I thrust back in, in, and...

I'm coming, coming inside her sweetness.

I stay there, empty myself inside her, and then I pull back out. "Sorry."

"For what?"

"I want you to come, Savannah."

She slides her fingers between her legs. "I can take care of that."

I'm breathing heavily, panting like a dog. "God, you drive me crazy when you play with yourself."

"This won't take long, Falcon."

"I'd like to help you along." I clamp my lips around one nipple.

She arches her back, groaning.

"Your nipples are so sweet," I say. "Like ripe blueberries."

I suck on her nipples, finger the other one, as she rubs her pussy.

The sighs from her throat, the moans, the groans...

"Yes," she says. "Suck them. Please."

I heed her words, until —

"Yes," she says on a soft sigh.

She rubs her clit fiercely, and even though I'm not inside her, not even so much as a finger, I feel her climax.

It jolts through me as if I'm having another.

As if we're connected on some visceral level.

I drop her nipple, squeeze her breasts, kiss her lips, shove my tongue into her mouth.

And as she groans into me, finishing her climax, I swear to God I fly along with her.

We lie for a moment in each other's arms until she rolls away, heads to the bathroom, and returns a few moments later.

"I could go for a cup of coffee," she says.

"Your wish is my command."

We put on the robes that we wore last night, and both of us pad out of the bedroom and into the kitchen.

I start a pot of coffee while Savannah hunts through the refrigerator, pulling out a carton of eggs.

"Bacon?" she asks.

"Always," I say.

She grabs the package of bacon and examines it, frowning. "What are we going to do when we run out of fresh food?"

"I told you, Vannah, I don't think we'll be here that long."

She presses her lips together. "How can you say that? I have no idea if anyone will be able to find Vinnie, and if they can't, I don't know how to get the information we're after."

"We'll figure it out, Savannah."

She nods and looks at me, but in her face, I'm not sure if she believes me.

She doesn't know my determination.

Determination to keep her safe.

She'll go back to her talking points about how we both have equal responsibilities to take care of each other, protect each other. While I objectively agree with her that in a perfect world that's how it would be, that's not the hand we've been dealt.

I will teach her to be strong, show her what she needs to do. Teach her how to fight.

But in the end, I will protect her, no matter what.

Savannah pulls out a frying pan and lays a few strips of bacon in it. Then she throws a few slices of bread into the toaster.

Once the coffee is brewing, I take a look around the

kitchen, figuring out where things are. There's enough fresh food to last a couple weeks. If we're here longer than that, we'll have to get into the survival food.

I doubt we'll be here longer than that. But I need to find resources. Leif, if he's up for it. If he's not, he'll know someone I can trust.

And Hawk.

He knows better than to tell Eagle any of this, but I need to find out what he tells my parents and sisters as to why I'm gone.

Technically, I'm not allowed to leave the county without telling my parole officer. Vannah, of course, is no longer my parole officer.

Shit. My parole meetings.

I've been reassigned. Vannah no longer works there.

And I'm definitely not going to be able to make my next meeting. Not if I'm here in the safe house with Vannah.

And there's no way in hell I'm going to leave her alone.

I might never leave her alone again.

Fuck.

I'll fix all of this somehow.

I just don't know how.

Savannah brings a plate of bacon, eggs, and toast to me at the table.

We eat together and I realize getting her into shape won't work.

I'm not sure what I was thinking, but that takes time. I had the advantage of being in awesome shape when I went to the slammer, and I only got stronger once I was there.

I'll start with an easy regimen for Savannah, because

starting out hard will only make her muscles sore. So we'll go slowly.

But there's something else I can teach her that won't take as much time.

Savannah's going to learn how to shoot.

10

SAVANNAH

"Learning to shoot a pistol safely and effectively involves a series of steps that should be followed with care and diligence."

I stare at Falcon. "Are you reading from an instruction manual? I've told you. I know how to shoot."

"This isn't a game, Vannah. I've seen what failing to know your surroundings when you're shooting can do, and you're out of practice. I'm going to take you through every part of your pistol as if you've never touched on before. First of all, treat every firearm as if it's loaded and the safety is off."

"Okay." My heart beats rapidly.

"Always keep the nose of the gun pointed in a safe direction and keep your finger away from the trigger until you're ready to shoot. Got it?"

"Yes, sir." I salute him.

"Are you going to take this seriously?" he demands.

"Yeah, of course. I'm sorry."

"Good. This will help you be able to take care of yourself. Keep yourself safe."

She points to the shelf full of firearms. "That small one. I'd like to try that one."

"Nope."

"Why not?"

"Smaller weapons tend to have harsher recoil." He picks up a pistol. "This is a basic nine millimeter."

He educates me on the parts of the pistol—the slide, the barrel, the trigger, the safety mechanism, and the magazine release.

"Got all that, Vannah?"

"Yes."

"Good. What's this?" He points to the long part of the gun.

"The barrel."

"And this?"

"The safety."

"This?"

"Falcon, I know them all."

"All right. We'll see." He grabs what look like bulky earmuffs and construction goggles and hands them to me. "Always wear ear protection and eye protection during target practice inside. Put these on."

I obey.

"Is the fit good?" he asks.

"I guess so." I fiddle with my eyewear. "I can't really tell."

He tightens my goggles and adjusts the earmuffs. "Good. You can take them off for now. Let's go into the shooting range."

Falcon opens the door and I step in ahead of him. The heavy door shuts behind me with a solid thud, sealing off the world outside. The air is cool and still, and two shooting lanes, each a narrow corridor with targets at the end, stand before me.

Fluorescent lights hum quietly overhead, casting a clinical glow on the two shooting stalls, their outlines marked by red paint.

"This targeting system is state-of-the-art," Falcon says.

Like I'd know, but I nod. Down the lanes, the paper targets hang still, their surfaces smooth and uninterrupted, the concentric circles unbroken by bullet holes. The quiet is profound, the kind of hush that feels almost heavy, expectant.

At each shooting station, there's a small bench. Falcon gestures to one and sets my gun and my protective gear down.

The ear protection seems superfluous in the silence, but I slip it on, the soft click of the muffs muting the already muffled world of this safe house.

"Watch me," Falcon says. He loads my gun with the first magazine. "Got that?"

"Yes."

"Now, let me show you the stance. I want your feet shoulder width apart."

"Okay." I obey.

"Make sure you distribute your weight evenly on the balls of your feet to counteract recoil."

I breathe in deeply. "Okay," I say again.

"It will be second nature to you before you know it."

Great. I'm not sure if that's good or bad. I never wanted firing a weapon to be second nature to me, but Falcon is right. This is something I need to practice in order to protect myself. And to protect him.

"Extend your arms fully without locking your elbows," he says.

"I don't have my gun yet."

"That's right. I want you to get familiar with everything before you actually pick up the gun."

He's acting like I've never done this before. I sigh. I get my arms into position, facing the target.

"Are you comfortable?" he asks.

"Literally or figuratively?"

"Both."

"I'm good."

He hands me the gun, careful to keep it pointing in a neutral direction. "Take this. Use your dominant hand to grip it, but keep those fingers off the trigger."

I take it from him, hold it.

"Vannah," he says gently.

"Yes?"

"I know you don't mean to, but you're pointing the gun directly at me."

"Shit!" I drop the gun, and it clatters to the floor. I truly *am* out of practice.

"And that's why we keep the safety on," he says, picking it up and handing it back to me. "No reason to freak out. I know you don't want to shoot me. But always be aware of where your gun is pointing. Never point it at something you don't want to shoot. Try again."

This time I'm more careful. I point the gun toward the target, adjust my stance, and grasp the grip with my right hand.

"Good. Now wrap your other hand around your dominant hand to secure your hold."

I nod, obeying.

"Good. Keep your head upright and level, not tilted or

turned, and bring the firearm up to your line of sight. Use your dominant eye to aim."

I nod, closing my left eye to bring the target into aim.

"Keep both eyes open, Vannah."

I nod, open the left eye. Good, I'm still trained on the target.

I cock my head a bit, careful to stay on target. "I wasn't supposed to learn to shoot, but my father insisted. He said you don't grow up in this kind of family without knowing how to handle a gun."

"Good on him. At least you weren't treated like a second class citizen when it came to protecting yourself."

"I suppose it sounds like we're treated that way, but when I think about it, that's not exactly the case. Not so much second-class citizens as...precious commodities."

He shakes his head. "How can you be living in this century, Savannah? This makes no sense at all."

"Tell me about it."

"You say women are treated like chattel, but you don't consider yourself a second-class citizen?"

"Kind of, but the term *second-class citizen* implies that we're thought of as having no value. That's not the case."

"I won't deny your value, Savannah. But I won't have you treated as a damned *commodity*. All the more reason for you to learn how to shoot."

I smile at him and re-aim the gun. "Is this the right stance?"

He nods. "Yup. Now, when you shoot the gun, you're going to get some kickback. Something you have to get used to. You're still lined up. You ready to shoot?"

The earmuffs are tight on my head, but I'm ready. I nod, without losing my target.

"Then go ahead."

I shoot.

The kickback is rougher than I remember, and the gun rises as the shell hits the floor.

But Falcon stares at the target. "Fuck it, you're a natural."

Sure enough. I hit right outside of dead center.

"Told you." I smirk.

"Do it again."

I aim again, shoot.

Slightly more off-center this time. "Was that first one a fluke?"

"Are you kidding me? This is still amazing. Again."

I go through eight more rounds, each one hitting right around the target, and one dead center. Everything comes back to me.

Then I watch Falcon shoot through his magazine, hitting dead center every damned time.

Falcon is still shaking his head when he takes off his protective gear. "I can't fucking believe it."

"Vinnie was a good shot," I say. "Dad always said he was better than he was. He also said I had potential."

"You've got more than potential," Falcon says. "What about Michael?"

"Michael was...different."

"What you mean?"

"Michael abhorred violence of any kind. He hated what our family was into, but once Vinnie left, he felt he had no choice but to stay in the family. He married Miles's cousin, and then ended up dead. He never got the chance to be happy, to live his life. To be with someone he truly loved."

"Was he in love with someone else?"

"I don't know." I purse my lips. "I always wondered if Michael might've been gay."

He raises an eyebrow. "And that's why he got killed?"

"No." I scratch my arm. "Nobody really cares what your sexuality is as long as you play your part. It's possible, though, that he wasn't sleeping with Elizabeth, and that was an issue. The idea behind alliances is that you have children. They anchor the families together."

"Was he effeminate or anything?"

I shake my head. "Not all gay men are feminine, Falcon. And not all straight men are alpha and macho."

"Hell, I know that. One of the guys in the cellblock over was gay, and he was nearly as tough as I am. No one laid a hand on him."

"Then you understand that there was no way of knowing without Michael telling us." I sigh. "I don't really know. It was a thought I had. His high school girlfriend always seemed a bit unsatisfied with him. They never really made physical contact when they were together, at least not in front of the family. And then later, there would be these unexplained absences. He'd say he was going out but gave no reason. This was after he finished school, so it's not like our parents could force him to tell them. But I always wondered what exactly he was hiding. He didn't like violence, but that's not why the thought occurred to me. It's something I've wondered about for a while. Just a feeling. And whether he was gay or not, he didn't get to live his own life, and that's what's the saddest."

"It's very sad," Falcon says. "As for hating violence, most

normal people hate violence. I hated what I had to do to survive in prison, what I had to do to protect others in prison. I hated every bit of it."

I look at Falcon's target. "But you're a great shot."

"That's part of being a Texan. You learn to shoot around the time you learn to walk around these parts."

I chuckle at his joke.

"You may laugh, but I'm not exaggerating that much. I was about ten when my dad taught me to shoot, and the next year he taught Robin and Raven."

"Really?"

"Hell, yeah. Women need to shoot more than men do sometimes. Guns are the great equalizer between the sexes."

"Yeah, you're right. Which is another reason why most families like mine don't teach women to shoot."

"Well, you're a natural."

"Like my father. And Vinnie."

"Did Michael ever learn to shoot?"

"Yeah, he did. I mean he was a guy in our family, so he had to. But he was never quite as good as Dad or Vinnie. I think he probably just hated it."

"If he was as much of a pacifist as you say he was, then yeah, I imagine he probably did."

"Is it wrong that I like it?" I ask.

He smiles at me. "It's not wrong at all, Vannah. Shooting is an art. You're a natural, and you're only going to get better. And I'll feel a lot better knowing you can protect yourself."

"You mean when you don't go all alpha and protect me yourself?"

"Baby, I will always protect you with my life if I have to. But if I'm not there, I want to know that you're prepared."

He puts his ear and eye gear back on. "Now let's go again."

*

After we shoot a few more rounds, Falcon takes me to the workout room.

"Tell me what kind of exercise you've done," he says.

"I told you. I hate exercise."

"You're lucky to have such a hot little body without resorting to exercise." He runs his hands up and down my back, making several chills run through my spine. "But exercise will help you keep it as you get older, Savannah. I'm going to make sure you get in shape. We're going to go slowly."

"We are?"

"It takes a while to get into shape, and if I push you too hard, you'll have a lot of muscle pain. I can't have you in pain, because we may need to leave quickly. But I'll start you on a few things. We'll start with some walking on the treadmill, just to get your heart rate up, and then I'll show you some very basic strength training exercises, gently so that you're not in any pain."

"Strength training?" I look in the mirror, imagining what I'd look like as a bodybuilder. "I don't want big muscles."

"First of all, I just told you, we're going to start slowly and gently. Second of all, women don't have the hormones to develop those big muscles. You don't need to worry about that anyway." He pokes me gently in my abs. "I'm talking about some core strength. I'm going to start you with a few planks, and some arm exercises with three-pounders. And we'll start easy on the planks. Only thirty seconds at first. I don't want your abs hurting."

"Trust me, I'm in favor of not hurting." I give him a smile.

"Absolutely. I can't have you in any pain." He narrows his gaze at me suggestively. "But I also want you in top-notch shape for all the exercise we're going to be doing in the bedroom while we're stuck here."

I smile then. "Now that's the kind of exercise I can get behind."

11

FALCON

Eagle freezes. "It's him. Diego Vega."

My pistol's in the back of my waistband, and I'm ever aware of it against my body.

"How do you know?" Hawk asks.

"I just know. Call it intuition. Call it whatever you want."

"We've got his fucking money. What else would he want?"

"My ass," Eagle says.

"We won't let anybody hurt you," I say.

Hawk glances around as the truck drives up to the old barn.

"Thank God," Eagle says. "It's not him. He sent two of his minions to pick up the money."

"Good enough." I glance at the duffel that contains a million in cash that I got from my grandmother. God, if she knew...

But she doesn't, and I'll make sure she gets paid back. It'll come straight out of Eagle's trust fund when he turns twenty-one. In the meantime, though, it'll come out of mine. Of the three of us, I'm the only one who has access to mine.

If I'd been able to get cash quickly, I wouldn't have gone to our grandmother at all.

God, Nana. And Lawrence, who knew exactly what I was up to. That man seems to have eyes in the back of his head.

We stay in the barn, and I watch from the doorway as two men get out of the truck.

They both have dark hair, and they're both wearing jeans and black T-shirts with work boots.

And of course, they're thugs. They have muscles on their muscles.

Luckily, Hawk and I are both in damned good shape. Eagle is still a scrawny teenager, but he's tall and broad.

Three against two, and we're armed.

Of course I'd be an idiot to think they're not.

I stand there, letting my broad shoulders take up the doorway. I don't speak.

They're going to have to make the first move.

"We're looking for Eagle," one of them says.

"You Eagle?" the other says.

I simply shake my head.

"Who the fuck are you then?"

"None of your damned business." I dig my heels into the ground. "But I've got what you want. You're going to take it, and then you're going to get the fuck out of here."

The bigger one of the two closes the distance between us until he's only about three feet away from me, his dark eyes glaring into mine. "You don't make the rules here, asshole."

I raise my arms to either side of my body. "This is my property, so I'm the only one who makes the rules here. I could have you arrested for trespassing, but I won't. I'm here to keep Eagle's end of the bargain. You're here to take it, and then get the fuck off my property and never return."

"I know who you are," the other one says. "Falcon Bellamy, Eagle's oldest brother. You think you're tough?"

"Is that a rhetorical question?"

"The fuck is that supposed to mean?" the other one asks.

Okay, I'm not dealing with bright people here. Of course I'm not. Smart people wouldn't get involved in the drug trade, or if they did, they wouldn't be acting as someone's delivery boy.

Which of course doesn't say much about my youngest brother.

"Stand back, and I'll get what you came after."

"We need to see Eagle."

"Eagle's not available."

"Diego says we've got to see Eagle."

"Did I stutter?" I take a step forward, holding my ground. "Eagle's not available. You came for the money. I've got the fucking money. Take it and scram."

Hawk walks in front of me, throwing the duffle outside the doorway. "Take it, and get out of here."

One of them turns to Hawk. "You Eagle?"

Hawk doesn't reply, but then I hear the click of a door.

A man gets out of the truck, and for a moment I'm not sure where he came from. He must have been hiding in the backseat. He's as muscled as the minions, and he wears steel-tipped cowboy boots, jeans, and a black button-down shirt. His features are sharp and pointed.

I know who I'm looking at, even though I've never seen him face-to-face.

This can only be Diego Vega.

"Where's Eagle?" he demands.

"He's not here." I grit my teeth. "Just take your fucking money and get out of here."

He narrows his eyes at the two of us. "You must be Falcon and

Hawk Bellamy." He laughs mockingly. "Birds of prey, both of you. You think you can take me on, tough guys?"

Hawk is rigid next to me. He hates violence, and he hates people who break the law even more. What Vega is doing is illegal, and he's doing it on our property.

He stalks toward me, but before I can brace myself to take whatever Diego thinks he's going to do, something pulls at my back.

Fuck. It's Eagle. He barrels through the doorway...and he's got my gun.

"Just take your money," Hawk says. "Take it and don't ever come back."

"I don't think so," Vega turns to Eagle. "This little shit and I have some unfinished business."

"It was my brothers," Eagle shouts. "They got rid of the stuff, man. It wasn't me. But we got the money and then some." His hand shakes.

"Oh, I'll take the fucking money," Diego says. "And then I'll take it out of your ass, you fuck-up."

Eagle raises his arm, trains the gun on Vega.

In a flash, both the minions have their pieces trained on Eagle.

"Eagle," I say, willing my voice not to shake. "Put down the gun."

"No, Fal." His entire body quivers. "He doesn't have any intention of letting me out of here alive. I tried to tell you guys. I tried to tell you."

"Eagle"—this time Hawk speaks—"you're going to be fine." He retrieves his gun and trains it on Vega. "Because once you put your gun down, I'm putting a bullet through his fucking head."

"Hawk doesn't miss," I say, as low and menacing as I can.

"He'll never stop," Eagle says. "He won't stop until he kills me. So I'm going to kill him first."

I gesture toward Vega's minions. "You two should get the hell out of here. Now."

I'm amazing even myself that my voice isn't cracking. Inside I'm a trembling mass of nerves, but on the outside? I'm standing tall, remembering the words of my father that have been jammed into my head since the day my sisters were born.

You're the oldest, Falcon. You must protect all your siblings.

And if my brothers—especially Eagle—ever needed protection, they need it now.

~

AFTER I SHOW Savannah how to exercise with the three-pound dumbbells, I join her in a half hour walk on the treadmill.

"We're going to do this every day?" she asks.

"The walking, yes. The strength training will only be every other day. Your muscles need to rest between workouts."

"What workouts do you do?"

"I do a lot of different ones. Different parts of my body each day, letting each part rest between days. Upper body one day, lower body the next."

"What about my lower body?"

"We're going stick with the walking for now. People don't realize this, but walking is a weight-bearing activity. And as a woman, you can use your own body weight as resistance. I need more than that."

"But you stayed in such great shape in..." She pauses and looks at her feet.

"Prison, Vannah. You can say the word. You were a parole officer, for God's sake."

"I just don't like to think of you there."

"I know you don't, but I would go there again to save you."

She doesn't speak.

And damn, this woman is stronger than I give her credit for. She was raised to be traded. To be used as a bargaining chip.

That didn't weaken her. Not by a longshot. And I know, if given the choice, she would do it again to save me.

I love her for it.

But I won't allow it.

"I'm going to finish my workout now," I say to her. "You go rest. Draw yourself a bath, add some Epsom bath salts."

"There are Epsom salts here?"

"Savannah, there is everything we need here."

She raises an eyebrow. "Are bath salts really a necessity?"

I shrug, "I would think so."

A small smile creeps across her lips. "Did you request them specifically?

"I might have."

She bursts into laughter.

"What is it?" I ask.

She looks me up and down. "I just...never took you for a bath guy."

I smirk. "Because I'm a big burly manly man, I can't enjoy a good bath now and then?"

She shakes her head quickly. "No, of course not. I just..."

She looks into my eyes. "You surprise me more and more every day, Falcon. Thank you for taking care of me."

I wrap her into a hug. "I always will, baby." I grab her face. "And if you spent as much time on the inside as I did, you'd realize what a luxury a hot bath is. Spending every morning in the cold-ass prison gang shower with a dozen other guys isn't the ideal way to get clean."

"I suppose it isn't." She gets on her tiptoes and kisses me on the cheek. "All right. I'll take a bath, soak my muscles. Then I'll make us some lunch."

"That sounds great. Thanks, baby."

She grabs a towel, throws it around her neck, and leaves the gym. I don't hear her walking up the stairs because everything is soundproofed.

But she's safe in the safe house.

If there's a breach, I'll know. I continue my workout, and by the end of it, I'm tired and hungry.

I walk upstairs, expecting to see Savannah in the kitchen fixing lunch.

But she's nowhere to be found.

"Savannah?"

No response.

My hackles rise.

There's no way she could even get out of this place. You need a code to do so, and I didn't give it to her.

I should give it to her.

She was locked in that room with Miles McAllister, and I don't want her to feel locked in again.

"Savannah?"

I find her in the bathroom, in the bathtub, her eyes closed. I stick my fingers in the water. It's lukewarm.

The poor thing fell asleep.

I nudge her on the arm. "Savannah. Wake up."

Her eyes pop open. "Shit." She moves around, splashing water. "Damn. Where am I, Falcon?"

"You fell asleep, Savannah. Don't you know you should never fall asleep in a tub full of water?"

"Of course I know that. God, I'm sorry."

"It's okay." I grab a towel and hand it to her. "The water's cool now. You need to get out before you catch a chill."

She stumbles out of the tub, and I get a good look at her naked body. God, she's so beautiful. Every part of her.

But right now, she's shivering. I wrap the towel around her and hug her close. "Promise me you'll never fall asleep in the tub again."

"I promise." She shivers. "That was really stupid."

I say nothing more. Just hold her.

She finally pulls away. "I was supposed to make you lunch."

"Don't worry about that. I'll throw together some sandwiches. You get dressed."

"What are we going to do for the rest of the day?"

I cast my gaze toward the bedroom. "I have an idea."

She chuckles. "That'll be great, but what about after that?"

"Savannah, I can do that for a long damned time." I kiss the top of her head and then I leave her in the bathroom, head through the bedroom and out, making my way to the kitchen.

My satellite phone rings on the table.

I take a look. It's Leif.

"What's up?"

"Just checking in to see if you're okay."

"So far so good. Good thing we've got a lot of books and movies here."

"I'm sure the two of you can find something to pass the time." The tone of his voice tells me he knows exactly what I'm planning on doing with Savannah.

"I taught her to shoot this morning. The girl's a natural."

"She should be, coming from her stock."

"Can you believe they don't teach their women how to shoot?"

"Doesn't surprise me. I don't know a lot about organized crime, but from what I do know, women are both coddled and treated poorly."

"That's kind of how Savannah was describing it." I tap my fingers on the kitchen counter. "Anyway, I know you're a newlywed, Leif, and I don't want to bother you and Kelly too much, but I need you to find someone for me. And seriously, if you can't take the time, give me the name of someone you trust."

"Depends on how quickly you need it done and on who you want me to find."

"Vincent Gallo Junior," I say. "Savannah's older brother."

"Okay. Where was he last seen?"

"That's just it. Nobody knows. According to Savannah, he left the family. Went to Europe. No one's heard from him since."

"Europe? That's a lot of ground to cover."

"I know. And he's probably using a different name."

"You got a photo?"

"Savannah might. I'll see if she does, and if so I'll send it to you by satellite."

"What's his middle name?"

"I don't know. Savannah's in the bathroom. Hold on. She should be out any minute."

Savannah comes walking out then, wearing yoga pants and a large T-shirt. Her hair falls in damp waves around her shoulders, and damn, she looks luscious.

"I've got Leif on the line," I say to her. "Does your brother have a middle name?"

"Same as my dad's. Lorenzo."

"Lorenzo," I say into the phone. "Just a minute. I'm going to put you on speaker." I push the button on the screen. "You there?"

"Yep," Leif responds.

"Vannah, do you have a picture of your brother?"

"I did. But my wallet is somewhere inside Miles's father's house."

"Shit."

"Can you describe him?" Leif asks.

"It's been years since I've seen him, but he looks a lot like my father. Dark hair and eyes. Tall. Around six two. Pretty muscular."

"You just described every Italian guy I've ever laid eyes on," Leif says.

"Yeah, I know. I'm not much help."

"Are there any pictures of him online? Did he have a social media profile or anything?"

She shakes her head. "He's been gone too long. My family always discouraged the use of social media, anyway. When you're in the line of work that we're in, you don't want to be so easily tracked. And my brother was pretty private anyway.

That's why it was so easy for him to disappear without a trace."

"Are there any pictures of him to speak of at all?"

"My family threw out everything they had of him when he went away, and it's not like they'd let you inside their house anyway." She scratches the side of her head. "But what you could do is check out his old high school yearbooks. He went to a private school on Long Island. It was called St. John's Academy for Boys. Maybe visit the school library and see if you can find a yearbook from when he attended."

"It's a start. When did he graduate?"

"Well, I guess it was fifteen years ago now." She wrinkles her forehead.

"You sure?"

"No, not really. He's eight years older than I am. And I graduated nine years ago, so I guess that's seventeen years ago."

"All right. That would make him about..."

"Thirty-five," Savannah says. "I think of him every year on his birthday."

"That'll be a help," Leif says. "What's his birthdate?"

"January seventeenth," Savannah says, closing her eyes.

"Good to have," Leif says. "I'll do what I can."

12

SAVANNAH

The days are beginning to drag.

Falcon and I have made love a lot, and that's been wonderful, but within two weeks, our supply of fresh food has dwindled, and we've had to resort to eating the survival food.

It's not terrible, but it's certainly not good by any stretch of the imagination. Everything we eat is either dehydrated and stored in a bag, or out of a can. Never in my life did I think I'd enjoy eating canned green beans, but the rehydrated beef stroganoff makes me wish I were a vegetarian.

The good news is that after two weeks, I'm in better shape than I've ever been in my life. I started slowly, as Falcon suggested, and without anything else to do, I've worked on my shooting and my strength.

I can't say my strength has improved much after only two weeks, but Falcon has taught me lots of self-defense moves, lots of punches and kicks, and I've been an eager and quick learner.

And my shooting has only gotten better.

The last time we practiced, I hit the target dead center four out of five times, and that fifth one was damned close.

Still though, as I boil water and pour it over freeze-dried macaroni and cheese for lunch, I'm starting to wonder if we'll ever get the hell out of here.

Until, for the first time in a couple days, Falcon's satellite phone buzzes.

I'm serving the bright orange concoction onto two plates when Falcon puts the phone to his ear.

"Yeah?"

Pause.

"Seriously? He's here?"

Pause.

Who's here? I bring the food to the table, set a plate in front of Falcon, and take a seat next to him, eagerly listening.

"That's great news!"

Pause.

"No, not here." He glances over at me. "I don't want to leave Savannah here alone though."

"Oh hell, no you're not leaving me here alone," I say.

He waves at me to be quiet.

I glare at him.

I love the man, but whatever's going on involves me as much as it does him. Moreso even.

Pause.

"Put it on speaker."

He nods, and then puts it on speaker, setting the phone on the table. "I've got you on speaker, Leif. Savannah's here."

"Hey, Savannah," Leif's voice. "How are you holding up?"

"I'm good. About ready to dig into some gloppy macaroni and cheese."

"Had to hit the survival food, huh?"

"Yeah. I've got a few eggs left for tomorrow's breakfast. A few apples and oranges here and there. They're the only fruits that would last more than a few weeks. There's also some pasta. But for the most part, the fresh food is gone."

"I can bring you a new stash."

"No," Falcon replies. "It's time we got the hell out of here. It's been two weeks, and no one has found us here."

"That doesn't mean they're not looking," I say.

"Oh, they're looking," Leif says. "I've been watching them. The McAllisters are furious. They've had their people out with dogs, combing every inch of the surrounding area, trying to track where we took you. Luckily they haven't come within a mile of here. At least, not yet. But here's the good news I was telling Falcon, Savannah. I found your brother."

My heart thumps wildly as happiness surges through me. "Vinnie? Is he all right?"

"He's good. I had to make an offer he couldn't refuse, though."

"You mean he wouldn't come for me?" I ask, the happiness lodging into my gut as a brick.

"That was the offer I had to make. Nothing swayed him. Not money, not a new identity so he could hide in plain sight. Nothing at all, Savannah, until I told them what they tried to do to you."

Happiness again. Happiness that my brother hasn't forsaken me.

"He's on a private plane now, traveling under an assumed identity. He's been living in Spain, going by the name Alejandro Martinez."

"Yeah, he could totally pass for Spanish," I say. "From what I remember, anyway."

"I've got a current picture of him," Leif says. "I sent it through the phone."

My heart nearly stops. I'm actually going to see my brother?

"He lands in Austin in an hour. I'm picking him up personally. Falcon says not to bring him to the safe house."

"The fewer people who know about it, the better," Falcon says. "We never know when we may have to use it again."

I look over at Falcon and grab his arm. "Will it be safe for me to leave this house to see him?"

"Since it's been two weeks, the McAllisters aren't looking quite as hard," Leif says. "At least not in this general area. At this point, they think you've fled the country. So we're going to let them think that."

"Then where should we meet you?"

"I rented a small furnished house in Giant Oak, the town over from Summer Creek," he says. "I'll text you the address. Meet us there at six this evening."

"Should I cut my hair?" I ask. "Color it?"

"Don't do anything that could draw attention to yourself," he says. "Keep your hair the way it is, and don't wear dark glasses or a scarf over your head. Nothing like that. But try to keep the bright colors to a minimum."

"That won't be a problem," I say. "All the clothes here in my size are beige and brown and nondescript."

"They're that way for a reason, Savannah," Falcon says.

"They sound perfect. What kind of car do you have available?"

"In the underground garage are two cars," Falcon says.

"Both electric, and both fully charged. A silver Nissan Leaf, and a navy blue Tesla S."

"Take the Leaf," Leif says. "It will look less assuming."

"That's what I was thinking, too," Falcon agrees.

"And I don't have to tell you." His voice adopts a dark edge. "You know what to do."

I nod. "We'll be there."

Falcon ends the call.

I run my hands through my hair. I can't help smiling. "I'm going to see my brother," I say. "I can't believe it."

Falcon's face is noncommittal. "We need to go down to the bunker, find you a holster, and get you armed."

"I have to be armed?"

"When Leif said, 'you know what to do,' that's code between him and me. It means we come armed."

"Why would I need to come armed to see my brother?"

"Savannah, your brother's been gone a long time." He lays a hand on my shoulder. "Do I think he's a threat to either one of us? No, I don't. But we can't take any chances. Besides, if something happens, and we don't make it to the meeting point, we need to be ready for anything."

I bite my lower lip. Then I nod. "I understand."

~

THE DRIVE IS about thirty minutes long, and I look behind and beside me everywhere I can the entire time while shielding my eyes from the sun. Staying inside two weeks with only artificial light really does a number on your eyes, and the sun...

The Texas sun is so damned bright.

I want to strip all my clothes off and just bask under the sun.

But of course that's not possible.

I can't even leave this car for fear that one of the McAllisters' spies will spot me and take me away from Falcon.

I quiver at the thought.

"Vannah, I've got this," Falcon says. "No one is here. No one can find us. No one's following us. Try to relax."

"I can't. I'm pretty antsy." I sigh and grab his arm. "I'm scared, Falcon."

"You don't have to be scared as long as I'm with you."

I believe him. I believe he'd move heaven and earth for me, just as I'd move heaven and earth for him. He doesn't want me to do that any more than I want him to do it for me. We each put the good of the other before our own. We've got our own little *Gift of the Magi* thing going. The irony of our gifts is a seductive sin, each of us giving up our heart's desire to find the true essence of our love in the depth of sacrifice. It's utterly beautiful.

But I think...

I think we need to work together a little more.

We slide into the open garage of a single-family dwelling in an unassuming neighborhood. As soon as we're in, the garage door closes behind us.

"How'd that happen?"

Then I see Leif standing in the doorway from the garage. He nods to Falcon.

Falcon and I leave the vehicle and go inside. The garage leads straight to a laundry room and then to the kitchen.

And at the kitchen table sits—

"My God, Vinnie!"

He has his back to me, but I'd know him anywhere.

My brother turns, looks at me, his eyes sunken and sad. Then he rises, rushes to me. "Oh my God, Savannah."

I burst into tears. "I'm okay. I'm okay, Vinnie."

"I'm so sorry I wasn't here to protect you," he says, grabbing me into a hug.

"No one blames you for that, Vinnie. I can't believe it's really you." I pull back and look at him. Leif sent me a picture, but it was nothing compared to seeing my brother in real life. He has a few wrinkles around his eyes, a few gray hairs at his temple, and he has a full beard, but it's my brother. It's Vinnie.

"I can't believe how you've grown," he says. "No longer a little beanpole. And so pretty, Sav."

"Anybody hungry?" Leif asks. "I've got fried chicken."

Then I inhale. Good old Texas fried chicken.

"All of a sudden, I'm actually starving," I say.

"Yeah, I could eat." Falcon holds his hand out to Vinnie. "Falcon Bellamy."

Vinnie shakes his hand heartily. "I understand that you've done a lot to protect my sister. Thank you."

Falcon looks at me and smiles. "I'd do anything for her, man."

Vinnie nods. He doesn't go all big brother on me, worrying that someone is having sex with his little sister. "You've proved that," he says. "I won't leave her again."

"You do what you have to do." I say. "I'm sorry you had to come back for me, Vinnie."

"I'm not. I shouldn't have left in the first place." He sighs and looks away from me. "If I'd taken my place at the head of the family, none of this would've happened."

I shake my head. "No."

"If I'd been here, maybe Mikey would still be alive, and maybe you wouldn't have been sold off to the McAllisters."

"I don't want you to think that way," I tell him. "None of this is your fault."

He doesn't reply. He thinks it *is* his fault, but it's not. It's not his fault any more than it is Michael's or mine. I'm not even sure it's Dad's fault.

Leif gets the food out, and we each take a plate and serve ourselves. I bite into a succulent drumstick, and my tastebuds go crazy. It's only been a few weeks on the survival food in the safe house, but I feel like I forgot how *good* fresh meat tastes. I can't believe how hungry I am in the midst of all this.

"Okay," Leif says, once we've all finished our dinner. "I don't know exactly what we're dealing with here. Falcon doesn't either. The two of you know more about your family and why they might be pushing this marriage between Savannah and Miles."

"It's got to be something big, Vinnie," I say. "They let me off when I was eighteen, and again when I was twenty-two. I did the family's bidding for five years out of college when I worked as a parole officer in Austin, and when I begged Dad to let me out a month ago, he finally agreed. But now, all of a sudden they want me again? There's got to be something more than a simple alliance at work here."

"I agree with you," Vinnie says. "I've been out of the family dynamic for a long time, but when I was in high school, Dad taught me everything I needed to know. He just assumed I'd be willing, and though I didn't want to know everything, I let them teach me. I was underage at that point, so there wasn't much I could do about it anyway. But the more I found out, the more I knew I didn't want to be any part of it."

"Do you remember anything that might be related to this situation?" Falcon asks.

"I remember every damned thing," Vinnie says. "It's not something you can easily forget. Finding out what your family is capable of."

"Oh God..." I swallow. "They're not into something besides drugs, are they?"

"They weren't then," Vinnie says. "Unless Dad held back on me. Once I turned eighteen right before I started my senior year of high school, I don't think he held back. For me, adulthood brought information I didn't want to know."

"The McAllisters. They traffic women and children." I shudder. "I found that out by accident."

Vinnie nods. "Yeah, they were just getting into it back then, and Dad promised me we would never ally with that family. Never in a million years."

"I'm afraid he broke that promise," I say.

"I know. First with Mikey, and then with you."

My stomach does a somersault. "Oh my God... Do you think..."

"Yeah," Vinnie says. "I think they killed Mikey. I think he threatened to go to the cops about the trafficking."

I place a hand over my mouth. "God, the drugs are bad enough."

"I know. So much fentanyl coming across the border, and all those fucking mules—"

Falcon drops his jaw, his eyes wide.

"You okay, Falcon?" I ask.

"Yeah, fine. I'm just putting a lot of things together in my mind right now. There are things..." He rakes his fingers through his hair. "Things I've never told anyone, Savannah. Things my attorneys didn't know eight years ago. Things only my brothers know."

"I'm sure I don't know what you're talking about, man." Leif says. "There's a bunch of shit you've never told me either."

"I made a promise a long time ago," Falcon says. "But I'm wondering... I'm wondering if I inadvertently got involved with your family, Savannah."

"Drugs?" I ask.

"Yeah, drugs." He looks over both shoulders and lowers his voice. "I'm trusting you people with this knowledge. Nothing leaves the room. Leif, I assume you checked for surveillance."

"Checked, double-checked, and triple-checked. You're good, man."

Falcon looks at Vinnie then. "Did you ever know a man named Diego Vega?"

Vinnie's eyes widen. "He's a *bad* guy."

"Don't I know it," Falcon agrees.

"All right," I say. "The two of you are going to have to tell us what the hell you're talking about."

13

FALCON

Diego Vega disappeared eight years ago.

No body was ever recovered, and the two men who were with him were apprehended at the border and never heard from again.

I'm about to break a promise I made to my brothers by telling a guy I just met. I trust Leif and Savannah with my life, but Vinnie? I don't know him from Adam.

"Did Diego Vega work for your family?" I ask.

"He did at the time I left," Vinnie says.

"If you talk to your father," I say, "you'll probably find out that Diego Vega disappeared about eight years ago. Into thin air. Along with a truckload full of merchandise."

Savannah's eyes go wide. "Falcon?"

"There's a lot more to my story than a young rookie cop getting accidentally killed," I tell her.

"Oh my God," she says.

The look on Savannah's face crushes my soul into fragments. Her mouth is agape, and she's looking at me quizzically. She wants to know the full story.

But I can't drag her into my history. Not when she's struggling to free herself from her own.

"Before I go any farther," I say, "I need to talk to my brothers."

"Both of them?" Leif asks.

"At least Hawk," I say. "I'm not sure I trust Eagle."

"Good enough," Leif says.

"In the meantime"—I turn to Vinnie—"is there any chance that your family may have decided to get into trafficking?"

"My father always swore he'd never do it," Vinnie says. "But he's not the head of the family. My grandfather is. Mario Bianchi, my mother's father."

Nausea claws at my throat. "My God, Savannah..."

"Are you saying," Savannah says, "that Grandpa may have decided to *join* our two families? That it's not a simple alliance anymore? They're going into business together?"

Vinnie shakes his head. "I'm not saying anything, Sav. I don't know. I've been gone. But there's something I should tell you about Grandpa."

"What about him?"

Vinnie closes his eyes and casts his gaze to the floor. He pauses for a good thirty seconds before speaking. "He's not a nice man."

Savannah's eyes go wide as circles. "He was always wonderful to me. You and Mikey, too."

"When we were little, yes. But he did something to me after I turned eighteen. Something that cemented my desire to leave. My guess is he did it to Mikey, too."

"What are you talking about?"

He inhales deeply and sighs. "Since you don't know what

I'm talking about, that means he didn't do it to you. And Savannah, I'm very glad to know that."

Savannah lips are parted, her eyes confused.

She doesn't have any idea what her brother is talking about.

But I do.

You don't spend eight years behind bars and *not* understand what Vinnie is leading up to.

"Man, I'm sorry," I say.

"Me too," Leif says.

I do a double take at my friend. How would he know such a thing?

"Fuck, Leif..."

He shakes his head. "Not me, thank God. My buddy Buck. Not pretty. But he's okay now. Happily married, working for the Wolfe family like I do."

"Thank God..."

"And you, Falcon?"

"Nope. More than one tried, but never."

"Could one of you please tell me what you're talking about?" Savannah demands.

"Oh, Savannah. It's not pretty," I say.

"Far from it," Vinnie agrees. "And it only happened once, Savannah. I was ashamed for a long time, but not anymore." Vinnie draws in a breath. "There's a lot to the story. About how I was tied up and couldn't fight back, because believe me, I would have fought back. I would have taken the old man down."

"Vinnie..." she says.

He draws in a breath. "Our grandfather raped me."

Savannah gasps. Then she clasps her hand over her mouth. "No. Vinnie. My God..."

"Not with his dick, and it was only one time. It was a power play. For some convoluted reason, he thought it would make me stay with the family. Show me how much power he had. Thought it would make me want that power so I'd take my place as the true head of the family once he died."

"Wouldn't that be Daddy?" Savannah asks.

"No. Dad was always just a placeholder. He doesn't have any Bianchi blood."

"God, Vinnie..." Savannah's eyes fill with tears.

"Sav, I'm okay. Believe me, I've hated myself for the last seventeen years knowing I wasn't there to protect you and Mikey from the same fate."

Savannah widens her eyes. "Oh my God. Don't you see? Grandpa *did* get into trafficking. If he could do that to his own grandson, why would he care about nameless and faceless others?"

"The man was always about the almighty buck," Vinnie says. "Even Dad said that. Said Grandpa valued money over people."

"I'm so sorry." Savannah sniffles. "He was always kind to me."

"And I thank God for that." Vinnie rubs his forehead. "I don't think Mikey was so lucky, and the fact that they married him to a McAllister makes me think Dad and Grandpa were getting into the trafficking scene. Why else would they ally with a family that practices such heinous things?"

"I don't know." Savannah gulps.

"There's still a lot I don't know." He closes his eyes again and winces. "I wish I'd had more strength. I wish I'd stayed instead of run. I should have been protecting you and Mikey."

Savannah wipes her eyes with a tissue. "Mikey's in a better place now. No one can hurt him there."

"Are you sure?" Vinnie says to Savannah, grabbing her arm. "Are you sure no one ever touched you? Did you block anything out?"

She shakes her head. "I'm sure. No one ever did anything to me."

"Damn good thing," I snarl.

Vinnie widens his eyes then. "Damn, I should've realized."

"Realized what?" she asks.

"You needed to be a virgin, Sav. A virgin for Miles McAllister."

"I hate to tell them, but I'm no virgin," Savannah says.

"But you were when you were eighteen, weren't you?"

Savannah shakes her head. "Yeah, but not for long. I lost my virginity in the back of Billy Conrad's car. It wasn't great, but my senior year of high school was hell. We left Long Island, moved to Austin, and all the friendships had already been forged at my new school. No one was interested in some newbie from New York. I was starved for attention and affection."

Listening about someone fucking Savannah gets my hackles moving. But I didn't know her then. I'm just glad her grandfather never laid a hand on her.

"How old is your grandfather?" I ask her.

"He's eighty," Savannah says. "But he's in excellent health and can easily pass for mid-sixties. I'd love to see old age get him, but it doesn't look like that will happen anytime soon."

Rage rises in me, and my jaw tenses.

Savannah looks at me. "Falcon, no."

"He's a fucking degenerate. A criminal. He needs to go down, Vannah."

Vinnie meets my gaze, angry fire as dark as mine in his eyes. "I couldn't agree more. If you have an idea, Falcon, I'm all in."

14

SAVANNAH

My entire world is shifting.

My brother, who I thought I'd never see again.

Finding out he'd been so cruelly violated at my grandfather's hands.

My grandfather…

I was always the apple of his eye.

Little cricket, he used to call me.

Come here and sit with me, my little cricket, he used to say.

I'd crawl into his lap, curl into him, relish the smell of cigar smoke.

He was a handsome silver-haired Italian man, and he always came over for Sunday dinner.

My grandmother died before I was born, and my mother was their only child.

My mother took her role as an organization wife seriously. Caroline Gallo was subdued and quiet for the most part. Always looked good, like a housewife in the fifties. Hair always done, makeup always on, and she rarely wore pants.

Today, her body is as good as mine is. She keeps herself beautiful so she can be adequate arm candy when my father needs to go out with her.

That's what I would've been groomed to be.

But at least with my father, I knew he wasn't mistreating my mother.

But can I really be sure that's the case?

"Vinnie," I say.

"Yeah, Sav?"

"Our father never…"

He shakes his head. "Nope. Not once. Hardly ever laid a hand on me. Only when I actually deserved it."

"And our mother?"

"You know as well as I do what a good mother she was, but she was a shadow compared to Dad."

"Do you think Daddy ever…"

"I don't know, but if he did, we'll never know." His face darkens. "Mom would never say a word."

I nod. "I can't believe all of this."

"It wasn't easy to say," Vinnie says.

I press my lips together. "I'm so naïve and innocent I didn't even know what you were talking about. But Falcon, you did."

He nods. "Naïve and innocent are two things that don't serve you well on the inside." He turns to Leif. "Or on the battlefield, I imagine."

"No," Leif says. "You learn quickly that man is the most dangerous animal out there."

My heart thrums wildly. "Thank God you guys rescued me from Miles."

"What the hell did he do to you?" Vinnie demands.

I look at Leif, who shakes his head slightly at me. He didn't tell Vinnie.

I clear my throat. "He was about three inches away from raping *me*."

Vinnie's cheeks turn red. Then he rises, bringing his fist down on the table.

"Easy," Leif says.

"Let him get it out," Falcon says. "I had to. God, the thought of it…"

Vinnie nods. "I did my share of smashing my fists into walls while I was away. Especially when Mikey died. Fuck. I'd smash a wall right now, except this isn't my place."

"Smash away," Leif says. "I get it. Trust me."

Vinnie breathes in slowly and lets it out. "I won't. I will bathe in my anger, and I will put my aggression to better use than taking out a wall." He breathes in again. "You think for one minute I haven't thought daily about the shit our own flesh and blood pulled? About what I went through, what I know Mikey went through? What I assumed you went through, Sav? It eats away at my soul. Every day. I can choose not to take part in it. I can choose to run from it. But that doesn't change this part of me."

I rise and walk to Falcon, wrap my arms around his neck, and look into his eyes. "For me, Falcon. Please. Do the same as my brother. Take that aggression, that anger, that rage, and channel it into something productive."

"Anything for you, Vannah."

Vinnie rises as well. "That's what we'll both do, Sav. I should've come back long before now. Hell, I should've never left, but I was a stupid kid. I wasn't thinking of you or Mikey. I was thinking only of getting myself out. It wasn't until I got older that I realized what I had doomed the two of you to. But by then, it was too late to do anything about it." He grabs my forearm. "But I swear to you, Sav. I'm going to do something about it now." He looks to Falcon. "I meant what I said. I'm all in."

"Man," Falcon says. "I got put away for killing someone. I was innocent, but I lied to save someone else. I served my time, but now, I've actually taken a life."

"Abel wasn't your fault," I say.

"Doesn't matter." He looks to the floor. "He'd still be alive but for me. The man's a psycho, and I won't mourn his loss, but I *did* do it, Savannah. And I'll do it again if I have to. I'll spend the rest of my life behind bars if I have to, if it means making things right."

I shake my head. "Falcon, I need you. And Vinnie, I just got you back. I don't want either of you going away, especially not because of our corrupt grandfather."

"And he is still your grandfather," Leif says. He nods to Vinnie. "Yours too. I've ended lives too, when I was on tour in Afghanistan. You learn to live with it. You learn to deal with it because you didn't have a choice. But this? Your own flesh and blood? I don't recommend it."

"I don't care," Vinnie says. "I wish I had come back sooner. Wish I'd had the strength to—"

I wave my hand to stop him. "No, Vinnie. I remember myself at eighteen. I wasn't in any position to do what Dad asked of you. What Grandpa asked of you. You were right to run. I'm glad you did. I wish Mikey had run too. Maybe he'd still be alive."

Vinnie simply shakes his head. "Maybe I wasn't wrong to

run," he says. "But I was certainly wrong to stay gone for so long."

"Dad and Grandpa looked for you," I say. "How did you stay so far off the radar?"

"I had documents."

"Where did you know to go for those?" I ask.

"I had money," Vinnie says. "When I turned eighteen, I got partial control of my trust fund. I cashed it out as soon as I could, purchased forged documents, and left. I moved around a lot at first. I was in Poland for a while. I wanted desperately to go to Italy, but that was a little too on the nose. So I ended up in Spain, since my documents had a Spanish name."

"What have you been doing?" Falcon asks.

"Odd jobs mostly. Remote work. I break into my stash of cash if I have to. But I hate living off the trust fund."

I nod. "I haven't touched mine at all."

"You're a better person than I am, Savannah."

I scratch the tingling nerves on my arm. "No, I'm not."

"You are," Vinnie says. "You basically told Dad no. You told Grandpa no. You told Miles McAllister no."

"A whole lot of good it did me." I meet Vinnie's gaze. "They need me for some reason, Vinnie. We need to figure out what it is."

"I'm pretty sure we already know," he says. "I think we were barking up the right tree earlier. Damn. I never thought I'd see the day when our family got into that kind of shit. Drugs are bad enough. We've got them flowing over the border like nothing else."

"How would you know that?" I ask. "You haven't been here."

"I know what goes on at the US border, and I know what was going on when I left. Two plus two will always equal four."

"It's all so weird," I say. "I'm wondering... I mean, if Dad and Grandpa really wanted to find you, they could have."

"You mean because you guys did?" He nods to Leif.

"Yeah," I say.

"No. You may as well know, Savannah, that your friends here? They have the resources our family could never hope to have."

"Remember, I work for the Wolfe family," Leif says. "They've got contacts everywhere, at every top government agency. Everywhere."

"You're freaking me out a little bit here," I say.

"No reason to be freaked out. We use our sources for good instead of evil," Leif says.

"You sure you're ready to take your grandfather out?" Falcon says to Vinnie.

"*I'm* sure as I've ever been about anything." He turns to me, his face concerned. "But I don't feel like *you're* in favor of this, Savannah."

I pause, taking a second to gather my thoughts. "Of course I'm not in favor of this. I hate what he did to you, Vinnie, but I don't want either of you getting put away. Falcon, you've already done time for something you didn't do. And Vinnie, you've been trapped in your own kind of prison for the last seventeen years. I'm happy you're back, but I sure as hell don't want *you* put away either."

"I'll do what I have to do, Sav," Vinnie says. "I owe it to you. And to Mikey."

"Mikey's in a better place. You don't owe him anything."

My brother shakes his head. "Unfortunately, I don't see it that way. He'd be alive if I had stayed back in the States. If I'd taken my place as the future head of the family."

I don't want my brother harboring so many demons, but I can't fault what he says. It's probably true.

"We're going to have to sleep on this," Falcon says. "I should get Vannah back to the safe house."

Then I look up, jerk at a pound on the door.

Falcon's eyes widen. "No one is supposed to know we're here."

"No one should," Leif says. "You know I took every precaution."

"Open up," someone yells from behind the door. "It's the police."

"Stay quiet," Leif says.

"Vinnie, take Savannah to the basement," Falcon says.

"I'm not leaving you," I say.

Falcon looks at me sternly. "You'll do as I say, Savannah. Is that clear?"

Vinnie darts his gaze at Falcon, and I see in his eyes that he doesn't like Falcon's command.

I step between them. "Vinnie, don't. He's only thinking of me. I'll go with you. We can't risk anyone seeing you. If Dad and Grandpa know you're here..." I shake my head. "I don't want to think about what will happen."

Vinnie glares at Falcon. "Fine. I'm doing this for her. For safety."

"Good. I'm doing it for both of yours."

Leif gestures. "That door leads to the basement."

I nod, give Falcon a quick kiss, and follow my brother through the door.

15

FALCON

Leif goes to the door, looks through the peephole. "It appears to be the cops," he says.

"Then I suppose you'd better open up, because if you don't, they're going to come in anyway."

"I need to see your badges," Leif says through the door. "Give me your names and your badge numbers so I can check you out."

"For Christ's sake..." one of them growls.

"It's okay, Bernie. He's just being cautious," the other says. "I'm Deputy Brent Mays from the sheriff's office. My badge number is..."

I stop listening as they both rattle off their names and badge numbers. Leif taps on his phone, and a few minutes later, he looks at me.

"They're legit."

I nod.

He opens the door. "Hello, Deputies. Thank you for your patience."

"Who are you?"

"Leif Ramsey. I rented this place for the next couple of months."

"Do you have documentation?"

"I did it through an app. I can pull up the information."

"Don't bother. We're here for him." One of the deputies nods to me.

I try not to react. "What the hell did I do?"

One of the cops looks at me. "You Falcon Bellamy?"

"Yeah."

He shoves a warrant in my face. "You're under arrest. For parole violation and on suspicion of the murder of Abel Kuhlman."

"That was self-defense," I say.

"You can tell that to your lawyer, and they'll figure out what to do about it. But you've missed your last two parole appointments."

Fuck.

I thought about that when Vannah and I first got to the safe house, and then it simmered on the back burner where I didn't notice it again.

"Look, I've got a damned good reason for all of this."

"You can tell it to your attorney, tell it to the investigator when they take your statement. We're just here to bring you in. Turn around please."

I take a look at Leif.

But he shakes his head slightly at me.

These cops are both armed. So are we, but our guns are hidden, and they can sure get to theirs quicker than we can get to ours. If I'm resisting arrest, they can shoot me in cold blood and no one will pay the price.

"Fine." I turn around.

And I wince at the click of the handcuffs in place again.

"You have the right to remain silent," the cop says, turning me around. "Anything you say can and will be held against you. You have the right to an attorney. If you cannot afford an attorney, one will be appointed to represent you. Do you understand these rights as I have read them to you?"

"Do I fucking ever," I say. I meet Leif's gaze. "Take care of her. Please."

"You got it. Who should I call?"

"Call my father. He'll get an attorney to see me right away."

"You got it."

I walk out, led by the two deputies. They open the back-seat of their squad car and shove me in. I resist the urge to bitch about the force that they're using.

How did they find me?

They couldn't have followed Leif or me. I was on high alert when Savannah and I drove here.

Doesn't fucking matter.

They've got me.

And they're right. I *have* violated the terms of my parole. Which means they can throw me back in the fucking slammer.

And then who will protect Savannah?

About twenty minutes later, we get to the local station. They take me in, put me through intake, take a mug shot and my prints.

Then into a holding cell I go. A couple of drunks and a meth head are in with me.

Christ.

A large bearded man sits on the steel toilet in the corner, farting and shitting. The putrid stench makes my eyes water.

Six cots altogether. I'm the sixth in the cell.

Guess they're thinking I'll be here all night.

They can think again.

I don't talk to the others. I just plunk my ass on an empty bed and lie down. Stare at the ceiling.

And wonder how the hell it came back to this.

~

Sharp rocks are a commodity.

I have one that looks like granite that I found a year ago during our outdoor time.

A few days later, I bought a new toothbrush from the prison commissary. I claimed to have lost mine in the bathroom. Things get stolen all the time in prison.

I began to whittle the end of the toothbrush into a sharp point using the rock and alternately filing it against the spalling concrete inside my cell.

It was slow and tedious work, but by the time I was done, I had a shiv that could rip the throat out of somebody.

I kept it on me as often as I could.

When they searched our cells for contraband, I hid it and the rock in a large crack in the concrete between my wall and the floor. I hid other things there too. I'm not a smoker, but I kept cigarettes on hand as much as I could. They helped me keep the other men in line.

No drugs, though. A few men are addicts, but I don't allow drugs on my cell block. Some of the addicts get transferred. Others go through a painful and torturous detox, but they're better off for it in the end.

Once Zion came to my cell block, I kept that shiv on me at all times.

I learned to hide it in different places. In the waistband of my underwear was the usual place, and with a little sleight-of-hand, I could move it during a body search.

I never put it up my ass. Was too damn sharp.

Plus, that's the first place those derelict guards would look.

I had one guard, Hoyt, for whom strip searches were a fetish. He loved doing them. In fact, he only *looked up our asses. He generally didn't look anywhere else.*

Fucking sicko.

But Hoyt's fingers were the only thing that ever got my ass during my years in the joint.

Zion wanted me, though. He was fucked up. Every time he met my gaze, he'd stick his tongue out and make a slurping sound like Hannibal Lecter in Silence of the Lambs.

Made me hate him all the more.

No way was that filthy bitch going to get anywhere near me.

And if he tried?

I had my fucking shiv.

"BELLAMY?"

My eyes shoot open.

God, the cell still smells like that guy's shit.

"Yeah?"

"Got an attorney here to see you."

They cuff me and take me out of the holding cell and into an interrogation room.

Lola Briggs, my attorney, wearing her signature tight-ass navy blue suit, sits there, along with two cups of coffee. "Nice going, Falcon," she says.

"I had my reasons, Lola."

"They're thinking of charging you in the death of that guy."

"That was self-defense and defense of another. He was armed, and he trespassed on my property. Besides, all I did was pistol whip him. That blow to the head could not have caused his death."

"That's for the medical examiners to determine."

"There's still self-defense," I say.

She shakes her head. "At the moment, I'm more concerned about your parole violation. You know they can revoke your parole, don't you?"

I say nothing.

"Was it worth it to go back to prison?" she asks.

I run my hands through my hair and sigh. "You don't know the whole story. Yeah, I missed some appointments, but I had a damned good reason. I was protecting someone."

"Who?"

"It's a long story, Lola."

She takes a sip of coffee. "Then you'd better start talking, because I can't help you if I don't know."

16

SAVANNAH

The basement is dark and dank. It's not finished, and the floors are concrete, the walls bare wood, with insulation tucked in between the two-by-fours.

A water heater and furnace stand in the corner, the furnace gyrating to make the air-conditioning unit go.

But no air-conditioning is needed in this basement. I rub my arms against the chill.

My brother stands next to me, his hands in the pockets of his jeans.

His full beard covers his handsome face, and it makes him look older, wiser.

And I imagine, after seventeen years in Europe on his own, he's gained some wisdom that I don't have.

On the other hand? Being here with my family? I've gained some wisdom *he* doesn't have.

And it's probably about time that we compared notes.

Besides, it'll give me something to do to keep my mind off what's happening with the police upstairs.

Because I already know why they're here.

And it's going to kill me when they take Falcon away.

It crossed my mind more than once while we were at the safe house for two weeks. Falcon is supposed to be going to parole meetings with his new parole officer.

I didn't mention it to him, because frankly I was afraid of him leaving me.

I should've mentioned it to him.

I should've seen that he did what he needed to do. I should've seen that he kept himself out of prison.

That's the reason I made the deal with that asshole Miles McAllister in the first place.

"Tell me what's going on, Sav," Vinnie says.

I pace the basement. "You know as much as I do. Falcon and I were in the safe house for two weeks. He and Leif rescued me from right under Miles McAllister's clutches. I don't know how they got into the house, but Leif seems to be able to do pretty much anything. They call him Phoenix. He always rises from the ashes. Gets out of scrapes, apparently."

"He technically hasn't done anything wrong," Vinnie says. "I mean other than the breaking and entering."

"According to Falcon, he's not going to get caught. He disabled all of their systems, and we got the hell out of there before they figured out what was going on."

"That's good." He looks at the floor. "God, Sav, I'm so sorry."

"You're sorry?" I shake my head. "Nothing happened to me, Vinnie. He didn't rape me. He tried, but he didn't. I puked all over him before he could get in."

"You and your quick-thinking stomach." Vinnie smiles weakly.

"Fight or flight, you know." I shrug. "I couldn't fly. He was stronger. So my body fought back the only way it could. By hurling at him."

"Hey, it worked."

The familiar feeling of nausea creeps up my throat, but now it's for a new reason.

"I can't believe Grandpa... And I understand if you don't want to talk about it, Vinnie..."

He lays a hand on my upper arm. "I can talk about it. It was a long time ago. It took me a while to get over it, but I'm whole."

"I just can't imagine. So Grandpa likes men?"

Vinnie shakes his head. "No, this had nothing to do with his sexuality. Like I said, he didn't use his own dick, thank God. It was a power play, pure and simple. A power play to get me in line, and he expected me to do it to others."

"He *said* that?"

Vinnie nods. "To whomever was next in line to lead the family, next in our bloodline. If I'd had a son, he would've expected me to do the same thing to him. And no way in hell was I going to do that." He sighs. "I knew then that I had to get the hell out."

"It's strange," I say. "When I went with Miles willingly, in exchange for him making any charges against Falcon go away, he took me to his father's house. And his mother, Maggie, is a really sweet woman but is unfortunately a product of the system. She told me I was safe for the night. That Miles wouldn't come to me until we were legally married. I took her at her word. Turned out she was wrong."

"Perhaps *her* husband didn't take her until they were married. I don't know," he says. "All I did know is that if I ever have a wife, she won't be some subservient little housewife like Mom." He frowns. "Don't get me wrong. I love Mom and I always have."

"You were her firstborn, Vinnie. It killed her when you left."

"I know, Sav. I know."

I rub my eyes to obscure the tears that are filling them. "It killed all of us."

"And it literally killed Mikey." He shakes his head. "When that news got to me, I came pretty close to jumping off a cliff."

"Oh God, Vinnie."

He slowly breathes in and out a few times. "But I didn't. I've done a lot of self-healing on this journey. I've read philosophy from the great masters, and I even studied with some of them. I've lived a nomadic life, and I've learned that suicide is never the answer. But I'm still on this earth for a reason. I have something to offer. When I heard from your friend Leif about what was going on, I knew it was time to return. I have a role to play in this family." He grabs my hand and squeezes it. "You do too, Savannah. I'm not quite sure what it is yet, but it certainly doesn't entail me heading the family, and doesn't entail you being married to Miles McAllister. We'll figure it out together."

I give my brother a hug, kiss him on the cheek. "I'm so glad you're home, Vinnie."

He looks around the drab surroundings of the basement. "This isn't home to me," he says. "We were still on Long Island when I left."

"I know. I'm still not clear on why we came to Texas. And why the McAllisters came as well."

"Easy enough," Vinnie says. "We're closer to the border. Closer to the source."

"But shouldn't we be far from the source? To keep fingers away from us?"

He sighs. "Hell if I know, Sav. If I knew how this whole business worked, I'd be in too damned deep."

The door opens to the basement, and Leif strides down the stairs.

My heart races. "Oh my God, where's Falcon?"

"The deputies took him. Suspicion of murder—"

I gasp.

"—and parole violation."

"Damn," I say. "They can shove him right back into a cell for that."

"I don't know why he didn't think of it," Leif says.

"I did," I say, "but there was so much else going on. And I just figured he had it taken care of." I bury my face in my hands. "I feel like a complete idiot."

"Don't blame yourself," Leif says. "Falcon wouldn't want you doing that."

"Don't blame yourself either," I say.

He frowns and looks up the basement stairs. "Yeah, well that ship has sailed."

"For me too." I nod.

"How do we get him out?" Vinnie asks.

"Falcon's father has the best attorneys in Texas. The problem is that they may not be able to get around is the parole violation. They'll probably be able to do something about the murder charges."

I sniffle. "That's why I went with Miles in the first place. And now I'm paying for that. For leaving."

"Don't even go there, Savannah," Leif says. "That is not what Falcon would want."

He's right, and I know it.

I still feel terrible though.

"What can we do?" I ask.

"I think the best thing to do is to get the two of you back to the safe house," Leif says. "I'm ordering supplies, and once they're here, we'll deliver you and the supplies back to the safe house in the Nissan Leaf."

"Then how will you get back?"

"I'm going to follow you with the supplies. We'll be careful."

I nod. "All right. If you're sure. But Leif, what about Kelly?"

"Kelly knows what I do for a living. She accepts it. And she knows how much Falcon means to me."

"I think you're married to a saint," I say.

Leif erupts into laughter then.

"I'm not sure I said anything funny."

"If you knew how Kelly was when we first met, you would know why I'm laughing." He stops chuckling, but a big smile remains on his face. "She's a great girl, and I love her more than anything, but a saint she is not." He walks toward the stairs. "Come on up. The supplies should be here shortly, and then we'll get you two back to the safe house."

"I don't think I should go to the safe house," Vinnie says. "I think I need to see my father."

"No, Vinnie." I grab his hand. "Please. Come with me. I don't want to be there alone."

"All right, for *you*, Sav. But as soon as Falcon is out and he's back with you, I need to talk to our father." Then his gaze burns into mine. "And our grandfather."

"I'd like to talk to the two of them as well."

"You will," he says, "but I've got first dibs. We have some unfinished business. We'll see if Grandpa can take what he dishes out."

I drop my jaw. "No, Vinnie, you're not going to—"

"Violate an eighty-year-old man?" He shudders. "Hell no, Savannah. I'm not a criminal, and that's just sick. But I've been thinking for seventeen years what I would do if I came face-to-face with him again."

"What could you do that's worse than rape?"

"I could kill him," Vinnie says, "but I'm not a killer. It's part of the reason I got out of this family in the first place." His demeanor hardens. "No, Savannah. I'm going to take the old man down. This family is going to topple, and I'm going to be the catalyst."

My jaw drops. "Vinnie, you're one man. I'm one woman. We can't take down our entire family."

"We *can*, Savannah. They all deserve to be in prison."

"Even Dad?"

"Especially Dad. He conspired to sell you off to the McAllisters." He looks away, disgust on his face. "I have no proof, but I bet he's taken some lives over the years."

"What about Mom?"

"Mama's innocent in all of this. Just like you are. Just like Mikey was." He swallows. "Mikey paid the price, and I'm going to make sure he didn't die in vain."

"How are you going to do it?"

He taps at his temple. "I've got a plan in the works. It's been percolating for years. And now that I'm back, it's time to put it into action."

"Hey, anything you need on my end, you got it," Leif says.

"Thanks, man." He takes Leif's hand and shakes it. "And

thanks so much for everything you've done for Savannah. But this is something I have to do myself."

"You're going to do it without me?" I ask.

"Savannah, I love you. You are smart and wonderful and I would love your help, but I don't want to drag you any further into this."

I let out a scoffing laugh. "I'm already in it. As soon as they find me, they're going to drag me back to Miles McAllister. So yeah, I'm as much in this as you are, Vin."

He pauses and cocks his head. "Tell you what. You and I will go back to the safe house, and we'll talk. We'll figure out a way."

"Falcon's going to hate this," Leif says.

"I love Falcon," I tell him. "And I know he loves me. I know he wants to protect me from everything, just like I want to protect him. But I couldn't protect him from the cops today, and I should have. I should have told him to leave the safe house and go to his parole appointment. So that's on me. But I can tell you one other thing." I cross my arms. "Falcon Bellamy doesn't own me, and if my family is going down, I want a hand in it."

Leif smiles at me then. "You remind me so much of Kelly. You're a handful, just like she was. And is. I wouldn't trade her for all the gold in the world. And I'm pretty sure Falcon feels the same way about you."

"And I feel the same way about him. Right now, I need to trust that his lawyers are going to take care of him, because I have to help my brother."

"All right."

"Falcon's satellite phone is at the safe house," I say. "I want you to call me there as soon as you have news about him."

"Absolutely, I will," Leif says.

We walk to the kitchen into the front room just as the truck is driving up.

Leif signals the driver over. "The supplies I ordered are here. You two get ready to go, and I'll get this all loaded."

I regard Leif, his light blond hair and blue eyes. Such a contrast to my brother, with his dark hair and dark eyes.

But the look in both of their gazes is unmistakable.

They both mean business.

"Vinnie?"

"Yeah?"

"Promise me," I say. "Promise me that we'll get our mother out of there. That we'll topple the Bianchis and the McAllisters for good, and that no woman will ever be forced into this life again."

17

FALCON

Here I am.

Sitting in an interrogation room with my attorney.

Something I swore would never happen again.

"You need to listen to me," Lola says. "Things don't look good."

"So I missed a few check-ins with my parole officer. Savannah was my parole officer until—"

She holds her hand up. "Until you whisked her away and put her in hiding. Yeah. Suffice it to say she's no longer employed with the county. You have a new parole officer, and he's not happy with you at the moment."

I rub my temples and look at the ceiling. "What are my options?"

"The most frequent parole violations for which revocation occurs are failure to report as required and failure to go to treatment programs. You were supposed to go to therapy, remember?"

"I've had a few other things on my mind," I say.

She stares me down. “You need to take this seriously. I can take this to the parole board, request a hearing. You’re already here in jail. It’s really up to the parole board how they proceed. They can modify your parole by adding new conditions, or they may require you to be taken to jail for sixty to one hundred and eighty days.”

I slam my hands down on the table. “A hundred and eighty days!”

“I told you this is serious. Plus, a man died after you pistol whipped him.”

A new thought occurs to me. *Fuck...*

“And I’m not supposed to have a firearm.”

She exhales sharply through her nose. “Give the man a gold star. What the hell did you think you were doing?”

“I think I was protecting the woman I love. Those two men trespassed, came onto my property. Threatened me, threatened Savannah.”

“I can make a case for that. But here’s the problem. You’re an ex-convict. You confessed to manslaughter eight years ago.”

“And you and I both know I didn’t do it.”

“You think that matters? You served eight years. You confessed to manslaughter, and then you got more years tacked onto your sentence for contraband.”

I grit my teeth. “And I’d either be dead or maimed if I hadn’t had that contraband.”

She waves her hand at me. “Hey, I get that. You’re preaching to the choir here. But you and I both know there are some rules you’re going to have to play by. You didn’t make the rules, and neither did I. Do I want to see you go back to prison? Hell, no. You didn't deserve to be there in the first place."

"I had my reasons."

"Which I hope you will one day open up about. But the fact of the matter is that as far as the system goes, you're an ex-convict. An ex-convict who violated parole by missing meetings and by possessing a firearm."

I open my mouth but she gestures to me again.

"Yes, we've been through it. It was self-defense, defense of another. And they were trespassing and they were armed. I will do my best to make that go away, and we certainly have a case to get you out of a manslaughter charge. But you've violated your parole."

I rake my fingers through my hair. "Sitting down with some idiot was the last thing on my mind for the last two weeks. And the guns are mine. I own them."

"I get that. I do."

I shake my head. "You don't know what was going on with Savannah, Lola. She was taken by the McAllister family, and she was going to be forced into marriage to Miles McAllister."

Lola's eyes widen.

"Yeah, Savannah is a member of the Bianchi family."

"Damn."

"Right? I wasn't going to let that happen. He was about to rape her when we found her."

She takes a deep breath then slowly exhales. "I'm sorry, Falcon."

"If you want to arrest somebody, get someone thrown in the slammer, go after Miles McAllister."

"He and his family live in Austin."

"So? Get them investigated."

"I work for *your* family, Falcon. I don't work for the state of Texas."

"I know that, but how have they been able to exist? Get away with this shit?"

She shrugs. "The same way organized crime has been existing for the past several centuries, Falcon. They buy people off."

"There should be some kind of punishment for all that."

"When the DA can catch them, there is. They go away for a long time. But these families are experts at laundering money, experts at buying off cops and judges. It shouldn't happen, but people aren't perfect. They see money, and they take it."

"Is it money? Or is it the barrel of a damned gun?"

"Sometimes it's both."

"It shouldn't be allowed to happen. This isn't Chicago in the twenties."

"No. It's a hell of a lot easier for these people to operate now," she says. "With the Internet, the dark web, all the technology they can use to protect themselves, they're virtually impossible to catch."

"I'll testify," I say.

"You can testify, and the two guys who trespassed—make that one, because the other's dead—will probably go down. But if that man is important to the family, they'll find a way to get rid of the witnesses." She narrows her gaze at me. "That's you, Falcon."

I cross my arms. "No one will touch me. No one touched me on the inside, and no one can touch me on the outside."

"There were rules on the inside, Falcon. You were able to figure them out and learn to play by them, make them work in your favor. But this is the real world. You and I both know that. And as far as these families go, there are no rules."

I shake my head. "I can't go back inside. I need to protect Savannah. I can't do that from the inside, Lola."

She shuffles through some paperwork. "I'll get the parole revocation hearing scheduled as soon as I can. But I can't get you out of jail right now. You're a convicted felon, and they're not going to release you on bail."

"So I'm just going to sit in here? Rot with these other miscreants?"

"You'll be moved to a different cell. And I can at least fix it so they don't send you back to prison. You'll be held here in the county jail until your parole revocation hearing."

"And when will that be?"

"Soon as I can get it scheduled."

"Jesus Christ, Lola. Doesn't *my* family own a judge or something?"

She raises an eyebrow. "I'm going to pretend you didn't say that, Falcon."

"Look, I know it's not right. But these Bianchis and McAllisters can pay off judges, and we have just as much money as they do. And ours is clean."

"If that were the case, do you think you would've gone to prison in the first place?" Lola asks.

"I know, I know. That was my choice. And I know you guys did the best you could to get me out of everything, but there was a dead cop involved."

"That's right."

"But there's no dead cop involved this time, Lola." I stand and pace the room. "I missed a couple parole meetings and I had a gun. That's it. Yeah, the guy died, but what I did was in self-defense."

She sighs. "This is complicated, Falcon. And you know why."

I rub my forehead. "Yeah, I know why."

And I wonder, for the first time ever, if it was worth it to save my brother's ass that day. To sacrifice eight years of my life for my little brother who got in over his head.

I breathe in.

Yes, it was.

Not only because he's my brother, but for one even more important reason.

The entire experience led me to Savannah.

And I will fucking burn down anything in my way before I let the McAllisters take her.

"I'll do what I can to get this hearing expedited," Lola says. "But I'm afraid you're stuck here in the county jail until it happens."

"First-class fucking accommodations," I say dryly.

"They're within their rights to send you back to prison," she says. "And trust me, there are people there who can't wait to get a shot at you."

"You think that scares me?"

"Falcon," she says, looking me straight in the eye, "I don't think there's a thing on this earth that scares you."

18

SAVANNAH

After I show Vinnie around the safe house, I make us a light dinner, and then I ask the age-old question that's on my mind.

"What's been going on for the last seventeen years, Vin?"

"I moved around a lot at first," he says. "Like I told you, I did odd jobs to make ends meet. I had plenty of money, but I couldn't *look* like I had money. Then I heard about Mikey."

I nod.

"I thought about coming back," he says. "I had a plane reservation and everything, made under my alias. I was at the gate, ready to board, and when they called my section, I stood."

"And?"

"I walked the other way."

"What changed your mind?" I ask.

He looks down. "I couldn't go back to it, Sav. I was scared to death. Especially with Mikey gone, they'd pull me back into the family, and I wasn't sure I had the strength to refuse. But I should've come back. I should've come back for you."

"I wish you had," she says. "But I don't fault you for not coming. You had to do what was right for *you*."

"No, I shouldn't have been so selfish. Sure, I wanted out of the whole racket, but I should've come back for you and then taken you with me."

"I would've gone gladly," I tell him, "but I think things worked out the way they should have. I met the love of my life, Vinnie."

Vinnie smiles. "He seems like a good guy, but not the type I thought you'd ever go for."

I cock my head at my brother. "It's interesting that you say that, Vinnie, since you really don't know me. I was ten when you left."

He smirks. "That doesn't mean I didn't keep tabs on you. I had some feelers out, got information when I needed it. When I heard that Dad actually allowed you to go to college without marrying you off, I was elated. And then, when I heard he didn't marry you off *after* college, I was even more elated."

"Yeah, but I clearly paid the price for that."

"You did what you had to do. You got a job you liked, you did a few favors for the family every now and then." He sighs. "It's what this life is about, Sav. It's why I left."

"I should've left as well, but if I had done one thing differently, I wouldn't have met Falcon."

He simply nods.

"But seventeen years, Vin." I grab his hand. "You said you came close to ending it all after Mikey died. You said you studied philosophy. Give me some details."

"I did. I actually spent six months in a Buddhist temple studying with monks."

"You're kidding."

"Yeah, it seems a little off brand for me, but I learned so much about myself. I did that right after I walked away from the flight that was going to bring me home after Mikey died. I felt terrible. It was like I had made all the wrong choices. I was thinking only of myself and not of you and Mikey. So I went to the Buddhist temple, studied with the monks. They put me on a strict vegan regimen."

I raise my eyebrows. "You're a vegan?"

"Only for those six months, but it gave me a sense of clarity. It was basically a fast."

"You went hungry?"

"No, but we would fast for twenty-four hour periods at least once a week. The fast makes you consider things. It makes you consider how lucky you are to *not* be hungry."

"True. Hell, we always lived in luxury."

"And I still did at that point. Like I said, I had plenty of money. I never went hungry, never went without food or clothing or shelter. But I felt an immense amount of guilt, wondered if I should just end my life. And that's why I went to the monastery."

"What did you find out?"

He places a hand over his heart. "I found out that I'm human, Savannah. That I'm not perfect. But I put my own needs before the needs of my siblings, and part of me regrets that very much."

"And the other part of you?"

"The other part of me has no regrets. I did what I had to do for my own well-being." His gaze falls. "I didn't want a life of crime. A life of always looking over my shoulder. A life where human lives had no more value than a business deal."

"I know," I say. "I hate that part. They say it's not personal, it's business. But you know what? Taking a life is personal. Taking a life is the most personal thing you can do."

He nods. "I know. I came to the conclusion that it was okay to do what I did. That it didn't make me a horrible person. It made me a person who took control of his own life, and that I had to trust you and Mikey to take control of yours as well."

"Except Mikey was already dead at that point."

"I know. But that's the life he chose, Savannah. He didn't have the strength to leave. Hell, maybe he never wanted to leave."

"I wish he could have been happy, Vin. He deserved that." I sigh. "But he's in a better place. It's Dad that confuses me more than ever. I've seen a side of him that I never thought I'd see. I never thought he would forsake me, but he locked me in a room once. He locked me in a room with his attorneys and the McAllister attorneys and Miles and his father. They were bartering for me. There was no landline going out, no cell phone service, and the door was locked from the outside. I couldn't escape, Vinnie. They had me trapped."

His eyes are wide. "God…"

"I couldn't believe it either. I basically told them I wasn't going to cooperate, and it must've tugged at Dad's heart-strings a bit, because he let me off. He let me off as long as I took a job as a parole officer and did the favors he asked."

"And you did?"

I bite my lip. "I did. For five years, and then I begged to be set free. And Dad made it happen. That's when I moved to Summer Creek, got a job as a parole officer, met Falcon. Only to find out that I was never truly free." I bury my face in my hands.

He reaches over and squeezes my shoulder. "I don't think either of us will ever be truly free, Sav. But I'm here now, and you and I together will figure out what Dad, Grandpa, and the McAllisters are up to. And then there's one other thing I need to do."

"What's that?"

His face darkens. "I'm going to see our esteemed grandfather behind bars if it's the last thing I do on this earth."

19

FALCON

Two nights.

Two nights of subsisting on Froot Loops for breakfast, peanut butter and jelly for lunch, and microwaveable macaroni and cheese for dinner.

At least I was moved out of the big holding cell.

I share a cell now with a meth head named Germs.

Seriously, he calls himself Germs. His actual name is Steve Germundson, and his teeth are rotted out, his eyes bloodshot.

He's skinny as a fucking rail, and he leaves half his Froot Loops every morning.

I gobble up the rest of them. They don't give me near enough food.

We don't get any outside time because this is the county jail and there's nowhere for them to put us. So I do what I can in the small cell. Sit-ups, push-ups, jogging in place. Working out until I'm a massive ball of sweat.

That of course just makes me hungrier.

"Man, Bellamy," Germs says. "You fucking stink."

I roll my eyes. “Funny, they didn’t give me any deodorant. You know, this being a five-star hotel and all.”

“Ease up, man. I just call ’em as I see ’em. Or smell ’em.” He erupts in laughter.

“Yeah?” I turn around and leer at him. “Well shut the fuck up. At least I don’t fart all night like you do.”

He shrugs. “Can’t help it, man. I’ve got IBS.”

“Yeah? Well I’ve got BO. Deal with it.”

A guard comes then, unlocks the cell. “Your lawyer’s here, Bellamy.”

“About fucking time.”

He cuffs my wrists and takes me to the interrogation room.

Lola’s already there with an iPad and a manila folder in front of her.

“Please tell me you have some good news,” I say.

“Please tell me you’re going to take a shower,” she says, waving her hand in front of her nose.

“God, you and my damned cellmate. I’ve been exercising, Lola. I’ve got to keep my strength up. They feed us crap. It’s not enough to keep a hummingbird going.”

“That notwithstanding, I’ve got good news for you, Falcon.” She opens the manila folder. “Your parole revocation hearing is this afternoon. I have permission to take you out of here and get you cleaned up. Which you clearly need.”

“Thank God. They only let us shower every three days here,” I say.

She pinches her nose. “And you need one. You’ll come with me. You’ll have an ankle monitor, of course, and I’ll take you to a hotel room with a police escort.”

“A hotel room? I want to go to my place.”

She shakes her head. "That'll take too long. The hearing's in a couple hours. I had your brother Hawk go over to your place to grab a suit and tie and everything else you need." She looks me up and down. "God, I hope he didn't forget the deodorant."

I give her a sarcastic scoff. "What's going to happen at this hearing?"

"They'll decide whether your parole will be revoked. I will argue the best I can on your behalf, and if they ask you questions, you will answer them honestly and succinctly."

"What kind of questions might they ask?"

"We're going to go over all of that." She waves me away. "But first, for the love of God, you need a shower."

"I WISH we'd had time to get you a haircut," Lola says as we walk into the county courthouse.

"What? This suit isn't enough?" I tug at the tie. Texas heat is not conducive to wearing a suit. Hawk ended up bringing one of his own, as I only had one at my place and apparently he found a stain on the lapel. Luckily, we're about the same size. The suit is dark gray, the shirt stark white, and the tie dark blue. The shiny black shoes are a little tight. Hawk's feet are slightly smaller than mine. I may lose a toenail by the end of the day, but if I can get the hell out of jail it'll be worth it.

Lola leads me into a somber courtroom. From the dark woods and aged brass accents to the benches that look like church pews, this room has seen the fate of many men like me. In the front is the judge's bench, with the American flag and the Lone Star flag on either side.

A young woman and an older man sit at one of the tables for legal counsel. Lola leads me to the other.

"The judge and the parole board will be in shortly," she says. "Stay here." She walks to the other table and shakes hands with the woman and the man, and then she returns to me.

"Who are they?"

"That's Marian Henley, the prosecutor, and Leo Ficus, your new parole officer and her star witness."

"Great," I say dryly.

"Marian is good people," Lola says. "We couldn't have asked for anyone better. Don't get your hopes up, but she won't nail you to the wall."

"That's good, right?"

"The ultimate decision lies with the parole board, but it'll help that she won't try to throw the book at you."

A uniformed bailiff enters with a court reporter. The reporter takes her seat.

"All rise," the bailiff says.

Lola tugs me to my feet.

"County court is now in session, the Honorable Fay Rodriguez presiding."

The judge walks in, followed by three others. The parole board, I assume, though they're different from the ones I recall when I first got parole.

"Please be seated," the judge says. "As you're aware, this is the parole revocation hearing for Mr. Falcon Bellamy. I'd like to welcome the parole board. Please state your names."

"Wanda Guzman," the women seated in the middle says.

"Barry Lane," the man to her right says.

"And Newman Franklin," the man to her left says.

"Counsel?" the judge says.

"Marian Henley for the prosecution."

Lola rises. "Lola Briggs for the parolee, Mr. Bellamy."

"Very good. Ms. Henley, please call your first witness."

Ms. Henley rises. "Good morning, Your Honor, members of the parole board. I'm here representing the state in the matter of the parole revocation of Mr. Falcon Bellamy. We believe that Mr. Bellamy has violated the terms of his parole, specifically the condition of attending weekly meetings with his parole officer and possession of a firearm. I'll call as my first and only witness Mr. Leo Ficus, Mr. Bellamy's current parole officer."

The questioning doesn't take long. All he says is that I've missed my last two weekly meetings, and I was involved in an incident with a firearm.

"We rest, your honor," Ms. Henley says.

"Do the members of the parole board have any questions for the witness?"

The board members confer for a moment until Ms. Guzman says, "No, your honor."

"Very well. Ms. Briggs, you may call your first witness."

"I call Mr. Falcon Bellamy," Lola says.

I rise and get sworn in by the bailiff.

Then I begin reciting what Lola told me. "Good afternoon, Your Honor, members of the parole board. I appreciate the opportunity to address these allegations. I want to start by saying that I take my parole seriously and have been working hard to reintegrate into society."

Lola asks questions, and I answer precisely and concisely, as she instructed, keeping my demeanor cool and collected. I tell them the story of the last few weeks of my life.

After that, I launch into my second recitation from Lola. "I fully understand the gravity of my actions, and I'm committed to making amends. Revoking my parole would be devastating to my efforts to rebuild my life. I'm willing to accept whatever sanctions the parole board deems necessary to address this lapse and prove that I can continue to rehabilitate successfully."

"Thank you, Mr. Bellamy," Lola says. "We rest, your honor."

"Does the board have any questions for the witness?" the judge asks.

They confer again, this time longer.

Fuck.

Finally, though, "No, your honor," Ms. Guzman says.

"Very well then." Judge Rodriquez bangs her gavel. "We'll recess until the board makes their decision."

"All rise." From the bailiff.

Once the judge leaves for her chambers, Lola and I head out of the courtroom.

"Well?" I ask.

"It could go either way, but the fact that the board didn't ask you to explain anything further is a good sign. All we can do is wait."

So the waiting begins.

It's the waiting that kills you.

The waiting each day on the inside, for your prison cell to click unlocked. To stand outside the door, waiting for inspection.

The waiting in line to get your shitty food.

And the waiting...

The waiting for a new prisoner to arrive—one that may

change the dynamic.

That's what Zion thought he was going to do that day.

~

THE DAY I broke Zion's jaw, I knew I'd have to watch it.

He'd been challenging me since he got here, despite his small stature, and he was strong for sure.

I knew the type. The kind who'd been picked on when he was little because of his size, so he learned to use it in his favor. He worked out, got strong, gained muscles... And then he became a bully. He bullied the bullies, and he became addicted to power. When there were no more bullies, he bullied everyone else. Beating up others made him feel strong. Made him feel like he was someone.

So he took it a step farther.

He started beating women. That made him feel even stronger because it took less work.

Then he graduated to rape.

Rape of both men and women.

Until he finally killed one and then another.

"I lost count after a while," he used to say with an evil grin on his face.

What kind of person loses count of the lives he takes?

I made it clear he wasn't touching me or anyone on my block. He tried to strike alliances, turn my men against me. When none of them took the bait, he started recruiting from other cellblocks, and pretty soon he had a nice gang of troublemakers—enough strength that he thought he could take out Savage.

One day, during our outdoor recreation time, he and two others jumped me on the asphalt.

They'd clearly paid off the guards not to intervene, and while a few of my men tried to, they didn't last long. They helped, though, taking the two minions out and leaving me with Zion.

I didn't come out smelling like a rose from that one. I had two black eyes, a broken nose, and a couple broken ribs. I felt like a truck had run over me.

Zion himself suffered the worst.

A broken jaw.

I never said a fucking word for the couple months he walked around with his jaw wired shut, having to drink his meals through a straw. Not being able to talk, but only being able to rage at me every time our gazes met, his skin turning red with anger.

I never said a fucking word.

My men did, though. They jeered at him at every chance they got.

And I didn't try to stop them.

But I knew...

I knew that when his jaw healed and he could talk again, I was in for it.

So I had to prepare.

I had to prepare myself and my men.

Because he was going to try to take out Savage.

And this time I'd have to stop him for good.

20

SAVANNAH

I take Vinnie downstairs, show him the shooting range, the workout area, and of course the bunker, in case of a true emergency.

"You up for some target practice?" he asks.

"Always."

I choose my firearm, load it, put on my ear and eye gear, and shoot ten bullets straight in the heart of the bullseye.

"Damn, Sav. Who taught you how to shoot?"

"Dad, to be honest, but I was out of practice. Then Falcon did a couple weeks ago, but he says I was a quick study."

"I'll say." He squints at the target. "I'm good, but I'm not that good."

I shrug. "I guess it comes naturally."

"Mikey was a terrible shot," Vinnie says. "But I was always good."

He loads up his gun, and shoots ten, right in the heart of his own bullseye.

"You're as good as I am," I say. "Maybe better."

He chuckles. "I've been shooting for twenty years, Sav. You've been shooting for what? Two weeks?"

"Mostly true. I'm not sure why I'm such a good shot."

"You should be entering contests," he says. "There's a lot of money to be made in shooting contests. Especially here in Texas."

"Maybe..."

"I'm serious."

"Vinnie, I can't even begin to think of anything like that until we take care of all this other stuff. Until we free me from the McAllisters, free Falcon from the county jail."

"He's in his hearing right now," Vinnie says.

"I know. That's why I wanted to do some target practice. Get my mind off of it." I look down at the gun in my hand. "I never thought about it before, but shooting makes me feel... I don't know. Stronger. Like if I'd had a gun, I could've gotten away from Miles McAllister."

"You *did* get away from Miles McAllister," Vinnie says. "You didn't need a gun. All you needed was your wits."

"And my projectile vomit," I say dryly. "And Falcon to save my ass when I got trapped in a different bedroom."

"Hey, it all worked out," he says. "I'm going to go another round."

I nod as Vinnie reloads his gun.

I load mine up, and together we go through a hundred rounds.

When we're done, he takes off his headgear and nods to all the empty shells on the floor. "We probably should have saved these."

"Nope," I say. "Falcon says we've got enough ammo down here to get through another war."

"So I suppose he wants us practiced and ready."

I nod. "Let me show you the gym now."

"Yeah, I need to stay in shape." He stretches his arms above his head. "I kept my muscles toned and strong except for those six months I spent in the monastery. I did what I could there, but that was more a journey of self-discovery and internal reflection."

I look him up and down. "You look good, then. You're broader than I remember."

"That's because I was only a little over eighteen when I left. I was strong and muscular, but I broadened over the next several years."

"Mikey was never as big as you," I say.

"I know. God..." His face twists. "If only..."

"Don't go there," I say.

He takes a deep breath and closes his eyes for a minute before speaking again. "I can't help it. I try not to be sad. The whole monastery thing really helped me. But in the end, I have to live with the fact that what I did was selfish."

"It's not selfish to not want to be a criminal," I say.

"Yeah, I know. I truly do." He sighs. "Still... He was my brother."

"He was my brother too." I grab his arm. "But I've got to tell you, Vinnie, it's good to have you back. I lost two brothers to this family. I'm glad I could at least get one of them back."

He pulls me into a hug, and I succumb to his brotherly embrace. I'm reminded of what it felt like when my father would hug me. Of course, knowing what I know now, I realize a hug from him will never feel the same way again.

I pull back. "Falcon taught me some self-defense. He's got

me on a regimen to tone my own muscles up. But we're going slowly, because he doesn't want me in pain."

"He's a smart man. You want to show me what he's taught you?"

"Absolutely."

I lead him into the gym in the basement. The center of the room is open, dedicated to bodyweight exercises and stretching. Interlocking rubber mats cover the floor, providing a forgiving surface for high-impact activities or the occasional dropped weight. This is where Falcon taught me self-defense, and this is where I'll show Vinnie.

I turn to face him, a wide grin spreading across my face. "I'm about to change your whole perception of your little sister."

He leans against the doorframe, arms crossed, an amused smirk playing on his lips. "All right, I'm all eyes."

I gesture for him to come closer. "First thing he taught me was stance and balance. You need a solid base, like this." I position my feet shoulder-width apart, knees slightly bent. "It makes all the difference whether you're throwing a punch or avoiding one."

Vinnie nods, stepping onto the rubber mats. "Sounds like you've got the right idea so far. Show me what you've got."

I start with a basic jab, the air whistling as my fist cuts through it. "Speed over power to begin with," I say, my voice steady, eyes fixed. "But then, you combine them."

"Let's make it a bit more interactive," Vinnie suggests, rolling his shoulders. "Pretend I'm your attacker."

"All right." I motion him forward. "Try to grab my shoulder."

He lunges, a bit theatrically, and I sidestep, redirecting his momentum and following through with a mock elbow strike to his ribs. "You use their energy, Vinnie. You don't fight against it, you guide it where you want."

He rubs his side, feigning injury. "Nice."

I giggle, feeling the adrenaline rush. "There's more. I learned how to get out of a chokehold. Want to see?"

"Yeah, but go easy on me." He places his hands loosely around my neck from behind.

With a swift movement, I drop down into a horse stance, making myself heavier and harder to hold. I shoot my arm up and hook it around his, pulling it away from my neck as I turn into him and push him back. "That's how you create space and escape."

Vinnie stumbles, seemingly impressed. "That's effective."

I can't help a proud smile. "But it's not all about escaping. Sometimes you have to disable your attacker to get away." I walk over to the padded wall with diagrams of pressure points and strike zones. "You aim for the vulnerabilities—eyes, throat, knees, solar plexus."

He follows, studying the diagrams. "This is serious stuff, Savannah."

"It is," I agree and point to a dummy in the corner. "I practice my strikes there. Accuracy is as important as strength."

Vinnie watches as I demonstrate, my fists thudding against the rubber torso. "Each hit has to have intent behind it."

After a minute, I step back, breathing heavily but controlled. "And when you can't punch"—I pant slightly—"you learn to grapple. Wrestling techniques, joint locks, using leverage."

"You could give those MMA fighters a run for their

money," Vinnie jokes, but there's a trace of real admiration in his voice.

I laugh, wiping sweat from my brow. "The point is not to fight in a ring, Vinnie. It's to make sure I can deal with our family—and the McAllisters—without being afraid."

He steps forward, putting a reassuring hand on my shoulder. "I know, and I'm proud of you. You've always been tough, but now, you're like... superhero tough."

"I don't know about superhero," I say, looking away, feeling a little bashful but happy. "But I do feel more in control. And that's a start."

Vinnie gives me a mock salute. "What's next in the training regimen?"

I roll my shoulders back. "Get ready, because next I'll teach you how to fall without getting hurt. It's all about rolling with it, literally."

He groans. "All right, let's do it."

We spend the next hour on the mats. I show Vinnie the art of falling, rolling, and getting back up again, the basement gym filled with our grunts of effort, a space where I'm not just learning to defend myself, but also teaching my brother to see me in a new light.

"I wouldn't want to run into you," he says, wiping the back of his neck with a towel.

I laugh softly. "You're not who concerns me." I grab a towel for myself. "But the next time Miles McAllister comes near me, I'm going to be more than ready. After all, you saw me shoot." I stand tall. "He won't get near me again."

21

FALCON

"You can come in now," the bailiff says.

I rise and follow Lola back into the room where the parole board sits.

"All rise," the bailiff says once more.

Once the judge is seated, she nods to the parole board. "Ms. Guzman, have you come to a decision?"

"We have, your honor."

"Very well. Go ahead. The defendant will rise."

Lola and I stand together.

Ms. Guzman clears her throat. "Good afternoon, everyone. We have just concluded the parole revocation hearing for Mr. Falcon Bellamy, who was facing allegations of parole violations, specifically missing required meetings with his parole officer and possession of a firearm. After careful consideration of the evidence and statements presented, it's time to discuss our decision regarding Mr. Bellamy's parole. Mr. Lane?"

The man to her right clears his throat. "I want to start by

acknowledging that Mr. Bellamy has shown genuine remorse for his actions. He admitted to the violation, explained the context, and expressed a strong commitment to his rehabilitation."

Oh God. Why do I feel there's a *but* coming?

My heart pounds in my chest and my vision blurs.

I blink several times and everything refocuses just in time for me to see Ms. Guzman nodding to the other board member.

Mr. Lane continues. "Mr. Bellamy's quick acknowledgment of his lapse in judgment and his efforts to seek counseling and support demonstrate that he understands the gravity of his actions and is taking steps to address the issue."

But he still broke his parole, and we're going to send him back to prison.

"That said, despite the context provided, Mr. Bellamy *did* violate his parole, and he was and has always been aware of the consequences of doing so. He has proven in his testimony that he is an intelligent man, one who is fully capable of understanding the ramifications of his actions."

Oh Jesus. I might throw up.

But unlike with Savannah, that won't get me out of this situation.

Ms. Guzman nods. But... Is that a small smile on her face?

Damn. I wish they would just spit it out instead of spouting all this legalese. Just tell me if I'm going to prison or not.

Lola knows what she's doing. She had me memorize all of those monologues and their extremely specific wording for a reason...

But I can't shake the feeling that something bad is going to happen. If not here in the courtroom, then somewhere else.

And soon.

"Given Mr. Bellamy's acknowledgment of the violation," Mr. Lane says, "his commitment to addressing the issue, and his otherwise good record, I propose that we do not revoke his parole."

A huge weight falls off my shoulders. My mind goes blank, and then confetti cannons go off in my brain. I could almost cry.

They're not sending me back.

"Instead, we could consider imposing additional conditions, such as more frequent meetings with his officer."

That's fair. I can handle that. It's bullshit and I won't get anything out of it, but that means I can stay out of prison. I can still see my sweet Savannah. Still make passionate love to her every night until the day I die.

"I agree with that approach," the third member of the board says.

Ms. Guzman nods. "I concur with my fellow board members, your honor. Let's give Mr. Bellamy the opportunity to prove that this was an isolated incident with special circumstances. I believe he can continue his rehabilitation successfully."

"Very well," the judge says. "Mr. Bellamy, your parole will not be revoked at this time. Do you wish to say anything to the board?"

"Yes," I say. "Thank you, members of the parole board. I appreciate your understanding, and I'm committed to demonstrating that I can succeed on parole and overcome this setback."

They all nod at me, and the bailiff clears the courtroom.

Lola pats me on the shoulder. "You ready to go home?" she asks.

I nod. "One second."

I run to the door of the courtroom. Leo Ficus, my new parole officer, is about to walk out.

"Mr. Ficus." I put my hand out. "I want to apologize for my absences. I've already explained myself in my testimony, so you know the story. Still, though, I don't want us getting off on the wrong foot."

Leo Ficus looks like he's about twenty years older than Savannah. He has a strong jaw and a bushy salt-and-pepper mustache that matches the mane of silver hair framing his face. His eyes are cold and no-nonsense.

He stares at my hand. "I gather you got away with a lot with your previous parole officer."

I swallow. "Yes, sir. We met before I realized who she was. And we fell in love."

He blinks. "Rest assured, Mr. Bellamy, that we will not be having as casual a relationship. I will expect you to report to your meetings on time. You got a second chance today. Don't waste it."

I shake my head. "I don't intend to, Mr. Ficus."

"Good." He turns away. "I'll shake your hand when I believe you've earned it. In the meantime, I expect you'll be returning to Ms. Gallo."

"I will, Mr. Ficus." I walk back toward Lola, but then turn back to him. "And I mean it. I look forward to our professional relationship."

He nods and exits.

Lola is packing her briefcase. She chuckles as I approach her.

"What?" I ask.

"Leo comes off gruff, but he's a good guy," she says. "Show up to your meetings and do the work and you'll get back in his good graces. Just do me a favor." She looks me dead in the eyes. "Stop fucking up your second shot at life, Falcon. My sanity, not to mention your father's checkbook, will thank you."

"You'd better believe I won't screw this up, Lola," I say. "Thank you, for everything."

She smiles. "So where are you headed now?"

"I'm going back to be with Savannah."

"Go wherever the hell you want, just get to your meetings with Leo every damn day he tells you to."

I nod vigorously. "I will."

"And you're going to have to give up the firearm."

"It's already in evidence. The cops took it that very day when they came to my place."

And that's fine. I have plenty more firearms if I need them.

"All right." She gives me a once over. "Keep your nose clean, Falcon. Hawk's got a car here for you to take you where you need to go. But the first stop is back to the county where they'll remove that ankle monitor."

"That's where I'm going. Thanks a lot, Lola."

"Thank your father. He pays my bills." Lola waves as she leaves the courthouse, but then looks over her shoulder. "And I mean it. You keep that nose *clean*."

I nod and wave.

Keep my nose clean.

She's covering her own ass. She knows what I'm up against. And she knows that my nose is going to be anything but clean.

22

SAVANNAH

Vinnie and I head upstairs, both of us still panting from the workout, when Falcon's satellite phone rings.

"Hello?" I say breathlessly.

"Vannah, it's me."

"Oh my God, Falcon. How did everything go?"

"Pretty good. They decided not to revoke my parole, except now I have to go to parole meetings twice a week and I have to do therapy."

"I told you about therapy at your first meeting."

"I know, Savannah. Therapy isn't going to do shit for me."

"Not with that attitude it sure won't."

"Savannah, I have no regrets. I did what I had to do, and I'd do it again."

I sigh. "It's precisely *because* you put your ass on the line that you should be in therapy. You have a lot of complicated emotions that a therapist could help you untangle."

He pauses. "Well, I have to go no matter what I think. So

maybe it'll help me. But I think the thing that will help me most is *you*."

I smile. His words make me feel so warm inside. "That's a sweet thing to say, Falcon, but maybe going to therapy *and* being with me will help you heal from your past. Maybe sometime soon you'll actually feel comfortable telling me what happened that day."

"Savannah, I love you. And I trust you. I will not keep any other secrets from you. But I'll be taking that one to the grave."

I say nothing. I try to understand.

"Anyway," Falcon says, "I'll be back as soon as I can, but I want to stop at my parents' house and see Raven."

"Yeah, of course. How is she?"

"According to Hawk, all recovered."

I can hear the smile in his voice. It makes my heart dance.

"Color is back in her face, and she's feeling great."

"I'm so glad to hear that." I scratch my arm. "I feel like I've been so selfish, not even thinking about her."

"We both had other things on our minds. I'm sure she'll understand, but I do need to see her."

"Sure."

"What have you and your brother been doing?"

"Some target practice, workouts, and we've done a lot of talking. Leif stocked us up with two more weeks of fresh food."

"I hope we won't have to be at the safe house that much longer."

"Well, Falcon, *you* don't have to be." I look at my brother and sigh. "Vinnie and I? First of all, my family can't know he's here. Not yet. Second of all, if Miles finds me, he'll take me."

"He will *not*," Falcon says.

I love Falcon Bellamy. I do. I love the fact that he thinks he can protect me from Miles.

Falcon may have been Savage in prison, but this isn't prison.

Miles McAllister has money and power on his side, and my father, for some reason, seems to think this is all okay.

Falcon can't protect me.

I have to protect myself.

"Give Raven my best," I say.

"I will. Love you, Savannah."

"I love you too."

"Who's Raven?" Vinnie asks when I set down the satellite phone.

"Falcon's sister. There's a lot you don't know."

"They both have bird names?"

"All five of them do."

"Why?"

"His mother loves birds. Her name is Starling."

"Really?" Vinnie smiles.

"His two brothers are Hawk and Eagle. His sisters are twins, Raven and Robin."

"Raven is actually a really beautiful name," Vinnie says.

"She's a beautiful woman. She's a year younger than Falcon, and she's had a rough time of it."

"Oh?"

"Yeah. She's in remission from leukemia."

His eyes widen. "Oh my God."

"Yeah. But things look good. And out of three brothers and a sister, only Falcon was a match for a bone marrow transplant. It's why he was able to get out of prison early."

He sits down and runs his hands over his beard. "You're right. There is a lot I don't know."

I open the refrigerator. "Well, Vinnie, we've got all the time in the world for me to catch you up. I'll make us a snack, and we'll start talking."

23

FALCON

"Hey, Ray."

Raven rises from the recliner and smiles at me, coming in for a hug. "Christ, Falcon. We've all been worried sick."

"I know. I'm sorry." I squeeze her tight, so grateful that she's still on this planet. "I wanted to reach out. I was so happy when your bloodwork came back normal."

"God, me too. Though, like I said in the hospital, I only felt sick. Not *sick* sick."

I nod. I don't understand what Raven means, and I'm glad I don't. On the other hand, I'd have gladly gone through the leukemia to spare her.

Raven and Robin are so different. They're fraternal, not identical twins, though they do look quite a bit alike. But Raven is softer, gentler. Robin followed me around as if she were my little brother rather than my little sister.

But not Raven. She stayed in the house with Mom, learned to do homemaking things from our traditional mother.

She learned to ride a horse, of course, but other than that, ranching wasn't really her thing.

Not so for Robin.

She never put a dress on until she hit puberty.

"You want an Orange Crush?" I ask.

"Just finished one, but help yourself."

I grab a water out of the refrigerator behind the bar. Orange Crush tastes like fake flavoring to me, but it's Raven's favorite. She always says it tastes like sunshine.

"Is Savannah okay?" she asks when I sit down next to her.

"So far, so good." I'm not sure how much I'm at liberty to tell Raven. "I had a parole revocation hearing this afternoon."

"Oh my God..."

"Hey, I'm here, aren't I? They didn't revoke my parole."

She cocks her head and smirks. "How'd you get out of that?"

"Lola. She wrote a script for me to memorize. It was the most obsequious thing you could imagine, but it did the job." I fiddle with the lapels of the suit jacket I'm wearing. "This is Hawk's tight-ass Armani suit, plus his shoes. They're too tight on my canoe feet." I lift one of my feet.

"Why don't you take them off?"

I sigh. "Because I can't stay long, Ray. I have to get back to Savannah."

"What's going on?" she asks. "Hawk won't tell me anything."

"Hawk only knows a little." I pat her hand. "I wish I could tell you, but for Savannah's safety—"

"Safety? What happened to her?"

I shake my head, take a swig of my water, and rise. "I've already said too much. Trust me. The less you know, the better off you are. But Leif, Hawk, and I will take care of everything. I don't want you worrying. You use your energy to continue kicking cancer's ass."

"How am I supposed to *not* worry about you?" She places her hand on her chest. "You're part of me now. You're why I'm no longer sick."

"That's exactly *why* you can't worry about me. You need to continue your recovery, get your immune system back up and running. I want you happy. Not stressed."

She rolls her eyes. "Right. Like I haven't been stressed for the last few years, fighting this damned thing."

"Raven, please. For me. Just focus and keep healing." I touch her head. "Hair's growing back."

"Yeah." She laughs sarcastically. "I look like a teenage boy from the fifties."

"Give it another week or two and you'll have one of those sleek and sexy short haircuts. You'll be gorgeous." I kiss the top of her fuzzy head. "I've got to go. Love you."

"Love you too. And Falcon?"

"Yeah?"

"Please stay out of trouble."

I nod. I want to do more, to tell her that of course I'll stay out of trouble.

But we both know that would be a lie.

Once I'm back in the car, ready to head for the safe house, I change my mind.

There's someone else I need to see. I need to put a face to the name, look into the eyes of the man who sold his daughter for God knows what.

I'm driving to Austin.

24

SAVANNAH

The phone buzzes again once Vinnie and I finish our snack.

"Hey," I say to Falcon. "Everything okay with Raven?"

"She looks good," he says.

I let out a sigh of relief. "I'm so glad. So you're on your way?"

"Well...not yet. There's someone else I want to see first, and I may not be home tonight."

My heart thuds. "You're leaving me here alone?"

"I'd never do that," he says. "But your brother is there, and the place is a fortress. There's something I need to do in Austin."

"What?"

"Just an errand that's really important."

My heart drops to my gut. "What errand?"

"Just something I have to do. It's family business, and I don't want you to worry about it. I'll be in touch." The line goes dead.

I gulp and look at Vinnie. "He's not coming home. Says there's something he has to do in Austin tonight."

Vinnie's jaw goes rigid. "He's not thinking..."

"No. He wouldn't. He'd never go back to the McAllisters' place. Would he?"

"You know him better than I do, sis." Vinny rubs his jawline.

"That's the problem," I say. "I know him. I know Falcon. But I also know Savage. And I'm pretty sure *he* is the one we're dealing with."

25

FALCON

I pull up to the wrought-iron gates of Savannah's father's mansion, my heart racing. The imposing metal stares down at me like a sentinel, daring me to take one step closer. Right. I don't have Leif here to break me in like I did at the McAllisters' place, but I *will* get in, and I *will* talk to Vincent Gallo.

Security cameras are trained on my every move. Every inch of this place is under surveillance. Thanks to Leif's tutorial when we broke into Declan McAllister's place, I know where to look and what I'm dealing with, except—

"Damn," I mutter to myself. "This might be more secure than the McAllisters' place."

I drive up to the gate and press the intercom button as sweat beads at my temples. I stare at the camera fixed on me as I wait for someone to answer.

"State your name and purpose," a voice crackles through the speaker.

"Falcon Bellamy," I reply, my tone firm and unwavering. "I'm here to see Vincent Gallo."

The voice pauses, and all I can hear is some rustling and crackling on the other end. My heart is beating more rapidly than normal, but not overly so. I'm not frightened.

I've faced worse than Vincent Gallo in the last eight years.

Of course, those inmates didn't have snipers trained on me. The same can't be said for Savannah's asshole father.

"You may enter," the voice finally responds.

The gates creak open, beckoning me forward.

I drive through, up a circular driveway, and an armed guard gestures me to a parking spot outside the mansion. I step out of the car, and an eerie silence hangs in the air, as if the whole of the estate is holding its breath.

The mansion itself is beautiful. The warm, earthy tones of the stucco walls are speckled with arched windows, and the entire structure is crowned with a red-tiled roof. Lush landscaping encircles the building, with beautifully trimmed gardens filled with classical Roman-style fountains, statues, and pathways. The whole house is probably gorgeous in the daytime.

However, in the black of night, it might as well be Dracula's castle, luring me in with the sole intention of bleeding me dry.

"This way," the guard says.

An armed escort.

Yeah, I've seen this before.

The mansion may look all glitzy and elegant from the outside, but the inside is a prison.

Just like the McAllister manse when Savannah was their prisoner.

Vincent Gallo's no prisoner, of course, but his wife most likely is.

Then again, this security isn't made to keep prisoners in. No, it's made to keep intruders out.

Potato po-tah-to.

The guard navigates me through a metal detector.

"Do you have anything in your pockets?" he asks.

"Just my phone, wallet, and keys."

"Give them to me."

I surrender the items out of my pockets. He looks them over, examining every inch of my wallet, even pulling out a few dollar bills and examining them closely.

He then looks at my phone, turning the screen on and off.

"All clear. Please walk through the metal detector."

I do so. It doesn't beep, thank God.

"Please put your arms out, sir."

For Christ's sake.

"Are you going to pat me down?"

"If you want to visit with Mr. Gallo, yes."

"But I went through the metal detector. It didn't beep."

"This is protocol, sir. Would you like to leave?"

I sigh. "No I wouldn't."

I put my arms out. The guard squats down and pats my legs, thighs, and hips thoroughly. He then looks over my chest and shoulders. When he's done, he takes a step back.

"Right this way, sir."

"Can I have my phone back?"

"Only once you leave. Mr. Gallo does not allow photos to be taken in his private residence."

"What if I promise not to take any photos?"

"You may still leave if you do not want to adhere to the rules of the house."

God damn it all.

"Fine."

It's worth it to talk to the piece of shit who calls himself Savannah's father.

Of course, I'm not laboring under any delusion that Gallo will tell me what's going on. Hell, he may not even listen to me. Mostly likely, he'll try strong-arming me into some kind of submission.

But he hasn't met Savage.

Once we reach the door, the guard rings the bell.

A tuxedoed butler answers.

"Mr. Falcon Bellamy," the guard says.

The butler nods. "Of course, Mr. Bellamy. Please come in. I'm Ferguson, the Gallos' butler."

Ferguson reminds me of Nana's old butler, Laurence. Is he even still alive? We never had a butler at our place. My father was a little more down to earth, though we did have a live-in housekeeper and nanny while we kids were little, though Mom felt that raising us was her responsibility.

I enter the opulent mansion, the air heavy with the scent of wealth and power. My footsteps echo off the marble floors as Ferguson leads me to a study where Savannah's father—presumably—sits behind a giant wooden desk.

"Mr. Bellamy," he says coolly, his expression guarded.

"Mr. Gallo," I reply, keeping my voice low and determined. *Thank you for seeing me* hovers on my tongue, but instead, "We need to talk."

He raises an eyebrow but remains tight-lipped, his face a mask of indifference. But his eyes betray a flicker of unease.

"About what?" he asks, his tone clipped.

"About Savannah's forced marriage," I say, my gaze never leaving his.

The tension in the room rises as we lock eyes, each of us unwilling to back down. But I know I must press further, break through his defenses, and get to the truth.

"Tell me," I demand. "Why are you doing this? What do you stand to gain?"

He speaks in an even tone. "I don't see how this is any of your business. It's between the McAllisters and my family."

"What about Savannah? What about what *she* wants?"

He stares me down. "You think I'd let her marry you? You're a criminal."

I let out a laughing scoff. "You really want to go there, Gallo? Don't you think that's the pot calling the kettle black?"

No reaction.

"Besides, if you've had me checked out, as I'm sure you have, you know I'm innocent."

"Doesn't matter. On paper, you're guilty." He shuffles through some paperwork. "You confessed. And I've never even been under arrest."

"You want to play that hand already? You kidnapped your own daughter."

"From what I understand, she went willingly."

She did, at that. "You sent armed thugs to my place to take her."

"Did I?" He widens his eyes in a ridiculous attempt to look innocent. "That's the first I've heard of such a thing."

"Right." I roll my eyes. "And I'm just that gullible. They may have been the McAllisters' men, but you and I both know what's going on here." I stand up and slam my hands on the desk, causing a few knickknacks to fall to the floor. "Tell me what it will take to free Savannah from whatever deal you made with the McAllisters. I'll pay anything. Do anything."

He eyes my fists but does not stand. "Stay out of what doesn't concern you."

"Come on, Gallo," I urge him, my voice low. "What *aren't* you telling me?"

Gallo's mask slips for a minute. Is that a flicker of regret I see in his dark eyes?

"You think I don't love my daughter," he finally says. "You're wrong."

I open my mouth to tell him he's full of shit, but then I think about Savannah.

Her father got her out of the marriage at eighteen. He somehow—after locking her into a meeting room with no means of communication—got her out of the marriage at twenty-two as well.

"Then what's really going on here?" I ask. "I love Savannah, and I swear to God I will not let her become some slave to Miles McAllister."

He sighs then, rises, and walks out from behind his desk. "This isn't something you'll understand, Mr. Bellamy. This isn't your world."

I grit my teeth. "Savannah *is* my world."

"And you think she's not mine? She's my only daughter. I've already lost both my sons. She's all I have left. My legacy."

"So you sold her to the highest bidder?"

"Damn it!" His fist comes down hard on his hardwood desk. "You really think this is that simple, don't you?"

I take a step toward him. I'm taller than he is, broader. But I don't underestimate him. He's powerful. And in his eyes is a hint of desperation.

That's what this is about.

Never underestimate a desperate man. He's already lost two sons. In organized crime, women are worth less than men. He may truly feel he's got nothing left to lose.

"Miles McAllister tried to rape her that night," I say quietly, taking another step. "My buddy and I got to her before that happened, thank God, and I swear to you, if that piece of shit ever lays another hand on her, I'll take care of him myself."

Gallo's gaze falls to a bookcase in his office.

Are there hidden cameras and microphones in this office?

Of course there are.

"Watch what you say in this office, Mr. Bellamy."

Yeah, not smart. The whole place is probably wired.

"Nothing I say here will ever be admissible in a court of law. You and I both know that."

"You think I give two shits about any court of law?"

Good point. This is a man who's selling his daughter into matrimony. Clearly the law doesn't trouble him. Not a bit.

"I want answers." I demand. "Savannah herself thinks there's more at play here. You let her off twice, and then you let her out of family obligations for good when she moved to Summer Creek. Why the fucking change of heart, Gallo?"

He stares at me, his face unchanging.

But he's not indifferent. Not by a longshot. His eyes flicker with unease. I can recognize almost any look on a person's face after my time inside. My life and the lives of the guys on my cellblock depended on it.

"Look, Bellamy," he says, his voice calm but strained. "There are things at play here that you don't understand.

Things that go beyond a simple marriage alliance between families."

I narrow my eyes, attempting to read between the lines. So Savannah was right. What is her father hiding?

"Enlighten me, then," I say, my tone firm. "You promised Savannah her freedom, and now you've reneged. You sent fucking gunmen to my place to take her."

He presses his lips together. "I had nothing to do with that."

"Do I look like I care?" I point at him. "This is all on you, Gallo. Your daughter's trauma is on *you*."

Gallo goes back behind his desk, sits in his chair, steepling his fingers.

"Listen," he says, his voice taking on a softer edge. "I know you care for Savannah. And I do too. But there are forces at work here that we can't control. And sometimes, sacrifices have to be made for the greater good."

I clench my hands into fists. Sacrifices? What kind of twisted logic is that?

"Savannah is *not* a sacrifice," I say through gritted teeth. "She's a woman. A person. A human being. She's your fucking daughter."

He opens his mouth to reply, but I hear nothing.

I see nothing.

Nothing but blackness.

26

SAVANNAH

Vinnie makes us a dinner of spaghetti and meatballs, but I can't eat. Worry about Falcon consumes me. It's nine o'clock, and he hasn't checked in.

He said he was going to Austin.

Where both my family and the McAllisters live.

I don't think he'd go back to the McAllisters' place. Why would he? He got me out, and they've surely enhanced their security since he broke through it.

Is he going to talk to my father? Give him a piece of his mind about everything that he's put me through since I got to my new job?

If that's the case, I'd like to think my father wouldn't harm him...but I'm not that naïve. Not anymore. I've been forced to see a side of my father that I'd blinded myself to by choice. My daddy. My daddy who I thought loved me.

Now I wonder if the man is even capable of love.

"Try to eat, Sav," Vinnie urges. "You won't be any good to anyone without adequate energy."

He's right, of course. It's the same reason I ate the salmon that night at the McAllisters'. I needed my strength, and it ended up saving me from a brutal rape.

I twist my spaghetti around my fork and bring it to my mouth. The pasta is cooked perfectly, and the sauce is robust and flavorful, but it's all mush in my mouth. Still, I chew and swallow and then twirl some more onto my fork.

"Good?" Vinnie asks.

I simply nod.

"You need to trust him," he says. "Trust that he's doing what he thinks is right."

"What if—"

He raises a hand to stop me. "No what ifs, Sav. It'll kill you. You think I haven't gone there a million times in my own head? It doesn't change a damned thing."

He's right, of course. I take another bite when—

Falcon's satellite phone vibrates.

"Thank God!" I grab it without looking at the number. "Falcon?"

Silence on the other end of the line.

I quickly put it on speaker and press my fingers to my lips so Vinnie knows not to speak.

"Falcon, are you there?" I glance at the number then.

It's not Falcon's.

Fuck.

"Who is this?" I demand.

"We have him," says a voice I don't recognize. "I'm sending an address. Get there as soon as you can."

My heart goes wild as fear slides into me. The few bites of spaghetti tumble in my stomach. "Don't you dare hurt him."

"That depends on you." The phone clicks off.

I gulp audibly. "Vinnie?" I whisper. "I don't know what to do."

He darts his gaze around the room. "He'd want you to stay here."

"Can they track me?"

He shakes his head. "That's a satellite phone. They can't track it. Otherwise they wouldn't have told you to come. They'd come after you."

Yes, yes. Of course he's right.

"How did they get this number?"

"They either held a gun to his head and he gave it to them..."

I shake my head. "No. He wouldn't do that. Not Falcon."

"Sav, when there's a gun to your head, and you're faced with—"

"Just shut up, Vinnie!" I yell. "Falcon wouldn't. He'd protect me at all costs."

Vinnie sighs. "You're sure?"

Am I? I'm not certain of anything anymore. I no longer know my father and grandfather. Do I know Falcon? "I don't know."

Vinnie nods. "If you're right, then he's unconscious and they hacked his phone."

The address comes through in a text. "It's somewhere outside Austin," I say.

"I'm going with you."

"No, Vinnie, you can't. If Dad and Grandpa are behind this, they'll never let you go."

He shakes his head. "It's not up for debate, Sav. I let you down once. I won't do it again."

27

FALCON

I wake up to a sharp pain in my head, and my eyes take a moment to adjust to the light. Where the fuck am I? I try to move, but my hands are tied behind my back, and my ankles are bound together. The rough rope is digging into my skin. When I inhale, I smell dust and mildew. A lightbulb hangs from a string overhead.

"Get up," someone commands from the shadows.

I don't recognize the voice. It sounds like it's coming through water or something.

I look up to see two blurred images.

"Where am I?" I ask, trying to keep my voice steady.

"Somewhere you won't be found easily," the same voice says. "Now, let's get down to business."

I struggle against the restraints. Fear grips me as I realize just how helpless I am.

I don't like the feeling. I don't like fear. I trained myself against it on the inside. But at least I knew where I was, what the rules were, and how to break them.

I don't know where I am or who I'm with. My hands are literally tied, and I don't know what my next move is.

What happened? How did I get here? I was... I had my parole revocation hearing. Went to see Raven. Then...

Drove to Austin to see Savannah's father.

Yes. Vincent Gallo. He talked about sacrifices. Talked about...

I can't remember any more.

"Let me go, Gallo." I growl through clenched teeth.

"He's not here," the same voice says, "but I am."

"Who the fuck are you, then?" I squint, trying to get my vision to become clear.

The man in front of me is dressed in a suit, and his hair is...gray. No, it's actually white. It's...

"Mario Bianchi," I say.

His wrinkled lips twist into a grin. "You're good, given we've never met. And this is Declan McAllister."

"Miles's father," I grit out.

"Good again," Bianchi says.

"What the fuck do you want with me?"

"We have no use for you," McAllister says, "although I could take out of your ass what you and your friend cost me after that break-in you orchestrated."

"Go right ahead," I tell him, "and I'll get you and your son for false imprisonment and attempted rape."

Bianchi chuckles. "You think it's all that simple. You're such an innocent."

I pull at my restraints. "I'm far from innocent."

"You think because you ruled your cellblock you can take us on?" Bianchi chuckles again. "You have a lot to learn, Savage."

"If you have no interest in me, why am I here?"

"Simple enough," McAllister says. "You're the bait."

No.

No, no, no!

"You leave her out of this, damn it. She's safe, and—"

A blow lands on my jaw before I can finish. I'm not sure which one did it. Probably McAllister. Bianchi's an old man. The ache jars me, makes my teeth rattle, but I'm good at hiding pain.

"You'll never find her," I grit out, spitting blood.

"No," McAllister says, "but she'll find us."

Fuck. My hands are bound, and they took my phone. Used facial recognition while I was out cold.

Savannah. They called her on my satellite phone.

"Seems she's very upset at the thought of us having you," McAllister continues.

"How can you do this?" I spit out. "She's your fucking granddaughter!"

Bianchi doesn't answer. Why would he? This is business to him. He violated his grandson in the name of business. Got one of them killed.

I'm dealing with vile criminals, not unlike Zion in prison. Only these creeps have the upper hand. They have money and power, and they're not locked up every night.

They're way more dangerous than Zion.

"She won't come," I say. "She'll know I don't want her here."

"Oh, she'll come," McAllister says. "She's already given herself up to save your ass, and this time, she knows we've got you."

My mind races as McAllister's words sink in.

Fuck.

Savannah *will* come, and there's not a thing I can do to stop her. She'll bring Vinnie with her, not because she wants to but because he'll insist.

That's the one light in this tunnel. If Bianchi gets Vinnie back, he'll finally have the natural heir to his legacy back. He may have no more need for Savannah.

And Vinnie…

With the guilt he feels, he'll sacrifice himself for Savannah.

Savannah and I would be free.

But she won't let him. And neither will I.

The ropes bite into my skin as I struggle against them, willing myself to stay strong. One of them is loose, but even if I get my hands free, my feet are still bound.

I'm utterly helpless, and I don't like that feeling. I hate it, in fact.

Another guy comes toward me with a cup of water. Must be one of their goons. He holds it against my lips, tilting it slightly. I eagerly lap up what I can, though a lot of the liquid dribbles down my chin. Once the cup is empty, the goon disappears.

"Make yourself comfortable," Bianchi says. "They won't be here for another hour at least."

Fuck.

I close my eyes.

Turn back, Vannah, I beg subliminally. *Please turn back.*

But my eyes pop open when two more goons grab me and put me in a chair, tying down my thighs so I can't move. "What's this about?" I demand.

"Not much," one of them says, his eyes gleaming. "The

boss said we could have some fun with you." He clocks my jaw.

I catapult back to the time when Zion and two of his goons attacked me—the time I broke his jaw.

That was three against one, but at least I could move.

This is two against one, and I'm fucking strapped down.

I take it. I take it all.

They batter and bloody me. Pain courses through every fiber of my being, but I grit my teeth and refuse to show any signs of weakness.

"Look at him," McAllister's voice echoes through the abandoned warehouse. "He thinks he's so tough. But we'll break him soon enough."

The goons surround me, taunting me with cruel words and delivering brutal blows to my already injured body. I fight against my restraints, desperately trying to loosen the rope at my wrists.

I spit blood onto the concrete floor. "Fuck all of you!"

Bianchi laughs, a crackling old man laugh that sends shivers down my spine. "You'll regret those words, Falcon. You see, I have a special plan for you. And my lovely granddaughter is going to watch."

Fueled by a surge of adrenaline, I fight against my restraints, determined to free myself and protect Savannah. But the pain is almost too much to bear.

A goon is just about to land another blow when McAllister stops him.

"Wait," he says. "She's here. And she's not alone."

28

SAVANNAH

I drive the Nissan Leaf to a small abandoned warehouse outside of Austin. In the darkness, it stands solitary in a stretch of arid land against the dusty trails that characterize the outskirts of the city. The paint peels on its exterior, and there's nothing around it.

The perfect place to hold someone captive.

Horrific images of what they've done to Falcon fly through my mind. I can't help but think about what my grandfather did to Vinnie. Will he do the same to Falcon?

Or—oh my God—something even worse?

Falcon isn't family. Maybe he has something even worse in mind. Torture…or worse.

My stomach twists into knots.

My brother sits beside me in the passenger seat, quiet and stern. He knows. He knows more than I do of what Falcon is up against inside this place.

And he hasn't enlightened me.

I pull into a parking spot, away from the other vehicles that are there, but close enough to the entrance that we can reach the car in a hurry. Vinnie and I leave the car and walk toward the front doors, which, oddly, are ajar.

They want me to come in. This is an invitation.

Vinnie shoves me behind him and takes the lead, opening the door slowly. The rusty hinges groan, announcing our arrival.

He walks inside ahead of me. When I follow, I inhale. The air is heavy with scents of mildew and dust. I expect rats to scutter by my feet, maybe stray cats as well.

I try to catch my breath, grasping Vinnie's hand, when a large man in black emerges from the shadows.

"Who are you?" Vinnie demands.

"Who the fuck are *you*?" the man hurls back.

"I'm Vincent Gallo, Junior," he says, his voice large and commanding. "I'm here to see my grandfather, Mario Bianchi."

The man's jaw drops.

"Where's Falcon?" I demand. "What have you done with him?"

But the man pays no attention to me. He's focused on Vinnie. "What the fuck?"

"Get my grandfather out here *now*," Vinnie says through clenched teeth.

"No can do, you lying asshole." He grabs Vinnie and frisks him, taking his gun.

Then he stalks toward me.

"Don't you fucking touch her," Vinnie says. "She's Savannah Gallo, my sister, and my family and the McAllisters will kill you if you lay a hand on her."

"She carrying?" he asks.

Vinnie scoffs. "A woman? Carrying? What do you think?"

The man cocks his head.

My pistol is strapped to my shoulder, hidden beneath a large black hoodie. It burns against my flesh as my heart thuds, but I keep my countenance calm.

Please don't take my gun. Please don't take my gun.

"Wait here," he says, and he walks through the first room of the warehouse and disappears behind a door.

Falcon. *Falcon* is behind that door.

"Thank God he—"

Vinnie grabs me, puts his finger to his mouth, indicating me to be quiet. Then he points.

I got it. It's probably bugged, and they can hear everything we say.

No need to let them know I'm armed.

He took Vinnie's gun. It's now on me to protect us. To protect Falcon.

As fear grips my heart, my brother's presence soothes me.

But only a little.

My palms are slick with sweat, and a shiver races down my spine, yet there's a fierce fire kindling within me, burning brighter with the acute awareness that I must shield both Falcon and Vinnie from harm. Each thud of my racing heart-beat echoes a solemn vow to stand as their guardian, to face whoever's in that next room head-on.

Is my father there?

My grandfather?

Miles?

Most likely all three, along with Miles's father, Declan McAllister.

Despite the trembling in my limbs, a steely resolve anchors me. I am the barricade against the storm, the unwavering protector. It can only be me, because I'm the only one who's armed.

It's a heavy responsibility, the weight of Falcon's safety on my shoulders, but it's one I bear with grim determination. I am frightened, yes—profoundly so—but I can't let the fear paralyze me. I can't let the fear define me.

Instead, I'll use it to sharpen my focus.

It's all I can do, because there is no other choice.

29

FALCON

The pain is a constant companion, throbbing in time with my pulse, a reminder of the beating I've endured. It's etched into every bruise and in every shallow breath that stings my broken ribs.

Blood trickles down my face, warm and sticky, as I struggle to keep my eyes open. The pain throbs in time with my heartbeat in a cruel, metronomic pulse that amplifies the agony of every bruise and cut on my body. My limbs are heavy, bound tightly by the rough ropes biting into my skin. There's no way for me to escape, not that I have the strength left to try.

I tilt my head upward, wincing at the effort it takes.

"You're a piece of shit," one of the goons says.

I want to spit back a retort, but my mouth is dry and raw from screaming earlier. So instead, I clench my teeth and glare at him, trying to convey my hatred through my gaze alone. It's all I have left.

Will they force Savannah to look upon my beaten and battered body?

Because I don't care what happens to me. Physical pain is far from new to me.

I endured it more than once on the inside.

What's new is the torment raging inside me—the helpless fury, the gnawing guilt. I'm shackled, powerless, my battered body a prison within a prison—a cage with more walls than the actual prison I endured for eight years.

Savannah is here, and she's going to walk into a battle she's not prepared for.

She'll be strong. There will be no piercing cries that I'm forced to hear. Instead, she'll show strength and defiance, even as they do God knows what to her.

She'll use what strength she has to save me.

And that's not what I want.

I would gladly battle against a thousand armed soldiers to save her from the McAllisters' clutches.

I see her then, through the blood that has trickled into my eyes, making them tear up and burn as if a hundred bees have sunk their stingers into my flesh.

She's wearing a black hoodie, one of mine, and—

Her brother. Vinnie is with her.

What the hell was he thinking?

Same thing I'd have been thinking. No way is Savannah coming here alone.

A defiant spark ignites within me.

I know the moment she sees me.

The look on her face is not shock. Not even horror or disbelief. She clearly knows what these people are capable of. Still, her mouth falls open and color drains from her pink cheeks. She closes her mouth and her jaw goes rigid.

A potent mixture of fear for me and anger at my captors.

Anger at how I've been treated. And anger that she couldn't prevent it.

Her lips tremble.

I open my mouth to speak, but I hear a gun cock behind me.

Someone else has entered the room.

I see two goons, Declan McAllister, and Mario Bianchi. Savannah and Vinnie. Mario and Vinnie seem to be whispering to each other.

So who is behind me, aiming to shoot? I don't dare turn to see the man who's threatening to kill me. He's most likely unhinged, but he won't do it. I'm the only bargaining chip they have with Savannah.

Still the fear slices into me like a sharp icicle. I endured eight years behind bars, and I have a new chance at life. I don't want it to be over.

"Miles, no!" Savannah shrieks.

Miles. So that's who's got a gun pointing to the back of my head. Such a coward. Can't even look me in the fucking eye.

One thing to say about Zion. He was a perverted motherfucker, but at least he wasn't a coward.

"Shut up, Savvy," comes Miles's voice from behind me. "Dad, hold this gun on him so I can fuck her right in front of him."

I furiously work the rope on my wrists, the friction making them raw. "The hell you will," I grit out.

But the attention of the senior McAllister and Bianchi is elsewhere.

On Vinnie.

Neither one looks pleased.

They take him to a corner and speak to him in hushed

whispers. Savannah attempts to come to me, but the goons hold her back.

"What have you done to him?" she demands. "Can't you see he needs a doctor?"

"Not for long." Miles's voice again.

"Why don't you show yourself, you yellow-assed pussy," I manage.

"Tough words from an ex-con who's tied up and beaten to a pulp." But he still doesn't come out from behind me.

"Words are all I've got at the moment," I say, "but if I could, I'd look you in your lily-livered eyes before I take your life. In fact, I will. I promise you." I strain against the ropes around my wrists. "I won't die at your hand. You'll die at mine, and I'll make sure I'm looking you straight in your fucking eyes when you do."

He laughs behind me.

"Miles, please..." From Savannah.

"Fuck off, bitch. You broke a promise. You came with me willingly, and then you refused me. I hate you. I fucking hate you, and I swear to God I'm going to make your life hell as my wife."

"She's not going to be your damned wife," I say through clenched teeth, my jaw hurting like a mother. "Now show yourself."

"Why would I give you the pleasure of looking at my face, Bellamy? Only a sweet, small thing like Savannah deserves such a privilege."

Savannah scowls at him. "I'll never look at your face with anything but disdain, Miles. You disgust me, and you'll never take the love of my life away from me."

She reaches under her T-shirt and quickly draws a gun, pointing it directly at Miles.

Miles gasps. "You're armed?"

I can't help a smile, though it hurts like hell. That's my girl.

Savannah smirks. "Your guard didn't think such a *sweet, small thing* could possibly be carrying a piece. Guess it's time we brought this family into the twenty-first century."

Miles scoffs. "Even if your boyfriend here got you a gun, you don't have the gall to shoot a man."

"You want to try me?" She cocks the gun.

Then Bianchi speaks. "Little cricket," he says, his voice low and gentle. "A nice girl like you doesn't need to use guns. Why don't you put that away and we'll talk this over?"

Savannah doesn't remove her gaze from above my head. She's looking that cowardly Miles McAllister in the eye. "You keep your mouth shut, *Grandpa*. I know how horrible a man you truly are, I know what awful things you've done. I'm not going to—"

Then a gunshot

And a shriek from Savannah.

30

SAVANNAH

"No! Not Falcon!" I drop my gun, rush past the goons, cradle Falcon's head, until—

"I'm okay, Vannah. I'm not shot."

I move backward a few inches.

"Then what—"

Miles's body is on the floor, blood draining from his head.

And behind him stands...

My father.

"Daddy?"

He turns to me, a single tear running down his cheek. "I'm sorry, baby. I'm sorry for everything."

Part of me wants to go to my father, wrap my arms around him, and thank him, but Falcon is my world, and he's hurting. They've hurt him.

"Please," I say to my father, "you've got to help him."

But the others are stalking toward us, and Declan McAllister is not happy. His gun is trained on my father. "I'm going to make you suffer, Gallo."

"No!" I shout. "Enough! Isn't this enough?"

"You'll do no such thing," my grandfather says, his voice completely steady, as if a dead man isn't lying ten feet away from him. "My son-in-law was avenging his daughter. Your son attempted to rape her before they were legally wed."

"He wouldn't," Declan says.

"He did," I yell. "He tried but I got away."

"Besides," my grandfather continues, "Miles and Savannah are no longer needed. My grandson Vincent has returned, and he will take his place as head of the family when I retire. He'll marry your daughter Belinda."

Declan's face shows not a hint of emotion. His son—a horrible man, but his son nonetheless—is dead at his feet, and there's no emotion. Even when he threatened my father, his voice was steady.

It's business.

I can already hear the words in my head.

"Belinda is eleven," Declan finally says.

"They'll be married when she turns eighteen," Grandpa says.

Nausea creeps into my mouth, sour and acidic. "No, Vinnie." I shake my head. "You can't."

"I can," my brother says, "and I will. This frees you, Sav. You and Falcon can have a life."

"But I just got you back!"

Vinnie raises his hand to quiet me. "I'm not going anywhere. I'll be here in Austin now. We'll be able to see each other whenever we want to."

"Vinnie, the girl is too young for you."

"It's my duty," he says, "and hers. Everything will be fine." He slightly shakes his head at me.

And I know.

He has no intention of marrying Belinda McAllister. No intention of taking over the family. He's saying what he must to free Falcon and me.

And God, I love him for it.

I nod back slightly at him, and I hope he knows what I mean—that Falcon and I will be there for him, that we'll help him bring these criminals down.

Grandpa nods to the goons. "Release Bellamy," he says. "And then, Savannah, you and he may go."

My gun lies on the floor a few feet away. I want to grab it, try to save Vinnie.

But my father also has a gun, and though I can't see them, I'm sure Grandpa and Declan are armed as well. And I know the two goons are.

I'd be risking my life and Falcon's, and I won't risk Falcon's. He needs a hospital, and I need to get him there as soon as possible.

"Untie him then," I say, my jaw clenched. "Falcon, we're going home."

31

FALCON

One of the goons whips out a knife and cuts the rope binding my wrists together. They're both bloody from the friction of the rope. My ribs ache, and my face hurts. My nose feels like someone shoved a sharp blade inside it, and my eyes sting from the blood that has trickled into them.

All in all, though, it's not too bad. The adrenaline has kept me out of major pain so far.

Once that subsides, I'm in for all of it.

Savannah offers her hand to help me from the chair, but I shake my head at her. I'm already appearing weak enough. I have to at least get up myself.

I rise, and—

I fall to the floor as my knees give out.

"Vinnie, Daddy, help me!" Savannah cries out.

But no help comes.

Vinnie, Savannah's father, Savannah's grandfather, and Declan McAllister are all gone. Only the two goons remain, and they're busy dealing with Miles's body.

"I can do it, Vannah," I grit out.

"I need to get you to a hospital," she says. "I have the Nissan Leaf outside."

I look back at where Vinnie was standing just a few minutes ago. "What about your brother?"

She gulps. "I can't help him right now, but I *can* help you."

I manage to get to my feet, and though it hurts like a mother, I stand.

~

A HALF HOUR later we're at the ER. My head throbs as I open my eyes to the chaotic scene—the sterile smell of antiseptic in my throbbing nose, and the cold, unforgiving surface of the gurney beneath me. Savannah stands by my side, her beautiful face a mix of worry and anger.

"It'll be okay," she whispers, gripping my hand tightly.

"Your family..." I mutter, finally grasping the gravity of the situation. The aching in my body intensifies as I recall the brutal beating at the hands of her family's goons.

I'm wheeled into an exam room, where a doctor sees me immediately. God, it must be bad.

His white coat is stark against the nurses' green scrubs.

"Hello, Mister..."

"Bellamy," Savannah says, "Mr. Falcon Bellamy. He's been badly beaten. Please help him."

"Mr. Bellamy, can you hear me?" He flashes a light into my eyes.

"Yeah," I say, my voice hoarse.

"Good. I'm Dr. Logan. I'm going to give you a quick examination to see if you need to go into surgery. If not, we'll get you bandaged up and your pain managed."

I wince as he pokes and prods me as he looks me over.

"Aside from the broken nose and surface contusions, you've suffered severe trauma to your head, most likely multiple rib fractures, and from the sound of your breath, I suspect a punctured lung. We'll get a chest X-ray and possibly a CAT scan to confirm diagnosis."

"A punctured lung?" Savannah's eyes widen. "Will he be okay?"

"The condition isn't uncommon." He grabs a form and starts filling it out. "I'll get the imaging tests ordered. In the meantime, I'm going to put you on oxygen, Mr. Bellamy, which will alleviate your shortness of breath and keep you comfortable until we can get the imaging done."

Comfortable? Is he kidding me? But I don't have the energy to say it. The adrenaline is wearing off, and I want some drugs. Pronto.

"Pain," I manage to eke out.

"Can you give him something for the pain?" Savannah asks.

"Of course. I'll order that and get it administered right away." He whisks out of the exam room, closing the curtain behind him.

Savannah squeezes my hand tighter, and I muster a weak smile, trying to comfort her. I can't let her know how much pain I'm in. Not when she's already grappling with the guilt of her family doing this to me.

"Hey," I whisper, forcing myself to sound more confident than I am. "I'm fine, all right? I've gotten through worse than this."

My words are a lie, of course. Even Zion and his two minions didn't get me this badly. I wasn't tied up then, and I was able to fight back. I fought back and I broke Zion's jaw.

Savannah nods, tears streaming down her cheeks. "Okay," she chokes out.

A nurse in green scrubs comes in. "I'm going to start your IV, Mr. Bellamy, and then administer the pain medication that Dr. Logan ordered. I'm going to get your oxygen started as well."

I sigh in relief through the oxygen mask she puts over my nose and mouth.

I breathe in, out, in again, attempting to regulate the pain through breath control.

Yeah, what a crock.

Savannah's warm hand in mine gives me comfort. The nurse stabs me with a needle to start the IV, but I don't even feel it.

A moment later, though, I see a river in my mind. A soothing river, and the pain... The pain...

I close my eyes and let it float away on sparkling water.

When I first got here, I measured the time in days.

Ever since Zion's jaw healed and he's back to taunting my men and me, I've measured it in minutes.

I know, at any minute, he'll come after me.

And I'll be ready.

My toothbrush shiv stays with me at all times, hidden in the waistband of my underwear, or under my arm. I've learned to move it quickly when I must so it's not detected.

The moment comes in the cafeteria.

I know it, because I feel the tension thickening in the air, like an electric current that prickles my skin. The shiv is with me, of course. I've spent the last week sharpening the plastic against the rough concrete walls of my cell. It isn't much, but it'll do the job.

Zion sits alone at a table. His lunchmates have left, and he's still working on his fruit cocktail.

I've finished my lunch, and I've told my men to leave and get outside for their recreation time.

I don't want them involved in this. This is between Zion and me.

I'm still sitting when Zion finally rises, takes his tray to the counter, and shoves it on the conveyer back to the kitchen.

He turns, and his gaze meets mine.

It's time.

I rise, stand tall, showing him the height I have on him. I take a deep breath, steadying myself for what comes next.

I won't go to him.

He has to come to me.

And he will.

He stalks toward me until he stands just inches away, his breath enough to make an alley cat gag. "We've got unfinished business, Savage."

I say nothing.

"You're going to just stand there?" he says. "Go ahead. Take your best shot, Savage."

But I won't strike first, and Zion knows it.

"Let's settle this right here, right now," he challenges, cracking his knuckles.

I can't help a chuckle. These criminals are all the same. They think cracking their knuckles is some kind of power play.

Again, I say nothing.

He lunges forward, and I react, swinging the shiv in an upward motion toward his throat. Time seems to slow down as I watch the sharpened plastic edge slice through the air, heading straight for its target.

Zion's eyes widen, but he quickly regains his composure, narrowly dodging the attack. He grabs my arm and twists it behind my back. The toothbrush shiv clatters to the ground, now out of my reach.

"Is that all you got?" Zion taunts, tightening his grip on my arm. "A makeshift weapon? Can't use your own fists to defend yourself?"

Oh. Hell. No.

All that time I spent making a weapon to use against this fucker, and now it's useless on the floor. But he's right. I can take this shithead out in my sleep, and it's about time I proved it. I don't need the shiv when it's only him against me.

He won't take what's mine. He won't take control of my cellblock.

I wrangle free from his grasp with little effort, slamming my elbow into his stomach so he lets me go.

I turn, face him, but he's fast. I ready myself, but instead, he scrambles to the floor and goes for my shiv.

Bitch!

Now he's got the weapon I made, but no way will he use it against me. I slam into him until his back is against the concrete wall. "You fucking son of a bitch. Thought you didn't need a weapon to take me out, you greasy cunt."

His eyes fire up, and he pushes at me, but I hold fast, knocking his bald head into the wall.

"Fuck you, Savage," he grits out.

"You wish." I knock his head into the wall once more.

Where are the guards? Usually they don't let a confrontation go on this long. I don't dare look away to see where they are or what they're doing.

I won't take my gaze from Zion's.

Until—

"Hey!" a guard rushes toward us.

Zion uses the split second my attention isn't focused on him to thrust the shiv against my stomach, but I'm too quick for him. I grab his hand, twist it, and shove it into his own flesh instead.

He squeals like a fucking pig as the guard grabs me by the arms and pulls me off him.

The guard grabs the toothbrush. "This yours?"

I blink. "No, I took it from Zion. He was about to fucking shiv me. Self-defense."

The guard looks me up and down, frowning. He then grabs his walkie-talkie from his waist. "Can I get medical over to Zion's block? He's been in a fight and is bleeding bad."

Some staticky response from the walkie talkie.

The guard looks at me. "You sure this wasn't your shiv, Savage?"

If I tell him the truth, it'll mean more time. Besides, he was using it against me. Not the other way around. In a way, I'm not even lying.

I swallow. "No."

The guard looks unconvinced. But then two medics come in with a stretcher. They hoist Zion onto it and wheel him away.

That was close.

Too close.

"Mr. Bellamy, I have it written here that you claimed that the weapon used in your altercation with Mr. Zion Flegler was his and not yours?"

I lean my face down to the microphone in the hearing room. "Yes, that is correct."

The woman cross examining me, a short-haired blonde named Ms. Waters, looks at me from across the space. "Mr. Bellamy, are you aware that the toothbrush in question was purchased from the prison commissary?"

I shrug. "I assume it was. I can't imagine anyone would sneak a toothbrush into prison."

"Then perhaps you are also aware that the prison keeps track of which toothbrushes are sold to which inmate."

My stomach clenches, but I don't respond.

Ms. Waters pulls out a piece of paper. "According to this copy of the commissary record, a few months ago, a toothbrush with the serial number matching the one on the weapon used by Mr. Flegler was purchased by you, Mr. Bellamy."

I sputter. "Who's to say Zion didn't fucking steal it from me*? I want an attorney."*

"First, Mr. Bellamy," Ms. Waters says, "I would advise you not to use that kind of language in a disciplinary hearing." She approaches me slowly. "Second, this is an administrative proceeding and you are not allowed to have counsel, as you well know. And third, it is entirely possible that the item in question is stolen. But then we examined your cell, Mr. Bellamy. Do you have any idea of what we might have discovered there?"

My throat closes. I can't speak.

"May the record show that Mr. Bellamy is not responding," Ms. Waters says. "In your cell, Mr. Bellamy, we found a small niche between the wall and the floor. Inside this niche we found a very

sharp rock, which we sent to forensics. On the rock, they discovered several microscopic pieces of plastic, the color of which match the weapon used in the assault with Mr. Flegler."

I still don't respond. I can't.

"We also found cigarettes in the niche. Also contraband."

Fuck. Fuck fuck fuck.

"It is clear, Mr. Bellamy, that the weapon of interest was in fact yours. Do you deny it?"

I should stay quiet. But my mind is a blur. I blurt out the first thing I can think.

"He was going to kill me! I had to have a weapon."

Ms. Waters nods curtly. "If you believed that you were in danger, you should have talked to a correctional officer. They would have helped you."

"They would have thrown me into solitary."

"Nonetheless, you would have been safe," Ms. Waters says. "Mr. Bellamy, I'm afraid that possession of dangerous contraband, in addition to lying under oath, is going to add a significant amount of time to your sentence."

And every last ounce of Falcon remaining in my body drains away.

Rage.

Wrath.

Ire.

I go rigid.

I'm Savage now. Only Savage.

Forever.

32

SAVANNAH

Falcon is sliding in and out of consciousness, and when the technicians arrive to take him for his imaging studies, I head to the front to fill out his paperwork as best I can. I have no idea what insurance he has or what his actual address is. My God, I don't even know his birthday.

I do the best I can, and then I sit in the waiting area.

I try to process what just went on.

How?

How did Falcon end up in that warehouse?

Last I heard, he didn't come home after his parole revocation hearing because he had something to do in Austin.

Next thing I know, I'm getting a phone call the next morning, telling me that they have him.

It was a goon, but was it my grandfather's goon or the McAllisters' goon?

Does it even matter at this point?

I call Leif and give him a quick update, and then I wait. I

grab a magazine but then put it back. Nothing can take my attention away from Falcon.

From this whole situation.

Falcon is my main concern.

Once he's out of danger, then I'll worry about Vinnie and the rest of the family.

Then I'll worry about my father shooting Miles.

Then I'll worry—

"Ms. Gallo?"

I jerk at the sound of my name. "Yeah?"

"Dr. Logan wanted me to tell you that Mr. Bellamy has returned from his imaging. We're admitting him and he'll be moved to a private room. You can be with him now."

"Thank God." I follow her back to the exam room, where Falcon is sleeping.

I kiss his bruised forehead. "Just sleep, babe. It's the best thing for you."

A couple orderlies begin moving the bed out of the ER stall and to an elevator.

I look around as we enter the actual hospital.

I was here when Ashley died.

When Raven was here.

Falcon and I made love here.

Though I guess it wasn't making *love* at that point.

Still, it was hot and passionate and needy and perfect.

And here we are again, back in this hospital, back where so much of our story began.

Sure, it began at that seedy bar Ashley picked out. Then it began again the next day at the parole office. And again that evening when I went to see Ashley and ran into Falcon when he was visiting Raven.

And so it all began...

We've come full circle.

Except we haven't.

Falcon may have won his parole revocation hearing, and I may be free from Miles McAllister, but this whole thing is far from over.

Vinnie has sacrificed himself for me. Agreed to marry a child. Granted, she won't be a child when they marry, but Vinnie will be forty-two to her eighteen.

Gross.

But Vinnie's going to try to bring them down from the inside.

If my grandfather finds out, he'll kill Vinnie. I already know Grandpa doesn't value human life at all.

And if Vinnie's gone...they'll come after me again.

I will not lose my brother. Not again. And I won't lose myself either.

Somehow... Some way... Vinnie's smart. He won't let Grandpa figure it out. I have to hold onto that belief.

We arrive at the room on the second floor of the hospital, and the orderlies wheel Falcon's bed inside and get him on the hospital bed.

He opens one eye.

"Hey," I say, being gentle as I caress his lacerated cheek. "You're going to be here for a while. At least until the doctors get your X-ray and CT results."

He nods and then falls back asleep.

"May I stay?" I ask the orderly.

"Of course." The orderly gestures to a weathered purple couch and recliner on the other side of the hospital room. "There's a pull-out couch if you want to spend the night with him. Or just use the recliner."

"I'll be spending the night," I say.

No way am I leaving his side.

Not when he's in here because of me.

God, the guilt.

The fucking guilt.

It's suffocating. The moment replays in my mind, a relentless loop of what I should have done differently. It's as if the air has thickened, and every breath is a struggle against the guilt that clings to me like a second skin. Its grip tightens with every beat of my heart.

What could I have done differently? Begged him not to go to Austin? Forced him to tell me what he was up to?

He wouldn't have told me.

Why did he go?

Who did he see?

And how the hell did he end up in that warehouse?

The sharp sting of regret pricks at my eyes as the tears form.

But I can't cry. Crying won't do Falcon any good. It won't do me any good.

I could call Vinnie, but I don't even know if he has a cell phone. I don't have his number.

But there's one number I do have.

My father's.

I push it into my phone, even as my body trembles. He killed Miles, and he didn't do it to save Falcon, although that was the result.

No.

He did it for me.

And I should thank him.

Of course he doesn't answer.

"This is Vincent Gallo. Please leave a message."

Short and succinct. What to say? I know better than to mention anything that happened. Every phone call is recorded by my father's staff, and I will not incriminate myself or Falcon.

Not that either of us has done anything wrong, but I don't trust my father anymore.

God, it's a knife in my heart to acknowledge that, but it's true.

"Hi, Daddy," I say. "It's Savannah. I'm with Falcon at the hospital. He's got a punctured lung and he's on oxygen, but the doctor is optimistic. Please call me."

I don't labor under any delusion that he'll actually return my call. He's no doubt in a meeting with Grandpa and Vinnie. Possibly even McAllister, for I already know my father won't be charged in Miles's death.

That's the way of these things.

It's just business.

I sigh.

Falcon lies on the bed, his eyes still closed, the oxygen mask over his nose and mouth.

I sit down in the recliner next to his bed and hold his hand. It's cold. So cold.

Everything is cold.

I grab my phone once more.

This time I call my mother.

And she answers.

"Hello?"

"Mom, it's me."

"Oh, Savannah," she says. "Don't you think you've done enough?"

My heart lurches. Her voice is venomous. I've never heard my sweet mother speak this way before. "What? What are you talking about?"

"Do you ever think, Savannah? Do you ever consider the consequences of your actions?"

"Mom? I don't understand what you mean. I haven't done anything. I'm in the hospital with someone I care for deeply, and—"

"Yes, the Bellamy boy."

"He's hardly a boy. I love him, and he loves me."

"He's a convict," she says.

"An *ex*-convict. Plus, he says he's innocent, and I believe him."

She sighs through the phone. "You have no idea what you've done."

"Mom, Vinnie's home. Vinnie. Your son."

"You think that makes me happy?" She's shouting now. "Vinnie had a life. A life away from all this. He came back because of *you.*"

"My God," I say. "Who are you and what have you done with my mother?"

"I lost my Michael, but at least I knew my Vincent was safe and happy. Far away from here."

"What about me, Mom? I was here, and I wasn't happy."

"You made a deal, Savannah. You agreed to go with Miles."

"How do you know about that?"

"I know everything that goes on in this family. I always have. I may look and act a certain part, I may have married a man I didn't know to do my duty to my family, but I've always known the truth of what's going on."

"And you were willing to forsake your only daughter?"

"Of course not! Your father let you out largely because of me. I went to bat for you, Savannah, not once, not twice, but three times, first getting out of marriage to Miles at eighteen and at twenty-two, but also freeing you from the business months ago when you moved to Summer Creek. You were home free, Savannah. *You* are the one who made the deal with Miles McAllister."

"That's not fair, Mom. He sent gunmen to Falcon's house to get me."

"But he didn't get you. And they would have been dealt with. This is on *you*, Savannah. You made a deal with the devil, and then you backed out. Vinnie, Falcon, Miles's death, your father... It's all on you."

I swallow against the rage inside me.

How dare she? Though Vinnie came back for me. And now...

And Falcon... He went to Austin for... I don't even know.

But Miles. What do I care about Miles? He was a vile rapist and a waste of human skin.

How dare—

"Wait. What? What happened to Daddy?"

My mother sobs through the phone. "He was arrested, Savannah. Arrested for the murder of Miles McAllister."

33

FALCON

"He'll never stop," Eagle says. "He won't stop until he kills me. So I'm going to kill him first."

I gesture toward Vega's minions. "You two should get the hell out of here. Now." I'm amazing even myself that my voice isn't cracking. Inside I'm a quivering mass of nerves, but on the outside? I'm standing tall, remembering the words of my father that have been jammed into my head since the day my sisters were born.

You're the oldest, Falcon. You must protect all your siblings.

And if my brothers—especially Eagle—ever needed protection, they need it now.

The minions don't respond to me. Not that I expect them to. Vega is most likely armed, but he can't reach for a weapon with Eagle's gun pointed at him.

Hawk is still trained on one of the minions, but I've got nothing. Eagle's holding my piece.

"Easy, boy," he says to Eagle. "You're in trouble enough already."

"Fuck you," Eagle spits out. "Fuck all of you."

"Eagle, come on," I say, keeping my voice calm. "You do this, your life is over, man."

"My life is already over, Fal."

"You're a kid," I say. "You got in with some bad people. You think you're the first kid to fuck up?"

Eagle scoffs. "You never fucked up. You and Hawk. Dad's perfect sons."

I raise my arm slowly. "Hey, I promised I'd help you, and I will, but I can't unless you put down that gun."

"You think those two shitheads won't pump me full of bullets the moment I do?" he says.

He's got a point. I turn instead to Vega.

"You've got your cash and then some," I say, again trying to stay calm. "Just get out of here. Leave our brother alone. You'll never hear from any of us again."

"Yeah," Vega says. "It'd be nice if it worked that way. But it doesn't. This kid caused me a lot of headaches, and I'm going to take it out of his skinny ass."

Hawk cocks his trigger. "Say goodbye to your friend, then."

Vega scoffs. "You think I care about either one of them? They're a dime a fucking dozen."

"Eagle..." I say. "Please."

Eagle's hand shakes. He's a good shot, but damn, a shaking hand with a gun in it never leads to anything good.

I take another step toward him. "Eagle, I'm going to put my hand over yours. I'm going to take back my gun."

I take another step, until only about four feet separate us. I'm ever aware of the four guns in play. Mine in Eagle's hand. Hawk's trained on the minion to my left. And both the minions', trained on Eagle.

If my brother shoots Vega, he's a dead man.

I can't let that happen.

"Please, Eagle. Think of Mom. You're her baby. This will kill her. Think of Nana. Think of—"

"Shut up, Falcon!" Eagle steadies his hand, takes aim—

And he fires, straight into Vega's heart.

34

SAVANNAH

The afternoon slides into evening. I hate leaving Falcon alone, but I have to go get some dinner in the cafeteria before it closes. I grab a pre-made chef's salad and bottle of water and hurry back up to Falcon's room, where I eat it robotically, alone with my thoughts—thoughts focusing mostly on Falcon but sliding every once in a while to my father's arrest and a side of my mother that's new to me and almost frightening.

A doctor in a white coat is there, but it's not Dr. Logan. She turns to me when I walk in.

"Hi, are you Ms. Gallo?"

"Yes. I'm Savannah Gallo."

"I'm Dr. Pinkman. I have Mr. Bellamy's imaging results."

My heart skips a beat. "And...?"

Dr. Pinkman smiles at me. "They look good. His punctured lung isn't serious and it should heal on its own. We'll keep him on oxygen through the night, but his vitals are good so he can probably go off it tomorrow."

"That's good." I look over at him in his hospital bed. "Why hasn't he woken up?"

"We're giving him Demerol for the pain. He's probably having a nice nap. It's good for him. But my guess is he'll wake up in the morning."

"Good."

"Will you be staying with him?"

I pat the arm of the recliner. "Yeah. I'm spending the night."

"That's fine. But you should know that the nurse will come in every hour to check his vitals. You may not get much sleep."

"Believe me. I'll get more than I would if I weren't here. I'd be a ball of worry."

She smiles. "I understand. He's doing just fine. I'm glad you're here for him."

Dr. Pinkman steps over to the computer monitor, makes some notes, and then leaves. A moment later a nurse steps in.

"I'm Nora. I'll be Falcon's nurse tonight." She lays a hand on my upper arm. "Do you need anything? A toothbrush?"

"That would be great if you have one."

"We do. We keep toiletries on hand for overnight visitors. I'll bring you a packet as soon as I make a note of his vitals."

She checks Falcon's oxygen and his IV, makes some notes on the computer, and leaves. Ten minutes later she returns and hands me a small paper bag. Inside is a toothbrush, toothpaste, some makeup remover wipes, and cotton swabs.

"Thank you."

"Not at all. If you need anything else, let us know. We'll help if we can."

"Just take care of Falcon. That's all I need."

"I will."

"Thank you, Nora."

She smiles and leaves, closing the door behind her.

I take the toiletries to the bathroom in Falcon's room and get ready for bed. I opt to sleep in the recliner so I can be next to him rather than pulling out the bed from the loveseat in the room. I fall asleep to his breaths through the oxygen mask.

~

"Sav." Someone nudges my shoulder. "Sav, wake up."

I jerk upward. "Falcon? Is he okay?" My vision adjusts and I see my brother's face. "Vinnie? What are you doing here?"

He darts his eyes around the room nervously. "I don't have much time. The sun's about to come up. I'm getting all my stuff together to move in with Mom and Dad." He frowns. "Well…Mom."

"What's this all about? What—"

"Shh. Don't wake Falcon." He kneels next to the recliner and lowers his voice. "I want to talk in here, where I know we won't be overheard. I told Grandpa I would check on Falcon this morning and also make sure you were okay. He's not happy with either of you, of course, but I told him if he wants me, then you two are off limits."

I grab his hand. "I never wanted that, Vinnie."

"I know that, but I made a choice at the time. I see the way you look at Falcon, the way he looks at you." He looks over at Falcon, who is still snoozing away. "The two of you deserve a chance. I'm not in love."

"But you're going to marry an eighteen-year-old?" I say. "And wait seven years to do it?"

"A lot can happen in seven years, Sav." His voice drops. "I mean a *lot*."

I nod. His eyes are laced with fire.

He's still determined to take them down from the inside.

"Vinnie, you've been gone for so long. What makes you think—"

He puts a finger to his lips, indicating for me to be quiet. "There's a lot I can't tell you for your own safety, but suffice it to say our theories were correct. They're combining the business. And getting into...new ventures."

God. I gulp. The Bianchis and the McAllisters are merging, and somehow Grandpa got talked into dealing not just in drugs.

But in people.

I swallow back the puke that feels like it will erupt at any moment.

"Vinnie..."

"Don't say it. I can only tell you this." His gaze burns into me. "Grandpa didn't have a choice."

"There's always a choice, Vinnie."

"In the abstract, I agree with you." He swallows. "But given the facts as I now understand them, if I were Grandpa, I would have done the same thing. Agreed to the same thing. Even if it meant marrying you to Miles McAllister."

I drop my jaw, ready to scream at him.

But he shakes his head. "Understand what I'm saying, Sav. This is big. Enormous, even. I can't give you the details. I don't even know all of them yet. Grandpa's an old man, and he's a product of his age, of his upbringing all those years ago. He didn't see any other way out."

"I can't believe you're taking his side," I hiss out in a whisper.

"I'm not. I said if I were *Grandpa*." He pounds a fist against his chest. "I'm not him, Sav. I would have made a different choice, but it's too late at this point. All I can do is go along for now."

"Christ, Vinnie."

"Listen to me. I can't tell you more. It would only put you in danger. I need you to trust me."

"How can I? You just said our family is getting into—"

"Shh. Don't even say it." He looks out the door of the hospital room. "Never say it out loud, Sav. You never know who is listening."

I gulp again.

"Seven years, Sav. I have seven years to figure out how to take down my own family."

"You'll have to work with someone in the government," I say. "Someone with the resources to help you from that side."

"I'm working on that. I figure I can probably find someone on our payroll who's willing to roll over to the right side for the right amount of money."

I shake my head. "Do you realize how fucked up that sounds?"

He scoffs quietly. "Yeah. It's fucked up, Sav. You think I don't know that? But this was always my fucking birthright. Not Mikey's, and not yours. It's mine, and I'm claiming it. Just not for the reasons Grandpa thinks I am."

"Do you think it's weird that he's welcomed you back with open arms after seventeen years?"

He shakes his head. "No. It was always supposed to be me. In his eyes, I'm the prodigal son."

I look at the ground and scoff. "I never understood that parable. One son leaves his family and lives a life of indulgence, while the other works his ass off for the family. Then the spoiled brat comes home and is welcomed."

"Calling me a spoiled brat, now?"

"You know that's not what I mean."

"It's a family thing," he says. "I was always supposed to be the one, and now I'm back."

"So Michael and I were sloppy seconds?"

"Not in my eyes, but in Grandpa's? Yeah, you were." He puts a hand up right as I'm about to respond. "I'm not saying it's right, Sav. What I am saying is that he's glad I'm back. I'll do what I have to do to earn his trust."

"And then use it against him?"

"Bingo," he says. "This *will* end, and it will end on my watch."

I open my mouth to respond when someone else walks into Falcon's room. Vinnie turns at the sound of the door.

"It's probably just the nurse," I say, standing.

But it's not the nurse.

It's Falcon's sister Raven.

And my brother can't stop staring at her.

"Hi, Savannah," she says to me. "How is he doing?"

"He's still asleep." I keep my voice low. "Raven, this is my brother Vinnie. Vinnie, this is Falcon's sister Raven."

"Nice to meet you." Vinnie holds out his hand.

Raven takes it. "You too."

"How are you feeling?" I ask Raven.

"All better. It was just a silly virus."

"I'm so glad," I say. "Vinnie and I can give you some time with Falcon. Come on, Vin." I drag my brother out of the room.

"We can't talk here," Vinnie says.

"I get it, but she deserves some time with her brother. He saved her life, after all."

"Yeah. Wow." He takes a slow breath in. "I wouldn't have expected a bald woman to be so damned beautiful."

"Everyone in their family is beautiful."

Vinnie stares at Raven through Falcon's door. She's sitting in the recliner I vacated, leaning over and talking to him. Is he awake?

"How will we stay in touch?" I ask Vinnie.

He tears his gaze away from Raven and meets mine. "I'll figure that out. I'm thinking a satellite phone. Falcon already has one, so you're covered on your end. I'll get one and make sure no one knows about it."

"Won't Grandpa be watching you like a hawk?"

Vinnie nods. "At first he will, so our communication will be minimal. But you'll be notified of anything important."

"And...Dad?"

"Dad made his bed. He knew what would happen if he offed Miles." Vinnie looks around. "We really shouldn't talk here."

"Where, then? I need to know about Dad."

He looks in the room again. "I hate to make her leave."

"We can't, Vinnie. That's her brother. I can't waltz in there and tell her she has to leave."

Vinnie breathes. "All right. Come to Mom and Dad's house tonight for dinner. It'll be just Mom and me, and after she goes to bed, we'll talk."

"And that's safe?"

"I'll make sure it is. I'll make some excuse to Mom and Grandpa that I need to spend some time with the only sibling I have left before I begin my work. Something like that. I'll find the right words."

"But Falcon..."

He lays a hand on my shoulder. "Falcon is fine here. No one will touch him. It's part of the deal I made with Grandpa and Declan McAllister."

"And you're sure?"

He nods. "Yeah. I sold my soul to the devil, so he'd better be good for it."

Vinnie's words don't exactly put me at ease.

"I've got to go now, Sav," he says, giving me a quick hug. "I'll see you tonight at Mom's house."

I nod.

And then I go back into Falcon's room.

35

FALCON

I *hate that mask.*

I wish I could see you.

I wish I could save you the way you saved me.

Words float around in my consciousness.

Am I asleep?

Awake?

My eyes open.

Two figures.

I try to talk but a mask is over my face. With one hand, I swipe it off.

"Falcon, no." A voice.

"I'll get the nurse." Another voice.

Then the image comes into focus. "Savannah?"

But it's not Savannah. "Ray, what are you doing here?"

"I came to see my big brother." Raven rubs my arm. "You look terrible, Falcon. I can't believe this happened to you."

What happened to me?

Right.

The McAllisters' goons.

Or the Bianchis' goons.

Same difference. They had muscles and fists. And of course the added advantage of tying my wrists together and my legs to a fucking chair so I couldn't move away from their blows or defend myself.

Cowards.

"Mr. Bellamy," another voice says, "how are you feeling?"

"Great," I eke out, my voice hoarse.

"Your oxygen saturation is excellent. We can get rid of the mask and use a nasal cannula for now. At the end of the day, we'll see if the doctor thinks you can go off of oxygen."

"Why am I on oxygen?"

"You have a punctured lung. It should heal on its own, but for now the doctor wants your oxygen supplemented."

"Okay," I say.

"Everything looks good. Your breakfast should be here soon."

Ugh. Breakfast. I can't eat. I'm hungry, but it will be too painful. My jaw isn't broken, or it would be wired shut like Zion's was. Still, it hurts like a mother just to open my mouth to talk.

"Broken?" I ask.

"What do you mean?" Raven asks.

"Do you remember what happened yesterday, Falcon?" Savannah asks. "What the doctor said?"

I open my mouth and wince at the pain.

"I'm sorry," Savannah says. "Don't try to talk. You have several fractured ribs, but no other broken bones. Other than the punctured lung, all the wounds are superficial."

Superficial. Right. They sure as hell don't feel superficial.

"You're a lucky man, Falcon." Raven's soft voice. "Now try to stay out of trouble, okay?"

I close my eyes.

36

SAVANNAH

Raven sat with Falcon most of the day, which allowed me to sneak out to the safehouse and get some clothes and an overnight bag.

One day I have to go shopping for new clothes. Most of mine were destroyed when Abel and Giancarlo ransacked my place, killing Mr. Shaw.

God... Poor Mrs. Shaw. She was released from the hospital and I haven't been to see her. In my defense, I was holed up at a safe house, but still... I should check in on her. I'll see about that tomorrow. Last I heard she was staying at her sister's place while the duplex is being renovated.

Now, though, I'm almost to my parent's place in Austin. I hope it won't be a late night because I have to drive back and spend the night with Falcon at the hospital. But I promised Vinnie I'd be here, and I need to be. I need to know what's going on. Of course, we have to wait for Mom to go to bed to speak privately. Someone should be with Falcon...

Why didn't I arrange for Leif or Hawk to be there?

I call Leif on my cell.

"Hey, Savannah," he says.

"Hey, I'm sorry to bother you, but I'm having dinner with my brother in Austin at my folks' house, and I may be late. Could I bother you to sit with Falcon tonight?"

"I'm actually here now. He's looking okay, all things considering. He's awake and alert."

"Thank God."

"The doc says he can go off oxygen, but he'll be here tonight and tomorrow night for observation. If all looks good with the lung after that, he can go home."

"That's good news." I bite my lip. "But about tonight…"

"It's taken care of," he says. "Raven is staying."

"Raven?"

"Yeah, I couldn't talk her out of it. She says—"

"May I speak to her, please?"

"Yeah, sure. Don't you want to talk to Falcon?"

"Not if it's still hurting him to talk."

"Yeah, it's still pretty difficult for him."

"Tell him I love him, and please let me talk to Raven."

"She loves you, Fal. Ray, she wants to talk to you."

"Savannah?" Raven's voice.

"Hi, Raven. I'm so sorry I'm not there, but are you sure you're up to staying with him?"

"Absolutely. He stayed with me when I needed him."

I sigh. "I should be there."

"It's okay. He understands. He says there are things he can't tell me. But are you okay, Savannah?"

"I'm fine."

"Take care of your business tonight," she says. "I have your number, and I'll call you if anything changes with Falcon."

I smile into the phone. "You're an angel, Raven. Truly."

"Falcon's my angel." Her voice cracks. "I'd do anything for him." She clears her throat. "When you get back though, you and I need to talk."

My heart jolts. "About what?"

"About that gorgeous brother of yours. I didn't even know you had a brother."

~

DINNER IS TENSE.

The coq au vin that Cook prepared looks and smells delicious, but the flavor is lost on me when I'm consumed with thoughts of Falcon and of the conversation Vinnie and I are going to have tonight.

My mother is sullen toward me.

Is this truly the same mother who took me on that mother-daughter day so long ago? That perfect memory that has been my safe space for so long? The mother who looks like me, with a fair complexion and a spray of freckles, so different from my darker-skinned brothers who resemble my father.

We eat mostly in silence, until finally I can't take it any longer.

"Mom, what's going on?"

She stops her fork midway to her mouth and glares at me. "What's going on, Savannah, is that your father—my husband—is not here. He's being held without bail for the murder of Miles McAllister, an action he committed to save *your* boyfriend."

"Exactly," I say. "So he shouldn't be charged with murder. He was defending someone. He was defending Falcon."

"You and your criminal justice background," she says. "Don't you know by now that the rules don't apply to us? He killed the son of a rival family. It doesn't matter *why* he did it. It doesn't matter if doing so prevented war, or famine, or the destruction of the universe. He will go down for it. Declan McAllister will see to that."

"Sav," Vinnie says, "there's more at work here than you understand."

"Then help me understand, Vinnie."

"Your father is expendable," Mom says. "Your father was *always* expendable, and your grandfather won't bargain for him because now Vinnie is back to take his place." Mom turns to Vinnie. "Not that I'm upset that you're back, honey. I've been dreaming of this day." Then she turns back to me, glaring. "But if you'd done as you agreed to—married Miles—none of this would be happening."

"So you'd prefer I be unhappy and married to a kidnapper and rapist?"

She slams her fork down on her plate. "Do you think it was any different from what I went through?"

"Are you telling us that Dad raped you?" Vinnie asks through clenched teeth.

"No," she says. "Your father was good to me. I was only eighteen, and we'd just met. He was gentle. Or he tried to be, anyway. He was kind and never laid a hand on me until I was ready." She looks down at the table. "Unlike my own father."

"Grandpa—"

"Don't look so surprised, Savannah," Mom snaps. "We all know what your grandfather is capable of."

I do now. Especially after Vinnie told me what Grandpa did to him when he turned eighteen. Except—

"He never touched me that way," I say.

"No, he didn't," Mom says. "He'd never soil his little cricket. He had a soft spot for you."

Vinnie twists his face in anger. "Christ, Mom. All these years—"

Mom pushes her plate away. "I'm done. I'm done with this pleasant dining experience. I'm blaming you for everything that's happened, Savannah."

"Mom, I—"

"Be quiet," she says. "Perhaps I'll see it another way eventually, but at the moment I'm no longer under my husband's care. I'm under my father's, and that is a very dangerous place to be. For all of us." She rises. "I'm retiring to my room." She whisks out of the formal dining room.

My heart is in shambles. My grandfather raped my mother? Wasn't she supposed to be a virgin like I was? So much I don't understand, and frankly I don't *want* to understand it. I ache for my mother, but her blame on me is misplaced.

Hedy, our maid, comes in to clear the dishes. "Do either of you need anything else?" she asks.

"Yeah," Vinnie says. "A bourbon. Neat."

"Make that two," I say.

When Hedy returns with our drinks, Vinnie rises. "We can use Dad's study. It's soundproof."

I nod and follow my brother out of the dining room and down the hallway to Dad's home office. It is indeed soundproof, and probably wired.

"You sure it's safe?" I ask once Vinnie shuts the door.

"Yeah. I had it checked out earlier today."

"By someone you trust?"

"Hell, Sav, I don't know who to trust." He rubs his temples. "The people here are loyal to Dad, not to me. But I have to assume, until I have the power to find out otherwise, that they're telling me the truth."

I take a seat on a leather chair in front of my father's massive desk.

I wonder if Falcon was here. I've been wanting to ask him since we got to the hospital, but first he was on that medication that made him sleep, and then I didn't want him to talk with his injured jaw. But I want to know if he came here to see my father that night he was taken to the warehouse. If my father had anything to do with it.

I don't know, and I can't waste my time wondering.

"Tell me everything," I say to Vinnie.

37

FALCON

"Please, Eagle. Think of Mom. You're her baby. This will kill her. Think of Nana. Think of—"

"Shut up, Falcon!" Eagle steadies his hand, takes aim—

And he fires, straight into Vega's heart.

Vega hits the ground with a thud.

Fuck.

Fuck, fuck, fuck.

"Eagle, get down!" I yell.

But there's no need. The two minions rush out, and within minutes, they're unloading a shit-ton of drugs out of their truck and onto our property.

"What the fuck?" Hawk races after them.

Eagle stands, the gun still pointing where Vega stood.

Vega's blood has soaked through his shirt, but I'm more concerned about my brother than trying to revive a drug lord.

"Eagle," I say, willing my voice to stay calm. "Please. Give me my gun."

He stares, trancelike, straight ahead as if Vega is still standing there.

"Eagle..."

Outside, I hear the truck engine start and then screech away, the four-wheel drive trudging over the bramble presumably back toward the border.

Shit. Those two will get back and tell the second-in-command what happened here, and they'll come after Eagle to avenge Vega.

Fuck.

Hawk returns. "They unloaded their cargo. Now what the hell do we do?"

Only then does Eagle look at me. "Falcon?"

I grab his shoulder. "Yeah, E. It's me. Everything's going to be okay. Just give me the gun."

He looks down at Vega's immobile body, the blood now soaking his entire shirt.

"It's okay. We'll fix it," I say. "Just give me the—"

Eagle escapes my grasp and darts out the door of the old barn.

Hawk and I follow, as Eagle shoots.

He shoots again.

"Eagle!" I shout. "Stop it. Stop it now!"

Hawk runs after him, but Eagle is quick. He shoots into thin air, in every direction.

Hawk and I watch our brother shooting like a lunatic.

Eagle continues to shoot until the cartridge is empty.

Still he shoots, clicking the trigger even though no more bullets rain down.

"Easy, Eagle," I say, keeping my voice as calm as I possibly can, even though my heart is thundering like a machine.

"What the fuck?" Hawk mutters.

"Eagle?"

I take a step forward.

"Watch out," Hawk says. "He's in shock or something."

"Yeah, but he doesn't have any more bullets—"

Eagle drops my pistol and then pulls his own out of a hidden holster. Damn it! He wasn't supposed to be armed.

My heart thumps like a galloping stallion.

"Eagle..."

He points the gun at me.

I'm unarmed. My pistol's at Eagle's feet.

Hawk stands, reaches for his own piece, but I gesture to him slightly with my head to back off.

Putting another gun on Eagle will just spook him more.

I have to believe our brother won't harm us. So I advance another step. Eagle still stands, holding the gun to me.

"Hawk, stay back," I say.

"I'm not moving," he says.

I take another tentative step toward my brother, who is still holding the gun.

"E? You need to put your gun down. There's not going to be anymore shooting tonight. No one's going to hurt you."

He cocks his head slightly, but he does not lower the gun.

My heart is thumping so quickly.

I take another step.

Eagle steps back a few inches then.

Damn. He's spooked.

Why shouldn't he be? He just shot a fucking drug lord.

"Come on, Eagle. You need to give me that gun."

I take one more step forward. Only about five feet separate us now.

One more step. "It's just me. It's Falcon." One more step.

Three feet. If I reach out, I can grab the gun. But I know better than to do that. I need to be closer to him.

One more step and then one more. We're face to face, and I hug him. I take my brother in my arms, and then I pull back slightly, retrieving his gun out of his grip.

Eagle falls back into my arms and lets out a sob.

"It's okay, brother. I got you."

Everything will be okay now.

Except everything's not okay. My brother just shot a fucking drug lord.

And he did it with my gun.

38

SAVANNAH

"*Everything* isn't on the table," Vinnie says to me. "You know that. But I'll tell you what I can. Everything will only make you unsafe, and I can't have that."

"Because you're doing this to keep me safe."

He nods. "This is my atonement. For you. For Michael."

I sigh. "You and I both know there's nothing you can do for Michael now."

"I know, but I feel it in my soul that I need to do this. That it's my calling."

"To bring down your own family?"

His face darkens. "To bring down Grandpa specifically. And if I find Dad has been his innocent pawn all this time? I'll see that he's set free."

"Did Dad know what Grandpa did to you?"

"I didn't tell him. I don't know what Mikey told him. For all we know, he did it to Dad before he let him marry Mom."

"God." I bury my face in my hands. "How much sicker can this get?"

"A lot," he says, "but I can't give you the gory details, and believe me, you don't want them."

I simply shake my head. There's nothing else I can say.

"Right now, Dad needs to be in prison awaiting trial for the murder of Miles McAllister. It's the only thing that's appeasing Declan at the moment, and according to Grandpa, we can't be working at cross purposes with Declan."

"Fuck them all," I say.

"Sav, you know I agree with you, but for now, I have to play the willing grandson. As far as they know, I'm seeking their forgiveness for my betrayal, and I'm going to have to prove myself."

My heart slams against my sternum. "By doing what?"

He draws in a breath, and before he speaks, I already know the answer.

"No, Vinnie. Don't."

He looks up to the ceiling and then darts his gaze around the room. He rises. "Let's go outside."

"Outside?"

"Like I said, I trust the security guys, but I don't want to take the chance. Come on."

We leave Dad's office and go out the French doors leading to my parents' large manicured lawn out back. Vinnie and I walk out into the middle of the yard, close to the pool house.

He nods to a camera mounted near the gate to the pool house. "They can see us out here, but they can't hear us."

"Won't they wonder what we're up to?"

"Yes, which is why I'm going to make this brief. As far as the camera knows, you're showing me around the back lawn, the pool house, everything else."

"Vinnie, it's all the same since you left."

"Yes, but I've been through a lot, and perhaps my memory has failed. That's what I'll tell them if they ask, but they probably won't ask." He takes my arm. "Come on."

We walk around the yard, stopping every couple of steps to make it look good.

"I have no intention of taking anyone's life," Vinnie says. "But that is what they'll expect of me."

"Then how will you prove your loyalty?" I ask.

"I'll fake it."

I shake my head, my mouth dropped open.

He nods slowly, breathing evenly. "Yeah, I don't have the details yet. But I'll get some blanks, send whoever I'm supposed to take care of out of the country. I don't know the specifics, Sav, but I promise you I won't kill anyone."

I want to believe my brother. With all my heart I do.

"Vinnie, please promise me one thing."

"If I can."

"If you can't figure out how to fake it, then run like hell. Go back to Europe. Do whatever you have to do to—"

"Sav." He grips my shoulders and stares into my eyes. "I will not abandon you again. Do you hear me? I will not. Don't worry about me. I got this."

"But Vinny—"

He releases his grip. "I've got a plan in motion to put them off for a few months. I'll say I need to be educated in all the inner workings, and I'm out of practice with a firearm so I need to get up to speed."

"I just saw you shoot a few days ago. You're hardly out of practice."

"They don't know that, and I'll use it to my advantage. Grandpa is so happy to have his blood back on board that I'll be able to subtly manipulate him. I'm not an idiot eighteen-year-old anymore. I've gained a lot of wisdom in the last seventeen years, and Grandpa's an old man. It won't be easy, Sav, but trust me. I can do this."

I nod.

I have to trust my brother.

I have no other choice.

"What can I do to help?"

"Nothing. This is on me, Sav." He grabs both of my hands. "You go. You live your life. Be with the man you love. Tell Falcon how sorry I am that he got brutalized so terribly, and that I'm happy he's on the road to recovery. This is your chance. Take it. Please."

39

FALCON

When I awake the next morning, I'm surprised to see Raven instead of Savannah in the room with me.

"Ray?" I say.

"Hey, you." She squeezes my hand. "How are you feeling today?"

"A little better. My breathing seems to feel normal, and it doesn't hurt quite so much to talk." I shrug. "How do I look?"

"Like you've been hit by a truck," she says, "but you look wonderful to me."

A doctor walks in briskly. "Good morning, Mr. Bellamy."

"Hey, Doc," I say.

"I have some excellent news for you." He looks down at a clipboard. "Your imaging results from yesterday afternoon look great. Your minor pneumothorax is healing nicely, and you should be able to go home later today. You'll need to take it easy, though. Full healing will take up to two weeks, which is why I'm going to want to see you back for imaging then. Your ribs are another story. The hairline fractures will heal on their own, and there's not much we can do except wait for them to heal. They will be painful for the next week or two."

"Great," I groan.

"It could have been a lot worse, Falcon," Raven says.

Yeah. I could be dead at the hand of that fucker Miles McAllister. But I can't say this to Raven. She doesn't even know the full story of what happened to me. I told her it had to do with Savannah's family, but that's it. So far she hasn't pressed it, but now that I'm feeling better, I know I'm in for it today.

"I'm going to sign your discharge papers today, and they'll be good for this afternoon. I just want to keep you here for the morning to make sure everything continues to go well."

"Thanks, Doc." I gingerly rub my jaw. "I think."

"Do you have any questions?"

"No."

"Good. The nurse will go over your discharge information with you after lunch." He looks at Raven then. "You're not the same woman who I met when Falcon was admitted."

"No. I'm his sister. Raven Bellamy. Savannah will be here as soon as she can."

"Good, good. As long as someone is here to drive your brother home," he says.

I raise an eyebrow. "You saying I can't drive?"

"You can drive as long as you're not taking your pain meds," he says, "but hospital protocol dictates that you must be released to an adult. After that, drive if you're comfortable, but my guess is it will be a few days before your pain is at a point where you can be off the meds for a bit."

"Got it," I say.

He looks at me as if he expects me to balk. I have no

intention of that. I spent eight years of my life locked up. Staying home and not driving for a few days is nothing—especially now that I know Savannah is safe.

"Good." He gently pats my shoulder. "You're a lucky man. This could have been a lot worse."

"You're telling me."

The doctor nods to Raven, makes a few notes on the computer, and then leaves.

Raven shuts the door behind the doctor and then sharply turns to me, her forehead wrinkled. "When are you going to tell me what's going on, Falcon?"

"Around the fifth of never."

She shakes her head. "You're part of me now, big brother. We have no secrets."

"We have some," I say. "And they're not my stories to tell, Ray. I'd tell you everything if I could." A yawn splits my face. "Ow! Damn, that hurts."

"Okay, okay. I can take a hint." She opens the door and puts a foot out. "You rest. We'll talk when it doesn't hurt you so much."

I nod and close my eyes. Savannah should be here soon, I hope. Raven said she went to Austin last night to have dinner with her mom and Vinnie, and she'd probably stay the night.

That's not like her...which means something's going on.

And I want to know what it is.

40

SAVANNAH

I leave my parents' home after spending the night in my old room. I say a quick goodbye to Vinnie, but I don't seek out my mother.

She's hurting now, and in her mind, it's my doing.

Vinnie tried to convince me over a quick breakfast that she doesn't know any better. That she did her duty by marrying Dad and believes that I should be willing to do the same. Funny. She and Dad eventually fell in love. Their marriage was a happy one as far as I could tell growing up.

So of course she's upset that her husband is gone and will likely spend the rest of his life in prison. But he did it to save the man her daughter loves.

Perhaps it's—

"Savannah!"

I'm ready to get into the car when I hear my mother's voice. I look up.

"Come here, please."

I draw in a breath. Be ready for anything. "What is it, Mom?"

"I need to say something to you."

I walk toward the doorway where she's standing. "I think you said enough last night."

She shakes her head. "You're my only daughter. I never wanted any of this for you."

"Then why the huge-ass guilt trip?"

"Because..." She dabs a tear away from her cheek with a handkerchief. "Because I love your father, Sav. I didn't when we met. I didn't when we got married. I didn't even when Vinnie was born. But I grew to, and I grew to need him as much as I needed to breathe. Can you understand that?"

I nod. "Yes. I know what that feels like."

"That's how you feel about your young man? This ex-convict?"

"He's innocent, Mom."

She begins to speak but I hold up a hand.

"You can think what you want about Falcon. I believe in him, and I love him. He loves me." I swallow. "I never wavered in my belief that you and Daddy loved me. Not until those gunmen came to Falcon's house looking for me. I knew what it meant. I knew Daddy was going back on his word. And I also knew, Mom, that he would never do that lightly."

"No, he wouldn't. And he didn't. His love for all his children always came first. That's why he killed Miles, Savannah."

"I know that."

"He chose you over everything else. His family. His wife. His son."

"That's not fair. He didn't even know Vinnie was back when he shot Miles."

"I adore Vinnie," Mom says. "I never thought I'd see him

again, and I'm over the moon that he's back. But he made your father expendable, Savannah. Your father is my heart. My lifeline. And he's going to be in prison until the day he dies."

I look at my mother. Truly look at her. At the fine lines around her eyes and her mouth. At the freckles, some of which have enlarged and morphed into age spots. She's still a beautiful woman, but she's nearing sixty.

"Your father grew to love me more than life itself," she continues. "And I him. He's the air I breathe, Savannah, but he's not coming back to this house."

"Mom, Vinnie will find a way."

Mom sighs. "I wish that were true, but you don't know my father the way I do. To you, he's the adoring Grandpa who used to bounce you on his knee. To me, he's a monster."

I nod. What can I say? She made clear last night what she was talking about, and I honestly don't want to know any more. A moment later, I glance around. "Mom, do you know why it was so important that I marry Miles?"

She pauses and then nods. "Yes, Savannah, I do. And I hate it. I hate what my father has become. I hate what he's done to our family. And I hate him for dragging Vinnie into it."

"Vinnie won't get sucked in. I trust him."

"He *will* get sucked in," Mom says. "I watched it happen to your father, and I watched it happen to Michael. The only thing that saved your father was his love for me and his children. Michael couldn't be saved. And Vincent... He has nothing to save himself for. All he has is an eleven-year-old fiancée and a betrayal he has to make up for." She starts to cry. "I'm frightened for him, Savannah. And I lashed out."

"At me."

"Yes. It was easy to blame you. In my eyes, all the family was asking of you was the same thing they asked of me."

"Miles wasn't Dad."

"No."

"He tried to rape me."

"I know. And I'm sorry." She buries her face in her hands.

I lay my hands on my mother's heaving shoulders. "Mom, you say Vinnie doesn't have anyone to keep him grounded. That's not true. He has you. And he has me. We'll be his strength. He's going to be okay, Mom. Trust in him."

She wipes her eyes and looks around, whimpering. "This house is so big. So empty now. Vincent will get his own place, and I'll be alone."

"Do you want me to move back in?"

"No. You have your young man. Be with him. I'm done being selfish." She walks back inside the house without saying another word.

I get in the car and drive back to Summer Creek.

Back to Falcon.

But first, I make a detour to visit my father.

~

He's in orange. My strong and handsome father is wearing orange.

Thank God I never had to look at Falcon like this. My father is big and strong, but he's no Savage. He hasn't been transferred to the prison yet, thank God. Right now he's being held in the county jail, and his attorneys arranged for him to have family visitors. We sit together in a small room, a guard watching us.

"This isn't like I expected," I say. "I figured you'd be behind glass and we'd be talking on one of those old fashioned telephones."

"Not here, in the jail," Dad says. "Once I'm arraigned, they'll either let me out on bail, which is unlikely, or they'll house me here or at the prison. The lawyers are working on it, but the McAllister lawyers are working just as hard against it." He draws in a breath. "And so is your grandfather."

I grab his hand. "Dad, I can't thank you enough for saving Falcon. Truly. He's the man I love."

"He came to see me," Dad says. "The night they beat him."

I nod. "I figured as much."

"I'm sorry for my hand in that. Please believe that I had no idea they would torture him like they did."

I look into my father's sunken eyes. He's sad, regretful. I believe him.

"What happened?" I ask.

"I sent your grandfather a text to let him know Falcon was here. Next thing I know, one of our staff members was hitting Falcon over the head and dragging him out of my office. Your grandfather clearly had someone in our house on his payroll."

"How did you know where they took him?"

"That old warehouse is where they do a lot of their dirty work," he says. "I was told to stay put, and that was my intention, originally, but I couldn't, Savannah. I couldn't let them kill someone you loved."

I love my father more in this moment than I ever have.

"I never wanted you with Miles McAllister," he continues. "But I didn't think there was any other way, Sav, and I'm sorry."

"You let me go so many times."

He looks into my eyes, his gaze soft. "You're my weakness. You and your mother. But your grandpa got into a mess with the McAllisters. He always said he'd never get into their line of business, and like a fool, I believed him. He's not a good man, Savannah."

"Yeah. I know that now."

"You tell your brother he needs to take care of your mother, okay? He's the head of the household now." Dad shakes his head. "God, I was so glad to see him, and then he got whisked away by your grandfather, and before I knew it, I was being arrested. My firstborn son comes home, and I go away."

"It's not fair, Daddy."

He looks at the bland walls in the visitation room. "Maybe it is. I drove him away all those years ago."

"That wasn't you. Vinnie told me some stuff."

"What?" His eyebrows are raised in question.

Does he truly not know?

I blink for a minute before I respond. "You'll have to ask him. He'll come see you."

"I'm not so sure of that." He sighs. "I'm not sure your grandfather will let him out of his sight."

"He's living at the house with Mom. I just had dinner with them last night."

"We'll see how long that lasts." He pats my hand. "Sweetheart, you take care of yourself."

"Thank you, Daddy. Thank you for everything."

"I made a lot of mistakes raising you kids, but one thing never wavered. My love for all three of you."

"I know, Daddy."

He stands and indicates to the guard that our visit is over. "Go now. Go home to the one you love. Make a life far away from all this, Savannah. Do it. For me."

41

FALCON

Raven and Savannah bring me back to my place on the ranch. After conferring with Vinnie, I agreed to come back here with Savannah instead of returning to the safehouse. After all, we need the safe house to stay safe, and if we're there, we risk people looking for us and finding it.

"You good here?" Raven asks.

"We are," I say.

"Would you like to stay for dinner?" Savannah asks Raven. "It won't be anything fancy. I ordered some groceries and I'm making spaghetti."

"No, no. I should get home." She gives me a hug. "You stay out of trouble, all right?'

"Ray, you know I never go looking for trouble."

She looks me up and down, smirking at my scars and bandages. "Right."

Savannah sees Raven to the door and then returns. "I should get dinner started."

"I love my sister," I say, "but I'm glad she didn't take you up on your invitation."

"I am too," she says. "I think the two of us need some quiet time alone."

"Not that quiet." I take her hand and lead her to the bedroom.

"Falcon..." She pulls back on my arm. "It's too soon. You're still all bruised up, and you're still recovering from your punctured lung. And those ribs. You can't possibly be comfortable."

"Vannah, I have never been too sick or injured to have sex, and I'm not about to start now."

She raises an eyebrow. "So you've had sex when you've been sick or injured before?"

I stare into her beautiful brown eyes. "Never with anyone who mattered."

She touches my cheek gently. "Does this hurt?"

"Your touch could never hurt me." Though it does sting just a bit.

She gently runs her fingers up my arm. "Tell me what to do. I don't want to hurt you."

"You won't." I cover her hand with my own. "I'd do anything for you. I think I've proved that."

"Why did you go see my father, Falcon?"

"For answers. To try to get you out of this arranged marriage." I sigh. "I was just so... so... angry, Vannah. Angry at what McAllister tried to do to you, what I knew he would do if he ever got his hands on you again." I look her in the eyes. "I'd lay down my life to protect you, but if I were gone, then what? I thought if I talked to your father, made him see reason..."

"Reason is different in my family."

I exhale sharply. "Yeah, I gathered that."

"We're here now," she says. "I don't want to talk about this anymore. Just for tonight, can we forget about it? Can we just love each other?"

I groan. "That's all I've ever wanted since the first moment I laid eyes on you in that dive-ass bar." I pull her to me and kiss her.

Hard and passionate, and damn, it hurts.

But it hurts so good.

We undress each other in a frenzy, although she takes special care with my chest. Then she leads me to my bed—our bed now, because she's never moving out of this house—and helps me lie down on my back.

"Vannah..."

"Quiet. You lie there and be still. I'm taking care of you tonight."

She slides down my body, trailing light and feathery kisses over my chest and abs until she gets to my hard cock. She grabs it at the base and slides her tongue over my cock head.

"Fuck," I growl.

She takes me into her mouth, about three quarters of the way, and then pulls back, sucking gently.

And then not so gently. With her other hand, she cups my balls. They scrunch up at her caress, and damn, I'm so ready.

"Easy, Vannah, or this will all be over too soon."

She moans against my cock, and the vibrations slide through me. She continues sucking me, and I watch her, gaze at her beautiful lips sliding up and down my cock, the perfect combination of pressure, warmth, and wetness.

It's like she's sucking the life force out of me in the most wonderful way. Tingles shoot through my spine, turning from icy to hot in mere seconds, until—

"Vannah, baby." I stretch my arms out toward her. "God... Come here. Come here and straddle me. I want to be inside you. I need to be inside you."

She lets my cock go with one more sweet suck to the head, crawls upward, and then sinks down on my hardness with a soft whimper.

"Feel good?" I grit out.

"So good, Falcon. I've missed this. I've missed you."

She leans down, and I grab her tits, taking one nipple between my lips and tugging while she undulates her hips, circling them, making me insane with her movements as I embed myself inside her warmth.

A moment later, she sits up, and her sweet nipple drops from my mouth. She finds her rhythm and she begins fucking me. Gliding up and down over my cock, her perfect suction driving me to the brink of madness.

"Yeah, Vannah. God, yeah. You're so tight. So sweet. God, I love you."

"I love you too, Falcon." She increases her speed, riding me like a bucking bronco, moaning, whimpering, until she slides her hand down her belly and touches her clit—

"Ah, God!" she cries.

Her pussy clamps around me, and I'm done for. I reach forward, grab her hips, and push her down hard onto my cock as I explode inside her.

And all the pain, the beating, the fear, the anguish...

It all fades away into the willing body of the woman I love.

Later, as we lie together, she snuggles into my shoulder. "I love you," she whispers.

I look deeply into her beautiful eyes, into her beautiful soul. "Then marry me, Savannah. Please. Make me the happiest man in the world."

She smiles wide. "And I'll be the happiest woman in the world. Yes, Falcon. I'll marry you."

We fall asleep in each other's arms.

EIGHT YEARS EARLIER...

I didn't sleep that night.

I stayed in Eagle's room, watching over him. He tossed and turned all night, and in the morning, I dragged him up, shoved him in the shower, and brought him cup after cup of coffee.

I already knew I wouldn't be going on my European wine tour with Mom or joining the Navy with Leif.

No. My life was laid out for this summer. I had to take care of my baby brother. Make sure he got the help he needed. And make sure this whole fucking thing went away.

Two days went by, and I thought maybe everything would be okay.

But then the sheriff came to our house.

Dead body found on your property.

Young rookie cop. Out hunting. Got shot.

The words buzzed in my ears—phrases and fragments.

A dead cop.

Someone was going to have to pay.

Without thinking, I started talking. I told them Hawk and I were out doing some target practice. A bullet must have gone off course and we didn't realize it.

Hawk and I both gave our pistols to the sheriff, and I lost more sleep, wondering if the bullet had actually come from Eagle's gun after he'd dropped mine.

Nope .

It came from my gun.

My brother had killed a cop. With my gun.

And I took the blame.

I AWAKE to the buzzing of my phone. The sun is setting through the window as I untangle myself from Savannah and find my pants to retrieve my phone.

It's Hawk.

"Hey," I say into the phone.

"Falcon, I'm sorry to bother you your first night home from the hospital, but I've got something important that can't wait."

"What is it?"

"Can you speak freely?"

Savannah is snoring softly, but I leave the room anyway, pulling on my pants as I go.

"I can now. What's up?"

He pauses a moment.

"For Christ's sake, Hawk. What is it?"

"It's bad, Fal. Really bad."

My pulse accelerates. "God, not Raven."

"No, no. Of course not. Last I heard she was helping Savannah bring you home."

"Yeah, she did. She left a while ago." I heave a sigh of relief. "What is it then?"

He pauses. "I just got out of a meeting with Dad, a couple of his foreman, and his land attorneys. He wants to expand, Falcon. He wants to begin clearing that parcel of land by the border…where that old barn sits."

My heart drops.

"Fuck," I say.

"I know. They're going to start taking some soil samples within the next week or so, check out water sources, make sure there aren't any wetlands issues that would violate the Clean Water Act."

"There aren't," I say dryly.

"I know. I didn't tell them that, of course, but you and I know that piece of land better than anyone."

"Fuck."

"Turns out, permits are already in place, so once they assess the property and determine that there are no legal issues, they're going to begin clearing. With bulldozers. And when they start digging…you and I *both* know what they're going to find."

THE BELLAMY BROTHERS CONTINUES SOON!

A NOTE FROM HELEN

Dear Reader,

Thank you for reading *Seductive Sin*. If you want to find out about my current backlist and future releases, please visit my website, like my Facebook page, and join my mailing list. If you're a fan, please join my Facebook street team (Hardt & Soul) to help spread the word about my books. I regularly do awesome giveaways for my street team members.

If you enjoyed the story, please take the time to leave a review. I welcome all feedback.

I wish you all the best!

Helen

Sign up for my newsletter here:

http://www.helenhardt.com/signup

P.S. Did you know I write historical romance as well? Turn the page for an excerpt!

EXCERPT FROM LILY AND THE DUKE

BRIDGERTON MEETS FIFTY SHADES IN THIS SPICY VICTORIAN SERIES BY #1 NEW YORK TIMES BESTSELLING AUTHOR HELEN HARDT!

Laurel Ridge, the Lybrook Estate, Wiltshire, England, 1845

Lady Lily Jameson set down her portable easel and palette of watercolors to smooth her mussed sable curls. The September day was sweltering, and beads of sweat trickled down her face. She gazed around the small alcove that appeared to be the remains of an old stone chapel. The long grass tickled her ankles under her skirt. White and yellow daisies poked cheerful heads through the lush green foliage, and yellow and magenta blooms dotted the abundant vegetation like confetti. A tiny brook babbled nearby.

Lily sighed, hoping she could capture the beauty of the alcove in watercolor before her mother and father noticed she was missing from the afternoon lawn party.

She tied on her painting smock, set a piece of thick cotton paper on the easel, and coated it with water. She started with the bright cerulean of the sky, and then the brook and the rich greenery behind it.

"That's quite good."

Lily jumped up, knocking over the small tin of water sitting in her lap. She turned and stared up into a golden face and striking green eyes. Her breath caught.

"I'm sorry," the young man said. "I didn't mean to frighten you."

"No, I'm fine." Lily, trembling, wiped her stained fingers on her apron.

His hair was the color of ripe wheat, and it fell to his shoulders in gleaming layers that brushed the collar of his brown jacket. He was tall—taller than her father or her brother—and his broad shoulders led down to slim hips and legs clad in tight tan trousers and brown riding boots. He wore no cravat, and a few tawny hairs peeked out of his crisp linen shirt. His face was handsome, with a strong jaw, full lips, and a Grecian nose. Long mahogany lashes adorned his arresting eyes.

Lily swallowed. Something new and uncomfortable churned in her stomach. Like butterflies. Or rolling water.

"How did you come to be here?" the man asked.

"I-I wanted to paint."

He smiled, revealing straight white teeth. "My mother likes to paint. I find her here often."

Lily clenched her clammy fists in her stained smock. "Your mother?"

"Yes. My mother. Your hostess. The duchess."

"Oh." Lily widened her eyes and willed herself not to stammer. "You're the marquess, then?"

"No. The marquess is my older brother, Morgan. I'm Lord Daniel Farnsworth." He smiled again. "And who might you be?"

"Lily, my lord." She offered a quick curtsy.

"Lily who?"

"Lady Lily Jameson."

"You're Ashford's daughter?"

"Yes, one of them."

"Is the other as pretty as you are?" he asked, winking.

Warmth crept into Lily's cheeks, and she hoped the young lord didn't notice. Imagining her blond-haired, blue-eyed sister, she said, "More so, I think."

"That, I doubt." He cleared his throat. "You have quite an eye for painting. I shall leave you to your work. I'd love to see it when you're finished."

"Yes, my lord."

He turned to leave, but looked over his shoulder. "How old are you, Lily?"

"Thirteen, my lord."

"Be sure to come back in five or six years," he said, and walked lazily out of the alcove.

Eight years later

"Now we'll never catch up with Mummy and Papa." Lady Rose Jameson tucked herself into her carriage seat. "Why you had to go searching for some old painting is beyond me."

"Because I want to take it back to the little alcove at Laurel Ridge and paint the scene again." Lily smoothed her sage green skirt. She remembered fondly the beauty of the Lybrook estate and planned to paint to her heart's content during the upcoming two-week house party. "Besides, we'll catch up. Won't we, Thomas?"

Her older brother, Viscount Jameson, nodded. "My team

can outrun those antiques of Papa's any day. We may even get there first."

"Thank goodness," Rose said, smiling. "I'm filled with excitement about spending the next few weeks at Laurel Ridge."

"I'm looking forward to it myself," Lily said.

Rose's sapphire eyes widened. "You want to meet the duke?"

"You know me better than that." Lily laughed. "I couldn't give two figs about His Grace. It's his art collection that intrigues me. It's rumored that he has a Vermeer!"

"Good God, Lily," her brother said, winking. "The most eligible men in England will be at Laurel Ridge, and you want to see a painting?"

"Thomas, darling, we all know that you have about as much appreciation for art as a tree toad." Lily smirked. "No doubt there will be plenty of beautiful women at Laurel Ridge who couldn't care less about Vermeer, and I'm sure His Grace will send hoards of castoffs your way. I, on the other hand, have better things to do than pant after the Duke of Lybrook like a bitch in heat."

Thomas laughed. "God help the duke if he crosses your path."

"Lily," Rose said, admonishing, "it's a good thing Mummy isn't around to hear you talk like that."

"Have you forgotten that he's only the duke by virtue of the untimely deaths of his father and brother? He's still a renowned rake. No self-respecting father would have dared allow his daughter to so much as blink in his presence." Lily rolled her eyes. "But now he's a duke, and all is forgotten and forgiven? The hypocrisy makes me want to cast my crumpets."

"Of course you're right, but—"

"He spent his entire mourning period touring the continent, no doubt visiting every whorehouse he came upon."

"I wish you wouldn't use such language."

"Brothel, then. House of ill repute. Is that better?"

"Lily..."

"He left his poor mother here alone to deal with her grief. He's nothing but a scoundrel."

"The duchess was in good hands, Lily," Thomas said.

"I suppose so. She was no doubt better off with her spinster sister than with that son of hers." Lily inhaled and fidgeted with her dress. "The duke does have a beautiful estate, though. I intend to spend a great deal of time admiring the artwork, strolling in the vineyards, and painting and writing."

"Don't you want to take part in any of the festivities?" Rose asked.

"Maybe some. But don't worry. Sophie and Alexandra will be there for you. We'll all spend time together. I'm sure Mummy won't hear of me going off alone as much as I wish to."

"I'm quite thankful for that."

"I'm not. What I wouldn't give for two weeks of freedom before I'm thrust into that barbaric meat market of a ritual that London calls a season."

"Lily," Rose said. "I'm not sure why Mummy and Papa made you wait until this year for your season. You could have started last year, and you would be happily married by now."

"Me, happily married?" Lily scoffed. "Of course I had to wait for you. Mummy and Papa know that you'll attract the right type of suitor, and they're hoping I can follow along on your tail."

"That's ridiculous and you know it."

"Ridiculous, maybe, since I have no desire to bind myself to some stuffy aristocrat for eternity, but true nonetheless."

"But you're just as beautiful as I. Perhaps more so."

"You know beauty has nothing to do with it." Lily turned to her brother, who was watching her intently. "I see you have that overprotective look in your eye, Thomas."

Lily adored her brother, but lately he had become a hindrance to her preferred way of life. Pretty soon he was likely to insist she have a chaperone to use the convenience!

He needed a hobby. Better yet, he needed a woman. If she could interest him in someone at Laurel Ridge... Yes, and then he would be occupied. She might as well find a man for Rose, as well. The Duke of Lybrook was out of the question, of course, but there would be no shortage of decent men at the estate. With both her brother and her sister out of the way, she would be free to paint and write to her heart's content.

A match for Thomas and a match for Rose. It would be startlingly easy. There wasn't a more beautiful woman alive than Rose, with her honey blond locks and vivid blue eyes, and she came with a generous dowry and the Ashford name. And Thomas was a wonderful catch, with handsome chiseled features and sleek sable hair, not to mention he was a viscount and heir to one of the most respected earldoms in England.

Lily smiled.

"What on earth have you got up your sleeve?" Rose asked.

"What makes you think I've anything up my sleeve?"

"I know that look, Lily. You're up to no good. I can tell."

"You're up to something, for sure," Thomas said. "Sometimes you forget you're a lady."

"I'm no more a lady than you are."

Thomas smiled lazily. "Most of my friends would beg to differ. Wentworth asks about you frequently."

"That balding fool? You only keep company with him because you have your eye on his sister. You can do much better, you know."

"I could do a lot worse than Lady Regina Wentworth. I find her quite engaging."

"Thomas, she has all the intelligence of a blood pudding. Whatever do you find to talk about?"

"I suppose she's not much of a conversationalist. But she has her charms."

"Dear God, if you're not exactly like every other man in England. Taken in by a pretty face and a pair of big... I suppose I expected more of you, Thomas. I've idolized you since I was a babe. How you can stand that phony is beyond me. If you're so taken with her, why didn't you offer for her last season?"

"I'm still young, Lily. No need to rush things."

"You're twenty-eight! I'm barely twenty-one, and Papa can't wait to marry me off."

"It's just the way it is. Do yourself a favor and accept it."

"Never! I want more than that, Thomas. I will not shackle myself to some peer and become his breeder."

"I won't let anyone make you his breeder. Papa and I will see that both you and Rose are treated kindly by any interested gentlemen."

"But I don't want to be courted. There are too many other things I want to do first." She sighed. "I absolutely must see that Vermeer."

"Sorry, Lily," Thomas said. "The Lybrook collection can only be viewed by private invitation."

"Perhaps the duke will invite me to see it. Surely he would appreciate my interest."

"I'm sure he'll appreciate many things about you," her brother said, "the least of which is your commitment to the arts."

Lily rolled her eyes at her brother and then closed them, remembering her previous visit to Laurel Ridge. When she had uncovered her painting, she had been surprised at how ghastly her technique had been a mere eight years earlier. But it had a cheerful innocence to it. She had never shown it to Lord Daniel, nor had she seen him again during her brief stay at the estate.

She would likely not see him this time either, as he would no doubt be busy with his many mistresses. Handsome Lord Daniel Farnsworth was now the Duke of Lybrook.

~

Daniel stepped out of his bath and into the towel held by his valet. He dried himself and held out his arms for the silk dressing gown. "Thank you, Putney," he said, taking a seat in his leather armchair for a shave.

The valet soaked a towel in a basin of steaming water, wrung it out, and wrapped it around Daniel's face. He tried to relax. He enjoyed a good shave, but right now all he could think about were the guests gathering below and how he had to begin his life as the Duke of Lybrook this evening.

Hosting a two-week house party at what was now his estate was a daunting concept. Thank goodness for his mother and Aunt Lucy. They were renowned hostesses and would see that everything went according to plan.

He felt a smile coming, but kept it at bay so as not to disturb Putney's shaving. Lady Amelia Gregory would be there. The attractive widow would no doubt be thrilled to warm his bed tonight. She could do marvelous things with her mouth. He stiffened.

Putney rubbed the last traces of shaving soap from Daniel's face and went to the wardrobe to prepare his garments.

"I think you'll find this acceptable." Putney held out a suit jacket of dark burgundy velvet and black trousers.

Daniel dressed and poured himself a small snifter of brandy.

"Do you require anything else, Your Grace?"

"No, Putney. You may go."

Putney bowed and left. Daniel drained the brandy in two gulps, left his chamber, and headed down the wide staircase to join the gentlemen who had congregated on the back terrace. *Here goes nothing.*

His father and brother had been good at this sort of small talk. Daniel had usually been debauching some willing widow or housemaid in a dark corner. His lips curved slightly upward at the thought. Those days were over, now that he was obliged to be the host of these blasted events. He pasted a smile on his face and joined the first group of gentlemen.

~

Fatigued from their journey, Lily and Rose fell into a slumber after a maid had shown them to their guest chamber. After what seemed like only seconds, Lily awoke to a knock on the chamber door. Quickly she flew off the bed, searching for her gown on the floor. "Who is it?"

"It's us! Let us in!"

Lily ran to the door and threw it open. "Ally, Sophie!" She grabbed her cousins in a hug.

"Lily, dear, you're in your undergarments," Sophie admonished.

"Rose and I were napping. We were tired and our bags hadn't been brought up yet."

"They're right outside the door," Alexandra said. "Sophie and I can get them for you."

"Oh, don't be silly, I'll get them."

"Lily, do not step one foot outside that door in your undergarments." Rose sat up in bed. "Sophie and Ally can get our bags."

"My God, what is in this one?" Alexandra asked, lugging in a huge leather case.

"Those are my art supplies." Lily grabbed the bag. "Do be careful."

"Don't tell me you're going to paint during your stay here," Alexandra said. "There are going to be lawn parties, and rides, and fancy dinners, and balls."

"You tell her, Ally," Rose said. "She's absolutely determined not to have any fun at all."

"You have your fun, and I'll have mine. This estate is breathtaking. I intend to brush every bit of it onto paint board and describe every last foot of it in my journal."

"I think that sounds lovely, Lily," Sophie said.

Lily looked at her small cousin with affection. Sophie had thick golden hair and large hazel eyes that could mesmerize a person. Her younger sister, Alexandra, had chestnut hair, golden eyes, and a flamboyant personality. Gentlemen would no doubt be queuing up for Ally's favors this very evening.

Their mother was Lady Ashford's older sister, Iris, the Countess of Longarry. Their father, an abusive Scottish earl, had died two years earlier, his lifetime of reckless spending leaving them penniless. The Ashfords had supported them since then and planned to bring the girls out for their first season with Lily and Rose.

"We have the chamber right next to yours," Alexandra said. "And mother is way down the hall. Where are Uncle Crispin and Auntie Flora?"

"I have no idea," Lily said. "Rose and I were so tired from the trip that we passed out as soon as we got here."

"Hopefully they're far away as well. Then we won't have any problem sneaking around." Alexandra winked.

"Now you're talking." Lily laughed. "I plan to do my share of sneaking around as well."

"Really? Who do you have your eye on?" Alexandra plunked down on the bed next to Rose. "I saw some exciting prospects out on the terrace when we came in."

"She has her eye on Vermeer," Rose said.

"Which one is he?" Alexandra widened her eyes. "Please tell me he's not that dashing tall one with the auburn hair."

"Really, Ally, Vermeer is an artist," Sophie said. "Didn't you pay any attention to Miss O'Hara's lessons?"

"You want to sneak out to look at a painting?" Alexandra burst out laughing. "You are mad, Lily."

"I'm certainly not going to sneak out to be debauched by some randy lord." Lily opened her valise and began to unfold her garments.

"I am." Alexandra curled her cherry lips upward. "Perhaps two or three. Perhaps even the duke himself!"

"He'll most likely be debauching everything in sight, knowing his reputation," Lily said.

"You had better watch your own reputation, Ally dear," Rose warned. "If anyone sees you get compromised, you'll be ruined and no decent man will ever offer for you."

"Then I won't be seen." Alexandra's sandy eyes gleamed.

"Ally," Rose said. "You don't really want to go down that path, do you?"

"I've been a good girl all my life," Alexandra said. "I'm tired of wondering what it's like. I want to be kissed."

"Yes, it would be heavenly, wouldn't it," Rose agreed dreamily.

"It's not all that much," Lily said.

"Lily, you haven't been kissed!" Alexandra stood. "Do tell all!"

"I knew it!" Rose said. "Why didn't you tell me? Wentworth stole one, didn't he?"

"Yes, just once, last Christmas," Lily said. "But it was nothing. His lips were pasty and clammy. If that's kissing, I need no part of it."

"Any kiss is better than nothing." Alexandra closed her eyes. "I'm quite envious."

"Darling Ally, please don't be. And you are welcome to Teddy if you want him. He's Thomas's age, and he's not too bad to look at, although his hair is receding. He does have nice hands and a good strong build. Not the smartest peacock, but he's got a sizeable fortune."

"He sounds fine. Introduce us, will you, Lily?"

"I'd be delighted, if he's here. But if he's not, there will certainly be better prospects to choose from, especially for a girl as pretty as you with your vivacious personality."

"What about Sophie?" Alexandra asked.

"There will be plenty for Sophie as well. And for Rose."

"And for you too, Lily," Rose said.

"I am definitely not concerned about that." Lily embraced her cousins again. "I'm so glad you two are here. The four of us are going to have such fun. Now, about tomorrow. There's a lawn party scheduled for the ladies after luncheon. What do you say that we sneak off and explore the estate a bit?"

"I don't know, Lily," Sophie said, nibbling on her lower lip.

"The men will be gone on a hunt all day," Lily continued.

"No men at the lawn party?" Alexandra scoffed. "Then count me in."

"All right, Lily," Rose agreed. "It might be fun."

"If the three of you are game, so am I," Sophie said.

Lily found, to her dismay, that the Wentworths were indeed at Laurel Ridge, and just her unfortunate luck, she was seated next to Theodore Wentworth at dinner. At least he was better than his lecherous uncle, Lord Ludley. On her other side sat Lord Victor Polk, whose height and silky auburn hair identified him as Alexandra's dashing knight. Thomas was seated across from her, between Regina Wentworth and a thin blond woman whom Lily did not recognize.

Both Wentworth and Polk took care of Lily, filling her wine glass and keeping the conversation lively as they feasted on Beluga caviar, vegetable chowder, poached cod, roast goose with apple-and-raisin dressing, creamed carrots and peas, and kidney pudding.

Polk's attentions flattered Lily. He was attractive and much more intelligent than Wentworth.

"I would be honored, Lady Lily," he said, "if you would save a dance for me at the ball."

"Of course. I would be delighted."

"The delight will be mine, I assure you. Tell me, where has Ashford been hiding you?"

"Hiding me?"

"I would remember you had we met before. I've seen your father and brother at many galas over the past few years."

"I'm afraid my father and brother are both quite protective. This will be my first season."

"Are you looking forward to it?

Lily took a swallow of wine and set her glass on the table. "Not in the slightest."

Polk's light brown eyes shone with amusement. "My, you certainly know your own mind. Tell me, what have you got against the season?"

"My lord, I'm sure you have no interest in my opinion on that subject."

"You would be mistaken. Please, elaborate." He smiled.

Lily knew she should hold her tongue. But— "Frankly, my lord, I consider the whole London season to be nothing more than a thinly veiled meat market."

Polk erupted in a gale of laughter. "Without a doubt, you are the first person I have ever heard describe the season in that manner."

"Well it's true, isn't it?" Lily gestured, nearly toppling her wine glass. "Men and women window shopping for a mate as if they were looking for the most sumptuous chops in the butcher shop. It's barbaric."

"You're opinionated, aren't you? It's rather refreshing, actually."

"Just remember, you asked."

"Yes, I certainly did. And I agree with your assessment, although I think there are some who prefer the richest chops to the most sumptuous." His eyes twinkled. "May I offer you some more wine?"

"No, thank you, my lord. I believe I've had enough. You wouldn't want me to become any more loose-tongued, would you?"

"I can't think of a more pleasant way to spend the evening," Polk said, his smile a bit devious, "than with a loose-tongued lovely like yourself."

Lily's cheeks warmed. Was Polk still speaking about her opinions?

~

Lily had chosen a gown of pale green for the opening ball that was fairly low cut. Thomas had shaken his head slightly when he came to the girls' chamber to escort them to the ball, but she didn't care. A maid had swept her dark hair into an elaborate chignon, leaving wisps of curls dangling around her face, framing her high cheekbones.

Thomas escorted Rose to the dance floor for a quadrille while Lily looked for a table. Before she sat down, Lord Wentworth approached her.

"Oh, Teddy, I'm so glad you're here. There is someone I would love for you to meet. Come with me." She took his arm and walked toward her cousins who had just entered, making the necessary introductions quickly and pushing Alexandra into Wentworth's arms for a dance.

When Thomas deposited Rose back at the table, Lily grabbed his arm. "Thomas, you must dance with me.

"All right, Lily. I never knew you were much for dancing."

"I'm not, but I need to keep Wentworth from asking me."

He laughed. "I see. Shall we, then?" He held out his arm and expertly led her in the next quadrille.

"Who was that lovely young woman sitting next to you at dinner?" Lily asked.

"The blonde? Her name was Emma Smith or Smythe. I can't remember."

"I see her over there." Lily motioned with her eyes. "You should ask her to dance."

"If I dance with someone else, how can I keep Wentworth from focusing on you?" He chuckled.

"I'll take care of Wentworth. I'm trying to get him interested in Ally."

"He's not good enough for you, but you'd shove him at Ally?"

"Don't be silly. He's not good enough for Ally either. But she wanted to meet him so I obliged. In fact, she's interested in meeting just about any eligible gentleman here. Do you have any ideas for her? And for Sophie and Rose?"

"I would suggest Lord Victor Polk, but he seemed quite taken with you at dinner."

"I think Ally would like to meet him also. Now, about Rose and Sophie."

"Good Lord, I'm no matchmaker." He looked around the dance floor. "There's Van Arden, his father is a viscount." He motioned to a gentleman of average height who was not exactly handsome, but had a striking head of pale blond hair.

"Hmm. He's too short for Rose, but he would do nicely for Sophie. Introduce them, will you?"

"Anything for you, dear sister."

"Now, you must find Rose a nice gentleman. I can't bear the thought of some rogue taking advantage of her."

"I'm not exactly comfortable with this, Lily."

"Yes, I know. You're just being overprotective, as usual. But wouldn't you like Rose to meet someone you approve of rather than some lecherous goat?"

"You have a point there. I'll introduce her to Lord Evan Xavier. He's quite intelligent, and I believe his intentions would be honorable."

"Which one is he?"

Thomas looked around. "He was here earlier. Don't worry, I'll find him. You'd recognize him if you saw him. He's tall with blondish hair, built like a tree trunk. He was an oarsman at school."

"Is he handsome?"

"I don't really know what you women consider handsome."

"Well, you're handsome, Thomas."

"Of course he can't compare to me." Thomas laughed. "But I don't think Rose will have any complaints. Now, if you're done telling me what to do, the dance has ended." He led her back to their table.

"Thank you, Thomas." Lily took a seat. "You dance divinely. Now, as soon as you make all the necessary introductions, I want you to ask Miss Smythe to dance."

"Aye, aye, Lily."

Lily sat, smiling, as the gentlemen came by and escorted her companions to the dance floor. When Thomas approached Miss Smythe, and her parents were busy dancing, she silently rose. No one would notice if she stole out of the ballroom in search of the Vermeer.

She crept along the back wall of the ballroom and headed to the double door that led out to the terrace. She'd sneak around to the front of the house and begin her quest there.

As she stepped onto the terrace, she delighted in a breath of fresh air. It was a gently warm night, and she had always preferred outdoors to indoors. Several couples chatted intimately in the shadows. No one seemed to notice as Lily crossed the terrace and descended the staircase to the lawn. Swiftly she walked around to the side of the mansion, giggling to herself. The manor was built onto the side of a hill. As she walked up the incline, she took care to stay in the shadows, away from the torch lights.

She smiled, humming to herself. This had been easier than she could have ever imagined. In less than an hour, she'd gotten her sister, her brother, and her cousins out of her hair. Pleased with her success, she began to skip a little. She was almost laughing out loud when a pair of strong arms grabbed her and pulled her behind a large flowering bush. Before she could scream, a mouth clamped down on hers.

Read more...

ALSO BY HELEN HARDT

Bellamy Brothers

Savage Sin

Sweet Sin

Seductive Sin

Follow Me Series:

Follow Me Darkly

Follow Me Under

Follow Me Always

Darkly

Under

Black Rose Series

Blush

Bloom

Blossom

Wolfes of Manhattan

Rebel

Recluse

Runaway

Rake

Reckoning

Escape

Moonstone

Raven

Garnet

Buck

Opal

Phoenix

Amethyst

Sex and the Season

Lily and the Duke

Rose in Bloom

Lady Alexandra's Lover

Sophie's Voice

Steel Brothers Saga:

Craving

Obsession

Possession

Melt

Burn

Surrender

Shattered

Twisted

Unraveled

Breathless

Ravenous

Insatiable

Fate

Legacy

Descent

Awakened

Cherished

Freed

Spark

Flame

Blaze

Smolder

Flare

Scorch

Chance

Fortune

Destiny

Melody

Harmony

Encore

Blood Bond Saga:

Unchained

Unhinged

Undaunted

Unmasked

Undefeated

Temptation Saga:

Tempting Dusty

Teasing Annie

Taking Catie

Taming Angelina

Treasuring Amber

Trusting Sydney

Tantalizing Maria

Non-Fiction:

got style?

Cooking with Hardt & Soul

ACKNOWLEDGMENTS

I'm so excited about this new series! For a while now, I've wanted to create a hero that is as compelling as Talon Steel, Rock Wolfe, and Braden Black combined. I believe I've found him in Falcon Bellamy. Falcon and Savannah's love story is complete, but the story of the Bellamys, the Gallos, and the Bianchis will go on!

Thank you so much to the following individuals who helped make this story shine: My editor (and son!), Eric McConnell; my cover artist, Amanda Shepard of Shepard Originals; Troy Duran and Angelina Rocca for loaning their amazing voices to Falcon and Savannah; and my awesome beta readers, Karen Aguilera, Meghan Curran, Serena Drummond, and Linda Pantlin Dunn. You all rock!

ABOUT THE AUTHOR

#1 *New York Times*, #1 *USA Today*, and #1 *Wall Street Journal* bestselling author Helen Hardt's passion for the written word began with the books her mother read to her at bedtime. She wrote her first story at age six and hasn't stopped since. In addition to being an award-winning author of romantic fiction, she's a mother, an attorney, a black belt in Taekwondo, a grammar geek, an appreciator of fine red wine, and a lover of Ben and Jerry's ice cream. She writes from her home in Colorado, where she lives with her family. Helen loves to hear from readers.

Please sign up for her newsletter here:

http://www.helenhardt.com/signup

Visit her here:

http://www.helenhardt.com

Printed in Great Britain
by Amazon

53649518R00175